Stay Magical!

ANTIQUE MAGIC

KAIT DISNEY-LEUGERS

ANTIQUE MAGIC

MAGIC, LOVE, AND MISCHIEF BOOK 1

4 Horsemen
Publications, Inc.

KAIT DISNEY-LEUGERS

4 Horsemen
Publications, Inc.

4 Horsemen Publications, Inc.
1497 Main St. Suite 169
Dunedin, FL 34698
4horsemenpublications.com
info@4horsemenpublications.com

Typesetting by Niki Tantillo

Library of Congress Control Number: 2022941300

Paperback ISBN-13: 978-1-64450-670-7
Hardcover ISBN-13: 978-1-64450-671-4
Audiobook ISBN-13: 978-1-64450-668-4
Ebook ISBN-13: 978-1-64450-669-1

For Linda Stewart - Best of friends and best of women.

ᴀCKNOWLEDGMENT

It's hard to believe this is real. I started *Antique Magic* while dealing with the sleepless nights of being a new mom, then continued working on it through the uncomfortable nights of being pregnant again. I would never have gotten this far without my good friend Linda. She has been with me every step of the way, cheering me on, giving me honest feedback, and pumping me up when I doubted myself. Just assume I put a *Star Trek* gif here.

To Greg, my partner in life, I fucking did it! Suck it, Trebek!

To my sister, Stormy, for always believing in me. It's been a privilege being your older sister. #SisterLeugers

All the Reylos out there, this one's for you. The internet is a strange place, but you all bolstered my writing confidence and made me feel like I had a community.

Shout out to the Last Word in Mount Airy, MD. You keep my bookshelves filled and have been so supportive. Please shop at your local indie bookstore.

And finally, to Mom and Dad, for giving me everything I needed to succeed. Dad, you gave me the gift of storytelling. And, Mom, not once in my life did you ever believe I wouldn't achieve my dreams. Thank you for believing.

TABLE OF CONTENTS

CHAPTER 1

The prospect of another school year living on ramen noodles and stale cereal did not appeal much to Bridget St. James. As a history graduate student at Central Connecticut State University, she already lived off too much caffeine and energy drinks. The thought of non-frozen or canned food was all the motivation she needed to search for a part-time job, not that she didn't already have enough on her plate.

Between her work on her thesis and teaching an introduction to history class to a bunch of clueless freshmen and bored seniors trying to get the last of their credits in before graduation, she wasn't quite sure how she would juggle her time. But the teaching assistant's pay was terrible, and her landlord raised the rent again on the two-bedroom apartment she shared with her adopted brother Wesley. Wes was already picking up more hours at the campus library, and classes hadn't even started.

Brie sighed as she scrolled further along the campus job board site.

Slim pickings, she thought as she tapped to the next page. It seemed like the same positions at the same fast-food places kept popping up on every page multiple times. Not exactly what she wanted to do, especially since she knew from other people those places didn't care about working around class schedules.

Her focus landed on a promising ad for a barista. During her first year of grad school, she had worked at a coffee shop for a few months. *Well, okay, it was more like a few weeks.* To work at a coffee shop, you need a lot more chill than Brie was capable of. They fired her after she threw an iced coffee in some guy's face when he got grossly suggestive about what he wanted to do with her. But at least she had the experience.

That job was a no-go, though. It was at the same coffee shop that had fired her years before. Doubtful they would hire her back.

Brie sighed. *Maybe Wes could get me a job somewhere in the library,* she thought. *Probably not, though.* Those jobs are super competitive, and her brother only got his position through luck.

She kept scrolling through her phone, only half focused on the postings. Ten pages through, she was well into last spring's postings, which were mostly still for the same fast-food places.

A break in the restaurant jobs caught her eye. It was posted back in April but still said it was open.

"Part-time shop assistant for an antique store," Brie read aloud, even though she was home alone. *That sounds promising.* She clicked the ad; it expanded with a few details. *Part-time only, hours flexible.* No phone number—just an address that wasn't far from her apartment.

Taking a pen from where she had shoved it between the back of her head and her hair tie, Brie quickly scribbled down the address on a post-it pad on her desk. She then pushed the pen back into place next to three others, likewise stuffed into her ginger ponytail.

"Any luck?" a voice asked from behind her. Brie jumped in her seat. She was so engrossed that she didn't hear him come home. "Sorry, didn't mean to freak you out," Wes said again.

Brie turned to see her brother standing in her open doorway. Wesley St. James, her adopted brother, and best friend, filled the space with his tall, athletic body. His black hair was shaved on one side while the rest hung to the top of his ears on the other side. There was no mistaking that they were not genetically related. Where Wes was deeply tan due to his Latino heritage, Brie was so pale she looked like she was haunting the place. Her fiery curls blazed next to his dark locks. Wes also wore the same band shirts he had owned in high school and refused to throw any out, no matter how ratty they got.

The one thing that they shared was the love they had received from their adoptive mother, Maddy. She was gone now, but she raised the two misfits like they were her own, and as a token of their love for her, they both changed their last names to St. James. Even if they didn't look it on the outside, Brie and Wes were siblings through and through.

Brie held up the lime green sticky note she had just written on. "Yeah, I think I'm going to try this place out. It's an antique shop. Posting is from a few months back, but I imagine it's not the sexiest place to work."

Wes shrugged. "If it means you can afford to buy real food instead of pizza rolls, who cares how boring it is? Want me to go with?" Her brother was like that, always willing to do anything for her. Wes would give her his right arm if it would even moderately improve her life. He kept it shy of being overbearing, but sometimes Brie buckled under the weight of his concern.

"Nah, it's just a few minutes from here. And I should probably shower first and not look like a starving college student." She stood from her slightly crooked desk chair and stretched. *Yeah, I definitely don't want to show up to an interview wearing a too-large shirt that says "Witch, Please" with shorts so small they are just shy of being underwear.*

"Shower, Little Witch, you smell," Wes said with an exaggerated waving of his hand before his nose.

"Oh, screw you." Brie gave him a playful shove as she walked past him toward their shared bathroom.

4

"Just for that, I'm staying in there as long as possible, so there'll be no hot water left," she called as she shut the door behind her.

"Joke's on you, I don't care if you're in the shower; I'll jump in too if it means avoiding a cold shower," he said through the door. From the other side, Brie laughed and locked the door.

An hour later, Brie stood before the full-length mirror in her room. Her ginger waves fell loosely down her back, no pens this time. She ran her hands down the knee-length, A-line, emerald dress she wore, debating whether she should put a cardigan over the thin straps. It was August and super hot; the cardigan would make her sweat. Then again, she wanted a job at an antique store that probably was owned by some old person who would take one look at the crow tattoos on her forearms and throw her right out of the store. Still, if she wore it, she would show up sweaty, which would be gross.

She went back and forth for several more minutes, pulling the cardigan on and off several times.

"You put that thing on one more time, and I'm going to burn it," Wes said, appearing at the doorway. "Leave it off and go."

Brie took a final look in the mirror before she tossed the offending garment on her bed. She picked up her silver and striped orange messenger bag from the desk and shoved her printed resume inside.

"Here, take this," Wes said as he handed her a rough unpolished red stone. "Garnet for career luck. Put it in your pocket and rub it before you go in."

The garnet felt warm in her palm and had a comfortable weight. She slipped it into the pocket of her dress, letting its weight settle against her hip. "I swear, rocks would constantly weigh me down if I let you do this as much as you wanted. Like a sink to the bottom of the harbor without any chance of escape kind of thing."

Wes laughed. "Then it's a good thing I'm giving you good luck stones instead of just plain old rocks. Now, get out of here and get a job." He gave her a playful shove toward the door.

"I'm going, I'm going," she said as she grabbed her house keys from the brass hook next to the door.

The walk over to the shop was quick, ten minutes tops. It was a blindingly bright, scorching hot day in August, and this part of New Britain was starting to fill up with students again. Brie passed more than a few moving trucks with people yelling at each other to pivot a couch or bed through a door.

At least living with my brother means I don't have to move every year, Brie thought as she passed two guys yelling at a third for taking too long of a break.

She checked the map on her phone to see that she was only half a block away. The residential area began to give way to more shops and businesses. Suddenly, there it was: the antique shop.

It didn't look like much from the outside, a little rundown, even compared to many of the other businesses on the street with their neon signs and vibrant paint. On one side sat a shuttered business with a "for lease" sign; on the other, a brightly lit flower shop with artfully arranged bouquets in the window. Above the door, an old wooden sign read "Spirit Antiques" in faded gold paint. A more modern blue plastic sign on the door's center glass panel was flipped to Open.

An odd assortment of knickknacks rested in the one large display window: gold pocket watches, silver letter openers, and old brass lighting fixtures attached to the top of the display. And sitting on the bottom left corner of the window was a little fluorescent flier that said, "Help Wanted. Inquire Within."

Looking through the glass panel of the door, it hardly looked like there were any lights on inside the shop, making Brie question if the place was really open for business. But the faded wooden door swung open when she turned the handle. A little bell tinkled overhead as she entered; although the shop wasn't brightly lit, it had an inviting, warm glow about it.

Stepping into the shop felt like entering into a space frozen in time: An antique shop that might very well be an antique itself with its worn yet sturdy mahogany counters and polished glass display cases. The floors were dark hardwood with lighter worn paths leading up to the counters. Crowding the space were shelves upon shelves crammed full of items from decades, maybe centuries, past.

The organization of the shelves was haphazard at best with seemingly unconnected items shoved next to each other. An entire shelf of faceless dolls made of cloth and straw sat next to another shelf full of an assortment of candelabra in an array of patinas, including one so tarnished that only a hint of silver was visible beneath the black. Everything in the shop looked aged, as if it had been sitting there for ages, yet the entire place was spotless. No dust settled on the shelves from what Brie could see; the floors had no dirt or scuffs beyond the well-worn paths.

Whoever owns the place is a clean freak, Brie thought as she walked up to the counter at the far back of the shop directly across from the door. A large mahogany counter was clear of everything but a newer model computer looking incredibly out of place among the relics on the shelves. Behind the counter, a simple wooden door stood slightly ajar; peeling gold letters in the middle identified it as the "Storage Room." No one was behind the counter; the whole shop seemed empty except for Brie.

"Hello? Anyone here?" Brie's voice seemed to echo loudly through the whole shop; she hoped it would carry through to the storage room. Several seconds passed, no reply came, and nobody stepped through the door. She waited, repeatedly reminding herself not to fidget with the strap of her bag.

Brie's gaze turned down toward the counter, searching for a bell or something that could alert a worker to her presence. Other than the computer, the counter was clear. She called out again and waited; maybe they just hadn't heard her the first time.

Another full minute went by, and nobody came. *Should have called first*, Brie thought as she turned from the storage room door, taking a step toward the door. *Oh, right, no phone number listed.*

"We're open by special appointment only. Come back another time," a voice said behind her.

Brie shrieked, the sound reverberating around the room. She had not heard any footsteps nor the sound of a door opening behind her. She turned to face the counter again with a deep, steadying breath. The man standing there was easily a foot taller than Brie, maybe six and a half feet tall and slim. He styled his blue-black hair in an undercut, the longer ends slicked back just a little. His light brown skin seemed to capture the soft glow of the room, giving it golden undertones. Jewel-green eyes pierced her face from under a drawn brow. The man was dressed head to toe in black, except for a small golden torch stitched into the breast pocket of his button-down shirt. The lack of lines on his face made it difficult to determine his age from sight.

Oh no, he's hot, Brie thought as she stared at the man, her brain running slower than usual.

The man's expression became just the slightest bit annoyed. "Can I help you with something?" His voice was black velvet to her ears; Brie shuddered all the way down to her core. She had never had a thing for voices before; that was new. It was easy enough to imagine spending all day staring at him. From his high cheekbones, full pouty lips, large, long-fingered hands all the way down his slim torso to the miles of leg clad in black, it was a sight she could drink in for a good long while. But then she remembered why she was here.

"Oh, yeah. I saw your 'help wanted' notice and wanted to apply." She mentally congratulated herself for managing to string a complete sentence together like a normal person.

"It's part-time only," the man responded, annoyance still coloring his features.

Brie smiled. *Be amiable*, she told herself. "That's fine. I'm a grad student, so I can't really do full-time right now."

The annoyance lessened just a tiny bit. "I need someone for evenings only. The shop has many regulars, and I accommodate their schedules. Will that be a problem?" He raised a questioning eyebrow. *Holy hell, are those eyebrows expressive and beautiful.*

How much business can an antique shop get that requires it to stay open late? she thought. But, instead, she let her smile widen. "No problem. All of my classes are in the morning, and the class I teach on Friday is at noon, so it shouldn't interfere."

"You will need to be here from six to ten Wednesday through Saturday. Those are the hours, non-negotiable," he said, his pointed look clearly saying he knew she would refuse, his green eyes boring into her grey ones. Almost like he was daring her to refuse. After all, what twenty-something college student wanted to give up part of both their Friday and Saturday nights for work?

One that was living off a teaching assistant salary and boxes of cereal, as Brie was currently doing. If it meant she got to spend the weekend with this man, well, it was a sacrifice she was willing to make.

"Totally fine with that. I'm not much of a partier anyway, so it doesn't bother me," she said. She really wasn't. Actually, she didn't have much of a social life at all these days.

Finally, the man smirked at her. It was small, more of a slight upturn of one side of his mouth. *A very nice mouth with soft-looking lips*, thought Brie before she could help herself. It had been a while since she had been with anyone. That look was spreading heat through her whole stomach.

"You start tomorrow, six o'clock sharp. If you have school work, you may bring it to work on during slow periods, though after eight, it usually isn't. There's no dress code or uniform. My only rule is don't be late. Come on time or don't come at all." His voice indicated a dismissal, and indeed he started to turn back toward the storage room door.

Brie stayed rooted to the spot, dumbfounded.

"Wait! That's it? So I got the job? Just like that?" She couldn't believe that was the entire interview.

The slight smirk still painted his face. "Just like that." The man turned back toward the door, waving her off with a hand. *Oh, that smile is more than enough to get her to agree with anything.*

This isn't how interviews are supposed to go, Brie's voice of reason screamed in her head. *People don't just give you a job.* That was enough to chill her lust for him. "Don't you need to see my resume or, like, check my references?"

"Do you have your resume?" he asked, the smirk slipping from his face. His long fingers drummed on the countertop; Brie's eyes flicked down to stare at his hand for a moment. He continued to stand at the counter and waited while Brie finished rooting through her bag.

She pulled out the copy of her resume she had stuffed in the bag before leaving the apartment. She walked back to the counter and handed it over.

He took the resume, glanced down for half a second, then set it on the counter. "I have everything I need to know. Six o'clock tomorrow."

"Um... okay. Cool. See you tomorrow, I guess," she said, furrowing her brow. She turned back toward the door starting to walk out.

She was halfway to the door when it dawned on her. "Wait, I don't know your name!" It seemed they had both missed several crucial steps in the hiring process. Even if the interview had been unorthodox, names were pretty important.

The man looked up at her. "I'm Ezra, and this is my shop."

"Ezra. I'm Bridget, but just Brie is fine." She gave him her biggest smile.

"I know," he said with finality, the smirk gone. Brie found herself missing the sight already.

She turned to leave when Ezra's voice sounded again. "An interesting name, not one I often hear anymore. If memory serves me correctly, Bridget was a Celtic goddess of healing and fire."

Brie faced him. "Poetry, too. I've always loved my name. When I was a kid, I went through this phase where I wanted to learn everything about the Celtic goddess, but almost all I could find was about Saint Brigid." Maddy always told her names have meaning behind them and that Brie would live up to her name. She never doubted anything Maddy said.

Ezra nodded his head. "Names have power. Until tomorrow, Bridget." Then he disappeared through the door with heavy audible footsteps this time, and the door clicked shut behind him.

Brie left the shop, puzzling over his response, really puzzling over the whole interaction. Just like that, she had a part-time job with no idea of the pay or what was actually expected of her. All she knew was that the antique shop kept odd hours and was owned by a ridiculously handsome man. *Not to mention the added bonus that it is only a few minutes' walk from my apartment building.* Brie wasn't going to question a good thing this time.

At least, she hoped it was a good thing.

CHAPTER 2

"So you didn't even ask how much it paid?" Wes stopped his chopsticks halfway into the takeout container.

Brie shrugged. "I guess I just assumed it was minimum wage. It's only a small shop; I doubt it could afford more than that."

Wes furrowed his black brows. "And that doesn't seem a bit weird to you? Pay is usually something that's discussed, and you said he barely glanced at your resume."

Brie chewed her dumpling in slow contemplation. The coffee table in front of them was laden with Chinese takeout containers from the restaurant on the ground floor of the building next door. It was one of their splurge foods, and Brie's new job seemed like occasion enough for it.

After telling Wes about her bizarre job interview, he seemed less enthusiastic. Wes was the pragmatist of the two. He never did anything without thoroughly thinking it through. In contrast, Brie was impulsive and prone to thinking in the moment, not before. An odd shop with basically no hiring standards definitely fell into the category of things Wes avoided.

"Oh, totally weird. But like, we're used to a little weird." She waved her chopsticks around to indicate their living space.

On top of the typical clutter of two grad students crammed into too small of a space, they managed to shove a massive overstuffed bookcase against one whole wall of the living room. Nestled against old textbooks and research materials was an extensive collection of books on the occult and pagan traditions. Crystals in a wide array of shades stood in place of bookends.

The bookcase and the non-school-related books were part of their inheritance from their adoptive mother, Maddy. Even before the two came to live with her, Maddy had acquired a large collection of books, crystals, and magical items over the years; she shared it freely with them when they were teenagers. The education on pagan traditions she gave them was thorough. Both had read every book she had, knew the uses of various crystals, and could identify magical plants by sight. More than anything, she made sure they knew they were loved.

Maddy died while Brie was finishing her bachelor's, and Brie and Wes had to go through her house before they selling it. They couldn't throw out the old bookcase with Maddy's books and magical objects. So they lugged the bookcase and all its contents with them through graduate school. It was a constant reminder of the mother who brought them together.

The rest of the apartment was taken over by plants, drying herbs, candles, and more crystals. A small altar sat in a corner near the threshold to the kitchen. Even with Maddy gone, they kept her traditions, even if they weren't active in the local community. They preferred to practice together.

"It's not weird; it's comforting. And a whole hell of a lot safer than some random shop with a tall, dark, and handsome proprietor," Wes responded before shoving a whole dumpling into his mouth.

Brie frowned. "I never said he was handsome." *Though he absolutely is*, she thought. But Wes didn't need to know that.

Her brother pointed a chopstick at her. "You didn't have to. I could tell by the way you talked about him. You literally described his face first and then his body. You nearly forgot to get his name. His name, Brie! Babies know to ask for a name first. And who agrees to take a job with absolutely no information unless they have been seduced by a handsome face and pretty eyes?" Wes rolled his eyes and picked up the container of rice.

"That's not why I agreed to take the job. Is he nice to look at? Absolutely. Are his eyes gorgeous? Totally.

But money is kind of the motivating factor here," she huffed as she grabbed the rice from Wes's hands.

This time Wes snorted. "Which, again, you don't know how much that's going to be, so that's a dumb excuse."

Brie threw a wrapped fortune cookie at him, which he dodged easily. "I'll ask about it tomorrow if it'll make you happy. But even minimum wage is better than nothing."

"Okay, fine! But I'll feel better if you at least bring some mugwort with you or something for protection. I'll make you a sachet." His tone sounded more serious than before, the playfulness gone.

Brie rolled her eyes. "Nettle would be better, but I get what you mean. You really are a rock head. Sure, you make me a protection pack, and I'll take it with me tomorrow just to make you happy."

"Thanks, Little Witch." Wes reached over and ruffled her ginger hair, making the strands fluff up into a mess.

"Whatever, mom," Brie responded, giving his shoulder a shove.

It was a quarter to six when Brie arrived in front of Spirit Antiques. She had barely gotten a block away from her apartment when the sky opened up and poured on her the rest of the way to the shop. She cursed herself for not thinking to check the weather on her way out as she stood to shake loose water from her body under the building's overhang.

Not that it helped; she was thoroughly soaked. It was going to be a soggy and uncomfortable first shift.

With the gray sky outside, the shop looked even darker through the window than it did the day before. Yet the blue, plastic sign said "Open." The little bell above the door tinkled as she walked across the threshold.

This time, Ezra stood behind the counter typing away on the computer. It looked so out of place amongst the old artifacts on the shelves. Brie scanned the shelves; she made a quick judgment that nothing in the shop was younger than fifty years old. Most of the pieces on display looked far older than a hundred or so years. Not exactly surprising for Connecticut.

"Try not to drip on any of the merchandise, please. Some of this stuff does not react well to water," Ezra called without looking away from the computer.

"Sorry," Brie sheepishly responded as she wiped her feet on the mat directly inside the door. It would do little good since she was still dripping, but at least it would keep her from tracking wet footprints through the shop as she walked up to her new boss.

"I'm in the process of digitizing my ledger book, so that's what I'm having you work on going forward," he said without preamble. "I will add customer interactions once you get more acquainted with the store and its clientele." There was no inflection to his voice. Ezra finally looked up and acknowledged her, taking in her sopping appearance. A ruby-colored t-shirt stuck to her curvy body and cutoff shorts that were now so thoroughly saturated by the storm they were practically a second skin. Her battered brown boots squelched with each step. The wild mane of ginger hair she had swept up into a ponytail was now plastered to her head; the ponytail dragged down. The only thing dry about her was the waterproof messenger bag slung across her body with her school stuff inside. Little was left to the imagination, her clothes clinging so close to her body.

Meanwhile, her impeccably dressed new boss was in all black: black jeans and another black button-down shirt with a small golden torch embroidered over the breast pocket. The sleeves of his shirt were rolled to his elbow, displaying his toned arms. He was also completely dry. Brie couldn't stop herself from drinking in the sight of him.

His gaze roamed over her, noticeably catching on her chest before moving upward, a slight blush appearing on his cheeks. Then he seemed to remember himself. "I can't have you out here looking like I tried to drown you; you'll scare away the customers. Wait here." He indicated a spot behind the counter for her to stand. Brie opened her mouth to call him rude, but then thought better of it. After all, it was her first day, and snapping at the boss was a one-way ticket to getting fired fast. Plus, he wasn't wrong; she did feel half-drowned. So she swallowed her retort and moved to stand where he had indicated.

Ezra disappeared behind the only door, the one behind them labeled Storage Room and pulled it shut behind him. Brie stood behind the counter shivering, her hands nervously fiddling with the strap of her bag. Her mind wandered to the nettle-mix sachet at the bottom of her bag. Wes had insisted again before she left, and to appease him, she bundled up the nettle with a few other herbs before tossing the whole thing into her bag.

She swept her gaze around the room again to keep herself occupied while she waited for Ezra to return. Some of the contents on the shelves looked like actual junk, bits of metal that would serve a purpose only as scrap. Other bits looked pristine, like the small Victorian gilt mirror that appeared so polished and shining it could almost be brand new.

After only a few minutes, Ezra slipped back through the door with a bundle in his hands. "Here," he said as he handed a pile of clothes over to Brie. "You're small, so these will be too big, but at least it's something dry. You can change in my office. Number one on the panel." He indicated a small brass panel next to the Storage Room door. There were six large buttons, each numbered. He turned away from her and went back to the computer.

Brie stood in the same spot, confused. She looked over at the panel, then the door.

"Just hit the button and open the door. It's not that difficult. And hurry up, I'm expecting a customer soon. I want to get you started before they show up." Ezra's voice had an edge of irritation in it, enough to spur Brie into moving her feet without questioning. *Hot and grumpy*, just how she liked her men. *So much work, but usually worth it for the sex*. Not that she was having much of that lately.

She tentatively reached out and pushed the One button on the brass panel. A small ding sounded from the door. Holding the bundle of clothes with one hand, she turned the doorknob to the Storage Room with her other hand.

Where she expected to find piles of junk and excess merchandise, instead was a sizable wood-paneled office with dim lighting. A large fireplace and mantel took up considerable space on the wall to her right; a cheery fire already burned in the grate. A deep burgundy leather couch took up a portion of the left wall directly across from the fireplace. Shelves lined the whole room, stuffed with books and trinkets in various states of wear. At the far back wall, directly across from Brie, sat a heavy redwood desk completely cluttered with papers, books, and an odd assortment of paperweights. Two padded chairs sat in front of the desk, and a high-back, worn-leather chair sat on the other side. The room had only two windows, both covered by heavy drapes.

Overall, it was a dark, yet cozy, room.

Brie walked to the leather couch and placed the dry clothes on the cushion while she stripped off her wet things with no small amount of difficulty. Goosebumps appeared on her arms as the warm air hit her damp skin and she shivered. She debated whether to take off her wet underwear for a moment but decided against it. Going commando and braless on her first day seemed like a bad idea, no matter how much more comfortable it would be.

Before pulling on the dry clothes, she stood in front of the fire, letting it heat her body up a little. It took only a minute for Brie to feel warmer and drier. Back at the couch, she pulled on the borrowed clothes. The black sweatpants were way too long, so she rolled the waist down and folded the legs up to her knees. The t-shirt was also black and so large that it went down to her mid-thigh. They were clearly Ezra's clothes; she couldn't stop herself from giving a small sniff of the shirt collar: *woodsmoke and vanilla*.

I could almost wear it as a dress, she thought as she pulled the loose fabric to the side and tied it off into a knot at the waistline. At least she wasn't wet anymore.

Luckily, Ezra was slim enough that she didn't have to worry about holding the pants up all night.

As she turned to face the fire again, Brie noticed a small drying rack that she was sure wasn't there before, but still, she draped her wet clothes over it and placed the whole thing in front of the fire.

Sockless, she pulled on her wet shoes. It wasn't ideal, but it wasn't like she could walk around barefoot no matter how lax Ezra was with the dress code. With some difficulty, she managed to pull her hair from the ruined ponytail and shook out her long tresses with no pens to worry about as she ran her fingers through her hair. Once she finished detangling her wet hair, she gathered it all up into a braid and threw it over one shoulder.

Emerging through the door in her dry clothes, she found Ezra speaking with a gaunt Asian man in a tailored three-piece suit. A crimson pocket square stood out in stark contrast to the charcoal gray of the suit. The customer was so exceedingly pale that if he closed his eyes, he would look dead, except for his lips, which were almost as red as his pocket square. His eyes were so black that his pupils were nearly invisible.

The door shut behind her with a slight click. The sound drew the attention of Ezra and the customer.

"Who is this, Ezra? I didn't expect you would have a snack ready for me in addition to my purchase," the pale man said, his tone flat and uninterested.

His voice sent a cold chill up Brie's spine, and she felt her skin prickle into goosebumps. She definitely didn't like the way he looked at her, like a hunter eyeing its prey.

Still, she wouldn't let anyone intimidate her.

"I'm not a snack," Brie said as she glared at him. She'd heard plenty of foul things from men about her appearance since she hit puberty. Maddy had taught her to never ignore words that made her uncomfortable.

"You live in this world, too, cher. Ain't nobody allowed to make you feel less than," Maddy would say to her, always giving her a chuck on the chin.

Three-Piece-Asshole, as she now called him in her head, gave her a wicked grin that showed off brilliantly white teeth. "And she's feisty, too. It's better when they put up a fight." His voice remained flat, almost bored, but it did nothing to diminish the threat behind the words.

Brie never considered herself a coward; however, Three-Piece Asshole's smile sent a flash of fear through her. It was instinct to hunch in on herself and clutch the messenger bag she had brought with her as she thought of the nettle buried at the bottom. The only comfort she had, and it felt woefully inadequate.

But then Ezra stepped in front of her, shielding her from view.

"She's my new assistant, Albert. You'll do well to leave her alone," he said with finality; Brie could see around him just enough to witness his words wipe the grin from Three-Piece-Asshole's face.

Albert sniffed loudly. "Just as well; she reeks of your scent. It's enough to spoil my appetite. Hmm–" Albert stopped and sniffed again. Brie peaked around Ezra just an inch or so and saw a small smirk return to Albert's face. "Nettle, how quaint. Seems you have yourself a little hedgewitch, Ezra. Adorable." Though his tone said it was anything but.

Brie watched as her new boss's hands curled into fists. "You got what you came for, Albert. Leave my assistant alone and get out." *Should I feel a thrill when he calls me his assistant? Probably not, considering the situation.*

Albert said nothing more. With a parting sneer in her direction, he turned on his heel and was gone. The bell tinkled his departure.

Ezra whirled around to face her. She looked up and up to see his face since he was so close. *Damn, I am going to have a sore neck just talking to this guy.* But there was so much to see on the way up. His button-down shirt sculpted to his body. And while he wasn't overly muscular, he was definitely very toned.

"First thing you need to know is that if Albert Hsu comes in when I'm not around, you must get through that door quickly. Use the number two button; you'll be safe there." His voice was commanding. This wasn't concern; he was demanding.

Brie felt a mix of confusion and fear course through her. "Does he hate women or something? If he's dangerous or whatever, why don't you just call the cops on him or ban him from the store?" *It is a reasonable thing to do if someone is potentially a risk*, she thought.

Ezra ran a hand through his hair. "It's complicated. He's kicking a habit right now, and it makes him moody, to say the least. He's a good customer, and he won't bother you if I'm around."

"And if you're not around?" Brie worried that if this guy was some recovering addict, he might just go berserk on her one day. *Isn't Ezra concerned about what that guy would do in his shop?*

"You will use the number two button on the door. But he's been doing well for several years now. The worst you will likely deal with when it comes to Albert is his attitude. Now, let me show you what you'll be doing first." He quickly changed the disturbing subject by walking back to the computer. An ancient ledger book sat next to it on the counter; Ezra pulled it closer to him, the whole interaction with Albert Hsu forgotten.

Brie walked to stand next to him. "So where do the other numbers go? On the door, I mean. Is it like mechanical or something?"

Ezra turned from the ledger to look at the wooden door behind them.

"Or something. One goes to my office, as you saw. Two goes to the Storage Room. Three is my personal

27

apartment; Albert would have to be invited through there, which he is not, so it's safe. Four is the back room, or I guess now the employee break room. I'll keep it stocked for you. Five is none of your business," he said the last more harshly than the others and with a pointed glare.

"And I haven't decided on six yet. Two and four are all you will need unless I say otherwise."

That didn't exactly answer her full question. "But how does it work?" A*re there going to be more questions than answers with this job?*

Ezra looked down at her, searching her face for a moment. "I will tell you now, Bridget St. James, there are many things in my shop that you may find unusual. The door is the least of them. Now, like I was saying, digitizing records."

Over the next hour, Ezra showed her how to enter records from the ledger book into a program on the computer. It wasn't the most exciting work. Actually, it was totally boring. But Ezra was adamant that the shop needed to pull itself into the modern era regarding its records. And really, Brie would listen to him read the phonebook if it meant she could hear his rich voice.

"After this, we can start work on keeping a digital inventory. I'm sure you'll find that more appealing, considering your dissertation on the importance of digitizing artifacts and manuscripts. I won't lie to you, Bridget; this project will take a very long time. There are things here that I've completely forgotten about, and I'm always adding new inventory. In all likelihood, these projects will outlast your time here, but I hope you are still up to the task."

He waited for her reaction, eyes drifting to hers and quickly away, but Brie didn't know what to say to that, so she just shrugged. It wasn't like she expected the job to be exciting or that she would stay at it forever.

"Okay, at least it'll keep me busy. I know you said I could work on my classwork while I'm here, but that feels a little like I'm taking advantage of your time and money. If I'm here, I should be doing shop work." That seemed fair, at least, though she might regret it once classes started.

Ezra ran a hand through his dark hair. "Very well. Gods know there is plenty to do around here. I've been putting off this update for far too long." The gesture made him look younger, and for a moment, Brie wondered what it would feel like to run her own hands through his hair.

The chime of the bell drew her attention away from such thoughts.

An elderly couple walked into the shop; both men wore matching brown leather fanny packs and white crew socks with sandals. They practically screamed antiquers into the room.

"Tourists come in occasionally. Try to get them to move along quickly whenever they do come in. They won't find anything they want here," Ezra bent to whisper a little too close to her ear, but his eyes didn't leave the customers.

Brie didn't look at him when she responded back in a whisper, though she was very aware of his closeness. "Why do you think they won't buy anything?" She didn't understand why it mattered if they just browsed. It wasn't like the shop was crowded; it was just the two customers and them.

He straightened and looked down at her. She was forced to look up to meet his gaze. "Because they won't find anything of interest. I've made sure of it. They come every time they return to New Britain and have yet to buy anything."

There was that finality to his voice that Brie took to mean that was all the answer she was going to get. So instead, she focused her attention on the couple slowly making their way around the shelves.

"Well?" Ezra looked down at her with a raised brow, his face betraying nothing else.

"Well, what?" she retorted, matching his look.

Ezra gestured toward the customers. "Are you going to do your job?" *Haughty tone and a hand wave... Yeah, he is the bossy type*, Brie thought with a smirk to herself.

"Oh, you meant for me to get them out now?" Not that she didn't expect it eventually, but she figured

Ezra would handle this first pair. And maybe she was messing with him. Just a little.

Ezra crossed his arms. "Obviously." He nodded toward the couple, clearly indicating that she better get moving. No smirk, but he wasn't impatient either.

Brie took a step, then another, around the counter. She turned to look back at Ezra, still standing in front of the computer, arms crossed. "It actually wasn't obvious, especially since you mentioned 'working up to customer interactions.'" She didn't wait for Ezra's response before she pushed away from the counter and walked toward the browsing couple. She did notice the tiniest of upturns on the side of his lips, however.

"Can I help you find anything?" She plastered on a smile. Her customer service skills were a little rusty since teaching undergrads didn't necessarily mean she had to be nice, let alone smile. But as it turned out, she could still make that fake smile. The couple seemed bewildered by her sudden appearance, as if they didn't expect the shop to have actual employees. She would bet good money that Ezra just ignored them every other time.

"Oh, no, we're just looking," one of the men said as he squeezed his partner's hand, pulling them both away from Brie.

"Um... we're closing soon ... so if you... uh... yeah. If you could just ... get out?" It came out as a question. *Nailed it*, she chastised herself. Heat flooded her face;

it was like she had completely forgotten how to talk to people.

The couple gave each other a quick look. "Ah, well, of course. Richard, it's getting late. We'll grab a cocoa from that cute cafe you love and head back to the B&B," the one who hadn't spoken to Brie said. The pair made a hasty exit with Richard giving Brie a last glance on the way out.

A laugh came from behind her, full-bodied and decadent to her ears. Well, it would have been if it wasn't at her expense. "Smooth," came Ezra's voice through the laughter.

Brie whirled around, her face red with embarrassment as she glared at him. "You can shut it," she said forcefully.

"I'm your boss, and while I would say I'm fairly lax, I don't think you get to tell the boss to 'shut it.'" The laughter was gone from his voice, but a hint of amusement remained. Brie had the choice to either push it or be cowed into respect. Brie was rarely cowed by anyone.

With her customer service smile back in place, if not a little mockingly, she replied, "Sorry. Shut it, sir." If she was honest with herself, she didn't even try to keep the smile from turning into a cocky smirk. Maddy always told her she was too mouthy for her own good, but then, Maddy would always smile at her when she said it.

Even though Ezra didn't exactly smile, a barebones grin formed on his face for just a second. "You're going to be a pain in the ass, I can tell," he said as she started to head back to the counter. Her smirk didn't slip.

Just as she made it to the side of the counter, the door opened, and the bell tinkled again. A fragrant wind blew through the shop, followed by a young dark-skinned woman in dirt-covered olive overalls. Tight, red-hued black curls fanned away from her head like a dark halo. A silver ring hung from her septum, settled below a splash of freckles across her nose. Down her exposed right arm was a full sleeve tattoo in gorgeous detail with swirling stems and blooming petals. A smile that could rival the sun flashed as she walked in, reaching all the way up to her sparkling amber eyes.

"Ezra! Nice to see you. You have my order?" she called out, eating up the space between them in a few quick strides. Brie couldn't help but stare at her. There are some people who just brighten up a room, and this woman seemed like one of them. Brie couldn't explain it.

"Hello, Lily. The aglaophotis just came in this morning. Just a second." Ezra turned and walked through the Storage Room door, leaving Brie and Lily alone at the counter.

Brie walked behind the counter. One of the legs of the too-long pants started to fall, and she bent down and rolled it back up again. When she stood up once more, Lily stood flush with the counter. The look she gave Brie made her feel warm and her soul stripped bare. It was both uncomfortable and pleasant.

Lily practically buzzed with excitement as she took in Brie's features. "A hedgewitch! I knew it! I knew it! I knew it! I told him you would be." She did a little dance in place, celebrating her own small victory that Brie didn't understand.

"Huh?" was Brie's dazzling reply as she managed to finally stop herself from staring at the woman.

Lily bounced on the balls of her feet. "I told Ezra you would be a hedgewitch. I saw you in my dreams months ago, and I told him! He didn't believe me, of course. Silly angel man rarely ever does." All Brie could do was blink in confusion; she had no idea what this person was talking about. And "angel man"? Well, that was a weird pet name.

One calloused brown hand stuck out toward Brie. "I'm Lily, by the way, Lily Everett. I'm here all the time; Ezra really has the best stock within a hundred miles." Brie took her hand, and that simple touch alone felt something akin to a hug as the two gripped hands. A fresh wave of scent—swamp milkweed, freshly turned earth, and peppermint tea—enveloped Brie, strong and comforting.

"I'm Brid—"

Lily cut her off excitedly. "Bridget, yes, I know. I told Ezra—" But whatever she was going to say was cut off by Ezra reemerging through the door. He looked at the two women still holding onto each other's hand.

"It's her first day, Lily. I'm easing her in," he huffed as he set what looked like a potted peony on the counter. Lily dropped Brie's hand, quickly turned her attention to the plant, and wrapped her hands around the plastic pot.

"Oh, you are gorgeous! You'll be a perfect addition to my garden," Lily crooned to the plant; she was already engrossed in examining the plant's leaves and petals, forgetting entirely about Ezra and Brie.

Brie bent her head to look closer at the plant sitting on the counter. Maddy had been a gardening fanatic and taught Brie all she knew. But what sat before her was something she had never seen in Maddy's garden or anywhere else. "I didn't think aglaophotis was a real plant. I've only heard about them in like mythology," she said as she brushed a finger gently along a petal.

"You can't find this beauty just anywhere. Only Ezra knows how to get them. He has connections with—" Again, she was cut off by Ezra.

"I'll put it on your tab. I'll have the moly next week. You'll get a message when it's in." Brie didn't miss the way his glance sharpened toward Lily as he spoke, as if he was trying to convey more behind his words.

Lily waved him away. "Fine, fine. Brie, once I get this planted, I'll bring you a starter clipping. Aglaophotis is great for protection and way more powerful than the nettle you have. Hedgewitches are so cute." Before Brie could say anything, Lily bounded around the side of the counter and threw her arms around Brie.

Brie was so stunned by the sudden contact that she barely managed to keep herself from flinching from the sudden contact. But then her whole body felt like it was wrapped in the warmest blanket, and her senses were suddenly filled with the smell of Maddy's garden and peppermint tea. Unbidden tears sprang forth; it felt like a happy memory. More than anything, it made her long for the woman she had called mom.

Lily pulled away from the embrace abruptly. "Hmm, that's odd. I thought I felt..." She stopped and searched Brie's eyes for a long moment, amber eyes gazing intently into gray ones. Brie tried not to squirm under her gaze or look away. She wasn't sure what was going on.

"Lily, don't," Ezra quietly warned or pleaded. Maybe both—Brie couldn't be sure.

Lily's eyes snapped to him with a look of understanding, then she drew Brie back into a rib-crushing hug once more. Then she and her plant were gone into the darkening evening with a parting floral breeze and one last blast of her sunny smile.

Brie stared at the door for several seconds after Lily's departure. "What was that about?" she asked as she turned back to face Ezra. The warmth from Lily's embrace still clung to her, but without the actual contact, she started to feel weird about being touched so abruptly.

Ezra heaved a deep sigh. "That's just Lily. She's a great customer, just a bit much. Likes to stick her nose too much in other people's business, though she means well. I'm sure she does," the last part he said like he was reassuring himself. "Anyway, I think that's it for today." He turned his attention back to the computer, a clear dismissal.

"I thought you needed me for four hours. It's like..." Brie pulled her phone from her pocket to check the time, "just after eight."

He didn't look away from the computer when he responded, "Don't worry about today. You'll be paid for the whole shift. Consider this a training day."

Now seemed like a good time to bring up pay, though she didn't particularly like talking about money since she grew up with very little of her own. This was her job now. Knowing how much she would be paid seemed like an important thing to know. Of course, Wes would be waiting at home to give her an "I told you so."

"Yeah, about pay. I know we didn't discuss it yesterday, but how's that working out?"

"You'll be paid every other Saturday at the end of your shift, and I'm sure you'll find I'm generous to my employees. Until tomorrow, Bridget." His tone was dismissive. Brie had a feeling she was going to have to get used to that. His eyes flicked over to her for an instant before darting away again; she knew challenging him was something he expected.

Brie didn't move toward the door; instead, she stayed rooted at the counter next to Ezra. "If it's all the same to you, I would rather work the full shift. I can work on the ledger now." She wanted to make a good impression, *well, at least an okay impression*, even if the boss was letting her leave. It was as good a time as any to prove she was a good and dedicated worker, especially since she knew with absolute certainty she would mouth off to him again. Not that he seemed to mind much.

Ezra finally turned his face from the computer and looked at her properly. "If you insist."

Brie nodded. "I do." Ezra just shrugged, took a few steps away from the computer, and allowed Brie to move into his unoccupied spot. He turned toward the Storage Room door, pressed the number two button on the panel, and pulled the door open a crack.

"I'll return before ten to see you out. I'm not expecting anyone else tonight, so just use that natural talent you have to usher out any tourists should they wander in." There was the barest trace of a smirk on his lips. *Is he actually teasing me?*

Before Brie could retort, Ezra slipped through the door with an audible click behind him.

The thick ledger book sat open on the counter. Brie settled herself on the only stool and pulled the book closer to begin the arduous task of adding data line by line to the computer program. The handwriting was in a neat hand, without flair, but perfectly legible. The pages were yellowed with age; it looked like earlier entries were written in old ink. *How much stuff does this place have?* she thought as she flipped through the pages of the ledger. There had to be thousands of entries, though she saw several lines crossed off, which were obviously sold merchandise.

"This is going to take years," she groaned as she thumbed back to the first entry and started to enter the data in to the computer. *One line at a time*, she repeated to herself.

At a quarter to ten, Ezra emerged from the Storage Room to find a bleary-eyed Brie still dutifully going line by line in the ledger. "Go home, Bridget. You can continue this tomorrow." His voice was gentle.

Brie stood with a stretch, her arms reaching high into the air until she felt her back pop. Her shirt rode up a little, and from the corner of her eye, she saw Ezra's gaze fall to the patch of exposed skin of her stomach. She shouldered her bag, hiding a smile. "See you tomorrow," she said, receiving a nod from Ezra in return before she walked out of the shop.

The rain had stopped at some point in the evening and the air still had that scent of petrichor. The walk home was uneventful, and she wasn't at all surprised to see Wes sitting on the couch waiting for her when she got home.

He flashed a smile her way as she walked in the door, then drew his brows in confusion. "Whose clothes are those?" Brie looked down. She was still in the sweatpants and oversized shirt Ezra had lent her. Her clothes were still on the rack in Ezra's office.

Well, that's not awkward, she thought as she took a seat next to her brother.

Chapter 3

On her second day at the shop, Brie made sure to double-check the weather report before she left her apartment. Rain wasn't expected, but she took her umbrella anyway. She had her bag strung across her chest with Ezra's freshly laundered clothes inside.

She arrived at the antique shop just before six. There were no visible customers as she slipped inside; neither was Ezra. Instead, a small sign sat upright on the counter that read "Ring Bell for Service"; below the sign sat a heavy bronze hand bell with a polished handle.

Brie walked around the counter and dropped her bag on the floor next to the stool. Taped to the computer was a note, the handwriting identical to that in the ledger book.

Bridget,

I'm working on a customer request in the Storage Room. Please continue on the records project. If a customer comes in, ring the bell.

-E

At least he wasn't the type to loom over her while she worked. Brie wasted no time in setting up the computer before she slid the ledger book closer. In the first hour, only one person came in. They looked through the shelves for a minute, or two, before Brie ushered them out quickly—with slightly more smoothness than the day before. A tourist was easy to spot now that Brie knew what to look for. Otherwise, she was left alone to make headway with the data entry. She hummed softly to herself as she did so. Maybe she could ask Ezra about playing some music while she worked, something to break the silence when no one was around. He seemed like the kind of guy who didn't go for loud, upbeat music.

The first hour passed, headed toward seven-thirty; still, Ezra remained in the back and nobody came through the door. Brie finally stood to stretch out her back. Just as she settled her arms at her sides, the bell tinkled to life, and a man walked in, catching Brie's eye.

"Man" was a loose term for the figure that stood in the doorway. He was tall, muscular, and golden all over from his sun-kissed skin to his bronzy hair that just touched his ears in a perfect wave. He looked as if he were made of sunbeams. The only deviations from the overall golden god look were his mesmerizing ocean blue eyes and full pink lips set in a seductive smirk. His clothing looked more suitable for a beach town rather than inland Conneticut with his navy Bermuda shorts, white tank top, and brown sandals. The expensive-looking wristwatch on his left wrist was the only thing that threw off the carefree look, and even then, only just.

When he spied Brie across the room, he practically ran toward her; his smirk blossomed into a full pearly white grin. There was something about his demeanor that instantly put Brie off. She couldn't quite figure out what it was. Maybe it was his smile, almost predatory, like he planned to do wicked things to her. The glint in his blue eyes offered a promise of mischief, or maybe it was the overall bronzed effect. It made him look like a manufactured Ken doll. Rather than smile back, she placed her hands firmly on the counter and kept her face neutral.

"Well, well, who do we have here? Are you new, darling, or has that cranky old angel been keeping you hostage somewhere in his dark Storage Room?" His voice was like honey, thick and sweet. It took all of her self-control not to roll her eyes.

"It's my second day, actually. Are you picking up or just browsing?" Brie planned to keep this interaction short, no pleasantries. But the newcomer had other ideas. He leaned against the counter, one arm resting on the wood, leaving the other free to gesticulate wildly.

"There will be time for business soon, lamb. I'm Apollo. What's your name, darling?" His eyelashes were obscenely long as they fluttered against his cheek. This was a man who knew how to lay it on thick.

She debated whether or not to give him her name, but she had a feeling he would badger her until she did. "Brie. And I'd rather you didn't call me darling or lamb." She crossed her arms over her chest defensively.

Apollo pouted for only a moment, then his saccharine smile returned. "And why is that, Brie dear?"

Brie's arms tightened against her chest, and she gritted her teeth in irritation. "It makes me uncomfortable. Now, are you picking up or just browsing? I have work to do if you just want to browse." His eyes roved over what he could see of her behind the counter. Brie distinctly felt like a piece of meat being sized up.

"Picking up, then. But that can wait just a little longer. Why don't we talk about me taking you—"

Wherever Apollo planned to take her was cut off by Brie picking up the hand bell on the counter and ringing it several times as hard as she could while keeping her eyes on him. Apollo's nose crinkled in mild annoyance, but it didn't displace his grin. "Oh, you didn't have to go and spoil our fun so soon," he said, looking directly at her before his gaze moved upward to a spot directly over her head.

Brie didn't need to turn around to know Ezra was there. She didn't hear the door open and close, nor did she hear his footsteps, but he was there, a solid presence at her back. Something she would have to get used to, she supposed. From the way Apollo's smile slipped just a fraction, she also knew Ezra was probably not happy to see him.

"Apollo, leave my assistant alone. She's not for you." Ezra's words were charged with an unspoken threat. He placed a heavy hand on Brie's shoulder, either to ward off Apollo or to reassure her; she wasn't sure which. His whole hand seemed to radiate electricity into the bare skin of her shoulder and through her body until she felt her entire self heat up. A few mental slaps to focus on the current situation and not on how good it felt to have Ezra touch her proved ineffectual. He gave her shoulder a slight squeeze. Brie had to stop herself from clenching her legs together and giving away her thoughts.

"You're no fun, my cranky angel. I wasn't going to do anything to her. At least, nothing she wouldn't beg me for eventually." He winked at Brie. His words made her feel sick. She couldn't decide if she wanted to punch him in his stupid smile or flee to the break room through the door behind her. Brie dismissed the second option; she wasn't going to give this Apollo creep the satisfaction of watching her walk away.

Instead, she crossed her arms and glared at him, hoping he would take the hint, get his business done, and leave. Unfortunately, this only caused Apollo's grin to widen. *Like the Cheshire Cat*, thought Brie. "She's even cuter when she's angry. So full of life! I could see us having a lot of fun together, lamb. I'll take my order now. So why don't you run to the back and get it, Arakiel dear? I'll keep little Brie here company. Take your time."

"Bridget, go to the break room." It came out as a command. "I'd rather not leave you alone with this monster." She couldn't see his face since he still stood behind her, but she knew without a doubt that a glare was fixed upon Apollo.

Brie kept her eyes trained on Apollo, tilting her chin up. "It's fine. I can handle him. Just hurry up and get what he needs so he can leave."

"Oh, I'm hardly a monster, Arak. Just a humble... Why are you shaking your head? You're giving me your 'Seriously Shut Up Face.' I haven't seen that face since my Fall." Confusion colored Apollo's face with maybe a hint of concern, though Brie wasn't certain. It was a startling change from his cocky demeanor, though it did nothing to diminish his golden beauty.

Brie noticed Ezra's free hand now gripped the counter; his knuckles had gone white from how tightly he was holding it. The hand still resting on her shoulder was gentle, just heavy and grounding. There was a feeling of safety in that touch. Brie wanted to relish in it.

Some kind of realization dawned on Apollo's face; the confusion melted away instantly, welcoming the knowing smirk once more. "I see now. She doesn't know what you are. Bet she thinks this is just a quirky little antique store and you the dreamy, yet unconventional, proprietor." He laughed.

"She is still standing here, asshole." Brie raised her voice, annoyed. Everything about this man got on her nerves. Nevertheless, what he said gave her pause. *Just who exactly is Ezra?*

Apollo's eyes turned to her now. Ezra's grip on the counter hadn't loosened from what she could see; she wondered if she had pushed it too far with Apollo. She couldn't see his face from where she stood, so she focused her attention on Apollo and hoped she wasn't about to get a reprimand on her second day for being rude to a customer. It was the coffee shop all over again.

Apollo locked his gaze with hers and leaned against the counter toward her. She glared right back. Then she noticed something unusual about his eyes. There seemed to be a glow emanating from behind those blue eyes, hypnotizing in their beauty.

"Apollo," Ezra growled. He removed his hand from Brie's shoulder finally. She felt the loss of his warmth and hated it. Apollo held up his hand to ward off Ezra, never breaking eye contact with Brie. She held his gaze.

"Little lamb, why don't we get out of here, and you let me take you to my place? By the end of the night, I'll have you screaming my name while you ride me." Apollo's eyes glowed brighter, his smile impossibly wide.

Brie kept her eyes locked on his, staring into the hypnotic glow that seemed to promise pure ecstasy if only she would follow him. She leaned across the counter toward him as if drawn to him. There was a look of triumph in his eyes.

Then she slapped him across the face.

A chuckle came from over her shoulder. In front of her, Apollo looked utterly gobsmacked, a red hand-print now adorning his handsome face. Brie was prepared for him to scream or get angry. What she did not expect was for Apollo to start laughing.

"Well, that's never happened before. Nobody has ever resisted the ol' charm. What are you, darling?" Apollo looked at her, now not with his lusty charm, but with wonder and maybe even respect. She didn't care for this kind of attention from him either.

Ezra spoke before she could respond, "She's a hedgewitch, Apollo, and my assistant. Now, do you want your shit or not?" He was annoyed. All traces of the amusement she had heard a moment ago were gone. Apollo kept his eyes trained on Brie, barely acknowledging Ezra.

"Hedgewitch? How common. Oh, I think you're more than that, lamb. But sure, go get my stuff, angel man. I have things to do anyway and people to seduce who will actually take me up on my offer." He directed that last with a wink toward Brie. She wanted to take offense at his tone. She may be a homebody, but she wasn't boring. Her mind, however, focused instead on what he called her. Hedgewitch. Lily had called her that, too. Did they both somehow know she was a practicing pagan? It wasn't like she openly advertised it. Maybe Lily was part of the local community or something. But that didn't explain why Ezra called her that or why Apollo seemed to know exactly what it meant. She didn't even know what it meant. Sure, she identified as a witch, practicing the craft Maddy had taught her, but she had never been called a hedgewitch before. She made a mental note to ask Ezra later. Then her thoughts shifted through Apollo's words. *He called Ezra an angel, same as Lily. Is it some pet name they all share? What if he is involved with both of them, like a throuple?* Something sank heavily in her stomach.

"Apollo, just stand right where you are and don't look at anything. Don't speak, either." Ezra pointed an accusing finger at Apollo for emphasis. Then he bent down to whisper to Brie, his breath tickling her ear, "If he tries anything, you have my permission to maim him in any way you see fit. You won't be fired. So long as you are here, I promise to protect you." Those words shouldn't sound as good as they did to Brie.

Then he went through the door, and Brie was left alone with Apollo once more. She tried to focus on the computer instead of the irritating man before her, but Apollo was not one to be ignored, it seemed. "He's a bit of an ass, but he loves me. Deep down. Somewhere in the dregs of his black heart, it's there. Probably."

Brie kept her focus on the computer screen while pretending to type. "Mm-hmm, sure." Her part in the conversation was over. After slapping him across the face, she hoped he would lose interest in her altogether.

That didn't seem to be the case because he kept talking. "Funny that Arakiel would keep a hedgewitch around. My cranky angel friend is getting soft in his old age." Apollo smiled to himself, as if he had told a private joke.

It seemed like a good moment to ask someone who knew. "Why do you keep calling me a—"

As she spoke, Ezra burst through the Storage Room door, an oblong package wrapped in brown paper in his arms. This time, he made plenty of noise as he came back into the room. He shoved the box into Apollo's arms. "There. Now get out," Ezra said with an edge in his voice.

Apollo flashed his perfectly white teeth. "Shouldn't I pay first?"

Ezra returned the smile with a stony glare. "I'll put it on your tab. Now go. Leave Bridget alone from now on, or I'm banning you from the store." Apollo was unfazed by Ezra's threat. With a grin and a little wave to Brie from under the package, he chimed, "Goodbye for now, darling. Maybe the next time we meet, I can use this on you." He indicated to the package and winked. Then he was gone.

For several moments after his departure, Ezra stood at the counter fuming while Brie watched him from the corner of her eye. She pretended to type while she gave him a minute to calm down. "Do I even want to know what's in that package?" she asked hesitantly.

"You really don't." Ezra shook his head. "I mean it, Bridget. If Apollo makes you uncomfortable or pisses you off, and he's exceptionally good at the second, do not be afraid to defend yourself. Your job here is safe. He won't call the police or anything. And really, he needs to be brought down a peg or three." Ezra looked directly at her now. Brie turned to face him, looking up to acknowledge his words. She nodded in response, feeling suddenly grateful.

"What's a hedgewitch?" she asked, though she wasn't sure why she asked that first. It wasn't that she didn't appreciate Ezra's words, but curiosity burned brighter and there was already plenty to pique her curiosity.

If the abrupt question caught him off guard, he didn't show it.

He looked away from her, though. "Simply that you are a solitary witch, one that channels with your intent rather than with any real magic." Brie hoped he didn't mean for it to sound as condescending as it did. She didn't know Ezra well, so she couldn't be sure. Still, she felt compelled to defend herself.

"Magic is what we send out into the world. Just because I don't practice with others or with a coven doesn't mean my magic is any less. There's power in herbs and green things, even if it's just for me." She finally gave up the pretense of typing and turned fully toward Ezra.

He wasn't impressed by her response, though. "The thing you call magic is merely happy thoughts you send out into the world. It's not real magic."

She rolled her eyes before she was even conscious of doing so. "It's real enough for me. There's no such thing like Gandalf-wizard magic."

Ezra's eyes rippled with confusion at her response. "I don't know what that means."

Brie raised her eyebrows; there was no way Ezra was that obtuse. He couldn't be older than thirty-five or so. He had to have seen the movies at least. "You don't know *Lord of the Rings*?"

"Is that the grey one or magic terrorist with the blue guy? Either way, it hardly pertains to work, which we are not doing. Records, Bridget. How is that coming along?" His face hardened into what Bridget now decided was his "boss" look.

So he is going to be like that, she thought.

Brie looked back at the computer, then down at the ledger on the counter. Before Apollo, arrived, she was making good progress. But the last thirty or so minutes had completely derailed her. "Coming along great, actually. I'll keep at it. But if more ... colorful characters keep coming in, I'm never getting anything done."

Was that an easing of his stern frown? Maybe. But his face remained impassible. "I know that a few of my Thursday regulars are out of town, so it should be quiet now. If you need me, ring the bell. I need to finish up in the Storage Room." Without another word, he turned to the Storage Room door, but before he disappeared, he turned toward her for a last parting glance. Then he was gone. Brie was left alone in the store.

Ezra was right; it was completely quiet for the remainder of her shift. It crossed her mind several times as she worked that he didn't seem to need the help when nobody came in during the later hours. Then again, she reasoned, it could have something to do with the Storage Room project, since her presence up front meant he could work in the back. Curiosity wiggled in the back of her brain, wondering what he was working on back there. She had yet to see inside the Storage Room; it had to be sizable enough, probably filled with more junk that didn't fit on the shelves out front.

Just before ten, Ezra popped through the door, a sheen of sweat on his brow. He looked exhausted. Whatever the customer request was, it was clearly labor intensive. "That will be all for today, Bridget," he said.

Brie blinked several times at the computer screen as if seeing the contents for the first time. Hours spent staring at all that text and neat handwriting had started to blur her vision. Still in a bit of a fog, she heaved herself from the stool and bent to grab her bag.

"Oh, I almost forgot. Here." She reached into her messenger bag and pulled out the clothes he had loaned her the day before. "Thanks again for the dry clothes. And don't worry—I washed them."

Ezra took the offered clothes from her hands, their fingers barely brushing, sending little waves of electricity up Brie's arm. He drew away and tucked the folded sweats under his arm. He nodded once. "I took the liberty of washing the clothes you left behind. They are under the counter there." He indicated with one finger a couple of shelves next to where Brie had been working.

A bundle wrapped neatly in brown paper and tied up with twine sat on the shelves; nothing else. Brie stared at the package for several seconds. It hadn't been there before. There had been nothing there before, not even shelves; she was sure of it. Well, mostly sure. Probably sure. With a shake of her head, she chalked it up to fatigue and picked up the wrapped clothes before shoving them into her bag. A sudden wave of relief overcame her as she reminded herself he didn't wash her underthings. Then she threw the bag's strap over her shoulder.

"Are all your customers so ... odd?" she asked, fumbling with the right words.

Ezra's smile was faint but there. "Yes, I daresay they are. Goodnight, Bridget."

Brie sucked in her bottom lip. "You can just call me Brie." If she was being honest with herself, hearing her full name out of his mouth with that voice was too much. It made her feel too heated.

Unaware of her thoughts on his voice, Ezra responded, "I prefer Bridget if that's alright with you. It's a beautiful name, and it suits you."

That was too much. There was no stopping the blush on her cheeks or the feeling of fire rushing straight to her core. She shrugged, playing it as cool as she could. "Sure, that's fine. I mean, I like my name, just most people call me Brie. So no big deal." It would be a very big deal if he continued to say her name like that.

"Goodnight, Bridget." He was amused, but it was still a dismissal.

"Goodnight," she said, then stepped away from the counter and out of the store.

The bell tinkled as she walked out into the night.

Chapter 4

"Don't forget the reading next week. The pages are on the syllabus. If you have any questions or topic ideas, you can post them to the discussion group page. You can also come see me during my office hours on Tuesday."

Brie shut her laptop and stuffed it into her bag as she watched her undergraduate students do the same. The older students were only a few years younger than Brie, something that weirded her out just a little. She enjoyed teaching, and since the class was in the late morning, people actually showed up.

For now, at least.

Today's class wasn't particularly exciting, though. Since it was the beginning of the term, there wasn't much going on other than syllabus review and the first bit of reading.

"Hey, Brie." A voice dragged her out of her head as she swung her bag over her shoulder. Standing across from the lecture table was one of her students, an easy smile on his face. She always asked her students to call her Brie. Being called Ms. St. James wigged her out.

"Hi, Craig. I didn't expect you to take another history class. You're a math major, right?" She recognized him from two classes she had taught the previous year, one each semester. He had a bad habit of making moon eyes at her and had always stopped by during her office hours.

Craig nervously scratched the back of his head and averted his eyes, cheeks pink. *So he continued carrying that torch over the summer.* "I needed to get some credit hours in, and I just really liked the way you teach. I only have classes for my major left."

Brie nodded distractedly; she didn't really care. "Well, cool. Glad to have you back. Did you have a question?" Pleasantries were definitely not her strong suit.

"Oh, uh, yeah. Some of us seniors were heading to the Union tonight. Would you like to come? For some start of the year chill. Not that you need to chill, but before the onslaught of bad papers, maybe," Craig rambled, grin faltering as he couldn't seem to stop his mouth. He looked up at her with hopeful eyes.

Brie had no interest in hanging out with him, or any of her students, for that matter. "Thanks, but I'm working tonight. Maybe some other time." She kept her tone casual. She should probably shut him down firmly, but he wasn't being pushy, and she didn't want to hurt his feelings.

"No worries. How about tomorrow? I hear there's this cool band playing at Casa. Could be fun," he persisted.

Brie sighed. "Can't. I work Friday and Saturday nights." If she had hoped that would put an end to it, she was wrong. He followed her as she headed toward the door.

"Damn, that must blow. Dr. Fry must be a real hardass to make you work over the weekend," he said with sympathy.

Dr. Catherine Fry, her dissertation advisor, and mentor, truly was a hardass, but the woman also valued time away from work and never pushed Brie to overdo it. "The best work is done when a mind is at ease," she always said.

"It's not her. I have a second job outside the university." Brie was tired of the conversation already. It was her fault it continued; she was being too friendly with him. She always felt like she had to be nice to her students. A fatal flaw, it seemed.

Craig nodded. "Cool, cool. Where do you work? Maybe I could drop by and say hey and bring some snacks or something this weekend." He was practically bouncing as he walked beside her. Brie was ready to scream for him to leave her alone. Instead, she kept herself neutral. After all, she was stuck with the guy in her class the whole semester.

"That's not a great idea. I just started, and I don't want my boss to think I'm not working or anything. Secondly, I don't date students. Let's just keep it professional." Craig looked like he was about to say something; she interrupted him. "Anyway, I have a meeting with Dr. Fry. I'll see you in class next week. Bye." Was she running away? Yes. She made her way quickly to her professor's office. She didn't actually have a meeting with her advisor, but it seemed like a good excuse to keep Craig from following her farther.

Dr. Fry was usually in her office when she wasn't teaching, so it wasn't a surprise to Brie when Dr. Fry called her in after she knocked. Behind the cluttered desk sat a small woman with gray-streaked brown hair cut into a fierce bob just past her chin. Coke-bottle glasses magnified her brown eyes. From Brie's vantage point, she could see Dr. Fry was wearing one of her signature knitted sweater vests. This one had several colorful leaves in browns, reds, and oranges with a crocheted squirrel.

She smiled warmly at Brie as the younger woman entered the cramped office. "Hello, Brie. Did we have a meeting scheduled? I didn't see anything on my calendar."

Brie shook her head. "No, sorry. I just thought I would drop in to let you know the first week with the class went great. This batch might be interested in learning something, too. We'll see how week two goes." *It wasn't my best excuse, but it should work all the same,* Brie thought. She wasn't about to tell her advisor she was avoiding a student.

Dr. Fry seemed to accept it. She smiled; the subtle lines around her mouth crinkled. "Very good. Maybe you'll convert a few of them to the history department. But please don't feel you have to give me status reports after every session. It's your class, Brie. I have the utmost confidence in you."

"Thanks, professor. That means a lot to me. Okay, well, I won't keep you then. I'll see you on Thursday next week." Brie didn't linger, just waved as Dr. Fry gave her another smile before returning her attention to the notes on her desk.

Brie stopped just outside Dr. Fry's closed door to check down both sides of the hallway. Satisfied that Craig had a decent head start and it was unlikely she would run into him again, she walked out of Bassett Hall and headed toward the campus library.

Wes was working at one of the reference desks when she arrived. As she approached him, Wes thrust a brown paper bag at her, which she gratefully took once she was within arm's reach.

"Forgot your lunch again, Little Witch. That's the third time this week, and it's only the first week of classes," he said with a reproachful look. But he laughed as Brie started to pick through the bag. He never really gave her too hard a time.

"Thanks. It's been a weird few days. But I think I just had the weirdest thing of all happen," she said as she pulled out a plastic-wrapped sandwich.

Wes tilted his head inquisitively. "Go on," he said.

"One of the guys in my lecture asked me out. He's not even a history student; he just keeps taking my classes anyway." Her tone implied that being a non-history student was the bigger offense.

"The one who's been making flirty eyes at you since last year? Aww, how sweet, you have an admirer—ouch!" Wes yelped dramatically as Brie punched his arm. "Fine, it's gross. You're not going out with him, right? You're like his teacher. That would be super awkward."

Brie started to unwrap the peanut butter and jelly sandwich. "So awkward! I told him I had to work this weekend and that I don't date students. I can't be more clear than that." She sighed.

"Good, because undergrads are nasty and immature. Don't date anyone under twenty-five." He waved his hand, indicating he was changing topics. "So, how is the job going so far? You didn't say much when you got home last night. Are you still packing the herbs like I asked?"

Brie took a large bite of the sandwich before responding. She leaned against the desk, sandwich still in hand. "The herbs have stayed at the bottom of my bag, so don't worry. And the work right now is just basic data entry. It's a little boring. But it's the customers that are the strange part. They're... I don't know what you would call them. Odd, maybe?"

"Odd how?" Wes's eyebrows drew together, his face morphing into a mask of concern. Brie waved him off and took another bite of sandwich to delay her response.

"Not like in a bad way. Well, most of them not in a really bad way. Just different. I don't know. It's hard to explain. But Ezra hasn't given me a reason to be concerned about them," she said with a shrug.

"Oh, so it's Ezra. First name basis and everything." Wes rolled his eyes in exasperation. He didn't approve of her lusting over her boss even a little.

She shrugged again. "He hasn't told me not to call him Ezra. And it's not like he gave me a last name. I can't just call him Mr. Whatever. He's been a good boss so far."

"Hold your judgment until you get through your performanc review. He might just decide to fire you," Wes tweaked her nose with a grin.

Brie flinched and wrinkled her nose. She shoved the last bite of sandwich into her mouth. "I highly doubt that." She swallowed. "Besides, he's nice to look at when he's not working in the back, so that's a good incentive to stick around with the odd things."

Wes pressed his hands together, pleading, "Please don't fuck your boss, Brie. That's almost as bad as dating your student."

Brie snorted. "I'm not going to sleep with him, Wes. He's just a cute guy and probably the least odd thing in that whole place so far. And he's age-appropriate." Wes glared. "And I like the job enough that I don't want to mess things up. Besides, he's way too broody for me."

"Good. Remember that." He pointed at her face. "Anyway, I have to get back to work. See you at home?"

Brie shoved the rest of the paper bag into her messenger bag. "Sure, I'll see you after work tonight." Brie turned from the desk and headed toward the exit.

"Make smart choices!" Wes called out to her.

Brie turned and flipped him off before leaving the library.

"Ezra! I have no idea what this says," Brie yelled through the slightly open door to the Storage Room. The ledger book was in her hands; she screwed up her face as she stared at the page again as if that would somehow help her understand what was written there.

Several seconds later, Ezra appeared at the door, crowding her until she backed up enough to let him pass through the threshold. "There are probably plenty of things in there that you may not know. Just type what you see. It's not that hard, Bridget." His tone was direct but not condescending.

Brie shot him her best annoyed look. "Yeah, I've been doing that. What I mean is that I literally can't read what this says because the letters are not from the Latin alphabet. I'm pretty sure it's Greek, which I don't know." Her focus returned to the book, hoping it would suddenly make sense. It didn't.

"Let me see." Ezra took the book from her hands and peered down at the entry she indicated with her finger. "? Oh, it's an urn. Origin's obviously Greek. I think it's from around the 5th-century common era. Shelf E, row 2. Usually. It likes to move sometimes, so it might not be there."

"Right, totally makes sense. Let me just add that in the notes: 'moves around a lot.'" Brie didn't hide the sarcasm in her voice; she thought his response was a little stupid.

It seemed that Ezra did not appreciate her tone. "Just make the note. If you have a problem with that, you can leave." His eyes were stern; there was no heat behind them. Still, Brie couldn't help but feel like a chastised child.

"Sorry, my default is sarcasm. You can blame foster care for that. It's your system, so I'll just make the note." She walked back to the computer with the ledger book, not making eye contact with Ezra to avoid feeling like she had just royally fucked up.

He sighed loudly. "It's fine. I'm just frustrated right now. It's not your fault." She gave him an understanding nod. His footsteps retreated through the Storage Room door, leaving her with only the ledger book and computer for company again.

Ezra stayed in the back for the next three hours. Occasionally, Brie thought she heard a distant clang or bang, but not much else. Not for the first time, she wondered just how expansive the Storage Room was. She still had not peeked inside, having decided that it was Ezra's domain until he gave her more responsibilities.

At a quarter past nine, the door opened and a cool breeze swept through the shop, despite it being a warm September evening. Brie looked up just as the bell tinkled only to find a woman standing directly in front of her, nearly causing her to tumble off her stool. *How did she cross the room so quickly?*

Standing before Brie was an incredibly tall, pale woman with auburn hair piled on top of her head in an elegant chignon with just the perfect number of wisps of hair to frame her angular face. Her eyes were shockingly dark for being so fair. The floor-length, forest green dress she wore still swished slightly from her movement.

"Goddess, you scared me." Brie clutched at her chest, feeling her heart beat quickly beneath her fingertips. The woman in green smiled. It wasn't a comforting sight. It was a wicked smile that didn't reach her dark eyes. That smile gave Brie a chill down her spine; it was unnerving. A primal instinct within her screamed danger.

"I tend to have that effect on people. Where's Ezra?" the woman asked in a clipped Scottish accent.

Brie steeled her nerves and tried to regain her composure, unsure why she was even feeling that way. "He's in the back. Are you picking up?"

"Yes, tell him it's for Helena. He'll know what to get." She waved her hand dismissively, her shining nails painted to match the dress.

The service hand bell still sat on the counter. Brie ignored it. Instead, she walked to the Storage Room door and shouted through the crack she made as she opened it. "Ezra, Helena is here. Can you bring up her order?" Brie did not look away from Helena as she called out; rather, she turned her head just enough that her voice carried through the door. In return, Helena smiled that wicked grin again. Brie had to suppress the shudder that threatened to overtake her body. Something told her not to turn her back on this woman.

Suddenly, the crack widened enough for Brie to be pulled through into the Storage Room. Ezra's strong grip dragged her into the room while still keeping her on her feet. "What the—" Brie started, then looked up at her boss's face; she shut her mouth.

Ezra looked down at her with genuine concern. His eyes roved over her face, neck, and arms quickly, even as he kept a firm hold of her upper arm. "Are you okay? She didn't hurt you or anything?" *Is that panic in his voice?*

Normally, Brie would have wrenched her arm back from anyone who grabbed at her, but she could see that he was a little panicked; that scared her all the more. "I'm fine. She didn't do anything other than be super pretty and super creepy. Who is she?"

His grip started to dig into her arm, causing some pain. She put her hand over Ezra's to coax him to loosen his fingers. He immediately released her arm, letting his hand fall to his side. His eyes fell to his hand, either in regret at hurting her or touching her in the first place.

"Helena. She usually comes in on Sundays. If I had known she was coming in today, I wouldn't have left you up there alone." He raked a hand through his hair, blowing out a breath.

"Is she dangerous? Why does it seem like half of your customers are, like, super creepy, possibly super dangerous people?" She tried for levity in her tone, but it bordered on hysterical.

Ezra ran a hand over his face. "She's not a good person, Bridget. But she won't do anything in my store."

"Then why sell to her at all? Does she really spend enough money to risk something happening?" Brie couldn't hide the confusion on her face.

"It's not about how much she spends. It's what I sell to her. It keeps her from really doing harm. You could say she's on the road to recovery, and I supply her with the means to kick the habit."

"And some antiques keep her from being a psycho with a drug problem?" she asked with a skeptically raised brow.

"Sure," Ezra said shortly, turning from Brie to look over at an industrial-sized shelf close to the door.

There was definitely something weird about the whole situation. "You know all this doesn't make a ton of sense." Her tone was accusatory.

"I know." He didn't elaborate.

She turned her head, finally taking in the Storage Room. The loud gasp that escaped her seemed to echo forever.

The Storage Room was large, impossibly large, cavernous large. Despite there being no steps between the front of the shop and the Storage Room, there was no mistaking that she was underground, deep underground. No matter how much Brie strained her eyes, she couldn't seem to see the back wall or even the side walls. From the few dimly illuminated rows she could see ahead of her, the entire area, as far as the eye could see, was filled with rows and rows of large industrial shelves packed with random items and tidy brown crates. She stood with Ezra on some type of small raised platform, only a foot or so off the ground. The only thing on the platform was the industrial shelf Ezra now stood before. This shelf was stuffed with neatly wrapped packages of various sizes and shapes. Each one had a small tag attached, presumably with the name of the person buying it.

The whole of the Storage Room was overwhelming and impossible. Brie could not comprehend how it existed just beyond a simple door in an antique shop in the middle of the city. "Wha... how... how is this possible?" She didn't even care that her jaw was hanging wide open in awe. Her eyes darted around to look at everything before her, finding no end in sight.

"It just is. Come on. Let's get this to Helena and get her out," Ezra said behind her. He grabbed Brie's arm again, gently this time, as he pulled her through the Storage Room door. Brie didn't take her eyes off the room until Ezra shut the door after they were through it. He let go of her arm, dropping the appendage as if it burned him. Her attention was drawn back to the woman in the green dress.

"Took you long enough," she said to Brie, not Ezra, drumming her perfectly manicured nails on the counter.

"I wasn't expecting you until Sunday, Helena. I only just got this ready earlier today," Ezra said with unchecked disdain. Instead of handing her a package, he slid a thin envelope over the counter. Helena picked it up quickly and put it in the purse she carried.

"I'm afraid I'll be busy Sunday. Moloc is in town, and he has need of me. Oh, don't look so stricken, Ezra. He'll be around to see you, too." Helena smiled at the glowering look Ezra shot her way. She extended her own envelope, which Ezra ripped from her hand and shoved into the back pocket of his black jeans.

"Tell him that's necessary. Now get out, Helena. And use the normal exit." His head nodded ever so slightly toward Brie, who had sat back at the computer pretending to type. She noticed the nod.

Helena grinned; this time it reached her eyes with a terrifying gleam. "How cute, Ezra. You've got yourself a pet. Well then, until next week. And be alert to his summons. He won't take no for an answer." She turned on her heel and walked slowly out of the store, hips swaying. Brie and Ezra watched her leave; Ezra with a glare while Brie stared in confusion, maybe fear. Her eyes were drawn to the bottom of Helena's dress, where her feet should have poked out with each step; however, Brie thought she saw the hooves of a deer instead of feet. When the shop door shut, Brie whirled to Ezra. "I have questions!"

Ezra massaged his temples, averting his gaze from her. "I figured you would. Save them for tomorrow. We'll discuss your questions at your one-month review."

"No, I want them answered now," she demanded.

"Go home, Bridget. That's all for today. I will see you at six tomorrow." Ezra turned and pressed the one button on the panel next to the Storage Room door. As soon as he was over the threshold, the door slammed shut behind him.

For five minutes, Brie stood at the counter, fuming and waiting—partially because she wanted to ensure Helena had a good head start and she wouldn't accidentally run into the woman on the street. Something told Brie that would not end well. And partially to see if Ezra would return to the shop front, which he didn't.

When enough time had passed, Brie grabbed her bag and headed home.

She walked through the door of her and Wes's apartment and was greeted by the sight of her brother on the couch with a book in his lap. He smiled warmly as she entered, but his brows instantly furrowed as he took in her face.

"Brie, what's wrong?"

"I think I might be in over my head, Wes." Goddess, her heart was racing.

Wes set his book aside and patted the space next to him on the couch. "Take a seat, Little Witch, and tell me all about it."

Brie dropped her bag next to the door, shucking off her shoes as she crossed the space. With an exaggerated thud, she planted herself on the couch and flung herself sideways, so her feet landed on Wes's lap.

"What's going on? Something happen at work?" Wes placed his hands over her ankles, resting them there as he looked at his sister with concern.

Brie sighed and ran a hand over her face. "I don't know. Nothing exactly happened. But like ... have you ever been in a situation where everyone seems to be in on something, but you're not?"

"Literally every day of my life." Wes deadpanned, then motioned for her to continue.

"Yeah, well, that's what it feels like right now. There are all of these regulars, and they're all pretty out there. Ezra said he would discuss it all with me tomorrow and answer my questions. But even he seems like a big ass mystery wrapped in a really good-looking package." She flopped back against the couch and stared at the ceiling.

She told him about the different people she had met so far and the impossibility of the Storage Room. He didn't say anything while he listened to her; he just nodded his head when it was appropriate.

Wes gave her ankle a reassuring squeeze. "You can always quit if you're uncomfortable. Maybe I can get you a job at the library instead."

This time Brie groaned. "You know those jobs are super competitive and hard to get. You got it on a fluke!"

"Blowing one of the librarians hardly seems like a fluke." Wes laughed.

One of Brie's feet lifted from his lap and shoved into his side. "I don't want to hear that! You're my big brother. You're supposed to pretend like you never have sex and keep my young mind chaste." She laughed.

With little ceremony, Wes pushed her ankles off his lap and let them fall to the floor, sending Brie off balance on the couch. "There is nothing young or chaste about your mind, or the rest of you, for that matter. And you heard worse when Maddy gave us The Talk in very thorough detail."

Brie gave an exaggerated shudder. "I still don't know why she felt the need to print off diagrams. Or why she had to do it with both of us together. That kind of thing seems like it should have been one-on-one."

Wes laughed. "She said it was easier to do it once than to have to repeat herself."

They sat chuckling together for a minute at the memory. "Goddess, I miss her so much," Brie said sadly.

With one arm thrown around her shoulder, Wes gave her a squeeze. "Me too, Little Witch." He paused, letting them have the moment to think of Maddy. "So, what are you going to do about the shop? It's really okay if you want to quit. I totally support your decision."

She shrugged. "I don't know. It's pretty weird, and some of the people there make me... Uncomfortable seems to only scratch the surface of what I feel, but yeah, that." She smoothed back her ponytail and plucked out the various writing tools she had stashed throughout the day, then she pulled off the elastic and let her hair tumble down in a mess of ginger waves.

"I'll sleep on it. Everything is better after sleep," she said as she stood up and stretched.

"How would you know? It's not like you sleep," Wes said and dodged the pillow Brie had picked up from the couch and threw at him. "You hungry? I think there are some Cheerios left in the box. Milk might be questionable."

A shrug was her answer as she padded over to their small open kitchen. The content of the refrigerator was sparse; neither had picked up groceries yet. Brie grabbed the carton of milk, gave it a shake, then opened it to sniff the contents. Good enough.

With a small bowl of stale Cheerios swimming in end-of-life milk, she bid her brother goodnight and shut herself in her room. With any luck, a decision would come to her quickly, and she could go straight to sleep. But it never worked out that way, even when she didn't have difficult decisions to make.

Once her cereal was done and the empty bowl sat on her desk, Brie laid down on her bed and stared at the ceiling. It was easy for her mind to conjure up the image of emerald eyes and the smell of woodsmoke and vanilla. But sleep did not come easy, even with her thoughts drifting toward Ezra. Several times now, she'd had an overwhelming sense of fear caused by the shop's patrons. Several instances in only a handful of weeks.

Am I safe working at the shop?

Ezra said he would protect me, but that isn't exactly comforting. And what about him? Clearly, there is something *+-more to him and his shop.

Brie had to ask herself if she could overlook the weirdness and keep the job she needed or if she should get the hell out.

The answer wasn't so easy; sleep evaded her for a long time.

CHAPTER 5

Brie stood outside of Spirit Antiques for a long time. It was already after six, but still, she stood in front of the door, unsure as to whether she was going in to quit or just not going in at all.

After speaking with Wes the night before, he had encouraged her to quit. Not because he believed her about the strange things and people she had met, but because he thought Ezra was drugging her or something9. At least, that was his latest theory. Brie knew that wasn't the case. There was no drugging. However, Ezra was definitely hiding something about the entire business. It wasn't drugs or hallucinations; there was something much more significant about the shop than she had been led to believe. *What if he is selling drugs?* she thought. *What if he has, like, a whole drug empire?* That would explain the weird people, including those that felt dangerous, even though he kept saying they were kicking an addiction.

There are things from stories that shop at the antique store. An impossibly large space occupies the back room in what should be a small space. In the middle of it all is my new boss, Ezra, who is obviously more than he seems. It sounded ridiculous, even as she thought it to herself. It was probably drugs. What else could it be?

Brie had so many questions, but she was also afraid of the answers. So she continued to stand outside the door, undecided. Ignorance was bliss; then again, Brie wasn't truly that ignorant anymore, was she? The burning need to know more, to slake her curiosity, overwhelmed her brain.

With a deep breath and a silent prayer to the goddess, she walked through the door into the shop. The little bell announced her arrival from above.

From across the room, her eyes met Ezra's. He stood behind the counter and stared straight at her. He had likely been staring at her through the glass in the door while she had stood undecided outside. Frozen at the doorway now, Brie could only stare at him.

"You're late," Ezra said, breaking the silence with an even voice, no judgment or irritation.

Brie started as if snapped from a trance. Compelling her feet to move toward him took a push of will. "I couldn't decide if it was better to come inside or run back home and stay in bed forever," she said, stopping short of the counter across from him.

Cocking his head slightly, Ezra didn't break his stare. "You stood outside for thirty minutes. After more than five minutes, you should have had your answer when you didn't run screaming home. Don't let it happen again."

"How do you know I'm going to stay?" There was a challenge in her voice, one she didn't immediately intend even as she lifted her chin.

Ezra smirked slightly, crossing his arms over his chest with an arrogant flair. "You will. You are curious; you have to know things." He turned, pressed the number two button on the panel, and opened the Storage Room door.

"I still have questions," she said as she walked around the counter.

"I know, and as I said yesterday, they will be answered at your review. We will do it at the end of your shift. Now, I'm heading back into the Storage Room. There's tea in the break room for you; just wait until the door is shut completely, then press four on the panel. And Bridget," he turned to fully face her, eyes intent, "I don't deal drugs in my shop." Then he was gone, the door clicking shut after him. Brie dropped her bag with little ceremony. Frustration filled her at the thought of working a whole shift before getting some answers. *What is he: a mind reader?* How could he know what she was thinking about?

Checking to ensure no one was coming in, she stomped over to the door, pressed the number four button with more force than was necessary, and walked through the door.

So far, Brie had only seen the Storage Room and Ezra's office, which were both impressive spaces, yet the break room was still unexpected. It was by far the smallest space she had seen yet. It looked more like a small solarium than a break room. Everywhere she looked, there seemed to be green plants and blooming flowers. The air smelled of flowers and turned earth. One wall was just floor-to-ceiling windows looking out on still more green and noonday spring sunshine, even though it was a gloomy September evening in the middle of a city. There was a simple wicker couch with a light floral patterned cushion against another wall with a matching wicker coffee table before it. The far back wall across from the entrance held a small kitchenette, complete with a single burner stove, a tiny sink, and a bit of counter space with cabinets above. Brie half expected the floor to be grass; instead, it was smooth, light wood.

Sitting on the kitchenette counter was a filled teacup and saucer, still steaming as if it had been freshly poured not a second before.

The room was impossible, of course. There was no way Ezra could have decorated it for himself if his office and personal style were indications of his tastes.

Is it possible he decorated this for me?

Tentatively, Brie crossed the small space and picked up the teacup. The china was white porcelain with little crows painted on both the cup and the saucer. The painted crows looked incredibly similar to the tattoos on her forearms. No, they were exactly the same.

How?

She sat down on the wicker couch, breathing in the scent of the tea once settled. Taking a small sip, she was delighted to discover it was a black tea prepared just to her liking: four sugars and a splash of milk. She downed the rest of the tea in less than a minute as she enjoyed the sensation of the hot liquid fortifying her. As she set the empty cup on the wicker table, she let out a loud gasp; the cup began to refill itself with the same type of tea she had just finished, perfectly prepared and steamy.

Brie stared at the cup for what must have been a solid minute before she dared to reach out a shaky hand and pick up the teacup.

The room now seemed utterly overwhelming. Brie made a hasty exit back to the familiar and took her place at the counter. The teacup and saucer she set on the countertop after taking another gulp. As strange and a little frightening as it may be, it was still full of tea.

For the next four hours, Brie found it incredibly hard to focus on the ledger book. Every time she finished the cup of tea, it simply refilled itself. No matter how long she ignored it, the tea was always the perfect temperature when she went to take a sip.

At ten o'clock on the dot, Ezra appeared from the Storage Room. Brie was off the stool in half a second, dancing in place in front of him. "Thank the goddess! Where's the bathroom?!" she practically yelled in his face. The time for dignity was gone when a full bladder was concerned.

"That was not the question I thought you would have for me." Ezra gave her an amused look.

Brie glared at him, her dancing becoming more frantic. "Ezra, I have had like seven cups of tea. Either tell me where the bathroom is, or I'm just going to piss myself right here on the floor!"

"There's one in the break room." He pointed to the door.

"Okay, I was in the break room earlier, and charming though it is, there was no bathroom. What are you—" She was cut off by Ezra as he actually shoved her through the door after pushing the four button. There, off to the side of the break room, was a door that most certainly wasn't there the last time Brie was in the room.

"There wasn't a bathroom in there earlier!" The Storage Room door slammed shut behind her as she stomped out of the break room.

"Why did you drink so much tea if you didn't know if there was a bathroom?" The glint of amusement in his eye further annoyed Brie.

Brie's eyes focused on the full teacup sitting where she had left it next to the computer. "I... uh... well, it kept refilling, and I didn't know how to make it stop." It sounded stupid now that she said it out loud. There was nothing compelling her to drink other than a compulsion to not waste. A byproduct of one of her foster homes, undoubtedly.

Ezra picked up the cup and drained it in one go. "That is entirely too sweet." He grimaced, then turned the teacup upside down onto the saucer. "Just flip it over when you are finished. Otherwise, the cup will keep refilling itself. This one especially gets a little overzealous."

"Okay, we are nearing the breaking point of my sanity. I think it's time you explained all this," she gestured to indicate the shop, "in detail. You can start with the teacup since it's the easiest." Widening her stance and crossing her arms, she waited for a response.

Ezra brushed past her, pushed the number one button on the panel, and opened the door to his office. "You'll want to get comfortable, and I can promise you will want something stronger than tea."

She glared at him for a long moment; he matched it with unnerving calm. She marched past him and through the door to sit down heavily on the leather couch in front of the lit fireplace. The office looked the same as it did the last time she was there. It had an Ezra vibe, unlike the break room. Brie's eyes swept the room. However, her attention was quickly drawn back toward Ezra as he nudged a glass into her hands. An amber liquid swirled inside; a small taste confirmed it was whiskey. Normally, Brie hated the taste of whiskey, but this one spread a pleasant warmth all the way down to her toes, not to mention its galvanizing effects.

With his own glass in one hand, Ezra used the other to pull one of the leather armchairs from his desk closer to the couch, keeping some distance between them. They sat in the glow of the fireplace in silence, Brie staring down into the glass, Ezra watching her, waiting. Under normal circumstances, the setting and privacy would have sent Brie's head hurdling into a lust-filled craze. Right now, she didn't know what to feel.

Brie took a deep breath, then gulped down the remainder of her whiskey before starting. "So... what is this place? Really, I mean."

"It's an antique shop." Ezra's face betrayed nothing. No hint of a smile or anything.

"And is that all it is?" Her voice was firm, accusing even, but she couldn't look at him directly.

"No, it's way more than that." There was a hint of wonder in his tone.

"And what about you? Are you just a shop owner, or a guy into weird stuff, or whatever?" It was harder than she had initially thought it would be to arrange her thoughts into cohesive questions.

"Are you sure want to know, Bridget? Once I tell you everything, there's no going back. There's no pretending all of this doesn't exist." He stared at her until she was forced to look up at him. His eyes seemed to emphasize the severity of his words. But then, she could see him begging; his eyes seemed to say "trust me." Strangely, she did.

"That Apollo guy kept calling you an angel, and so did Lily. Is that what you are?" She didn't avert her gaze this time; instead she kept her eyes locked on his as she sucked in her bottom lip. Ezra's eyes shifted to her mouth; he looked away and took a sip of his whiskey before responding.

"Yes," he paused, "and no."

"That's hardly an answer, Ezra," Brie huffed. Patience was not one of her virtues. Ezra sighed and drained his glass before he started to speak again.

"I was an angel once. But then I had my Fall and I came to live among humans. Technically, I guess I am still an angel, just a fallen one. Any angel that makes the Fall is considered a fallen angel. By your human standards, I have lived countless lifetimes. Most angels don't stay down here this long. It's unheard of really to be a permanent resident."

"Why?" she asked. Not that she actually believed him, but she was willing to go along with it for now.

"Why what?" He raised a brow at the question.

"Why did you fall? Is there like a heaven you rebelled against or something?" She was vaguely familiar with biblical stories. Several of the homes she had stayed in as a kid were ultra-religious, but it wasn't for Brie.

Ezra's face became thoughtful. "Not heaven, exactly. It's more like the place where all things begin and end. We call it the Above. It's a complicated story, really. There wasn't some catastrophic Fall like in human stories. Any angel can Fall at any time for any reason. I wanted more than what the Above could give me. I wanted to spread knowledge to humans. There were some more personal reasons, but those are my own to keep."

Brie didn't push him further.

"And how long have you been running this place?" Brie figured that Ezra and the store were a package deal, so she wanted to know its history as well. If she even got the true history from him.

Ezra was thoughtful for a moment, as if trying to remember. "This particular incarnation has been at this location for about a hundred years, give or take. But I have run similar places, either as storefronts or stands for, I would say, five hundred years."

It was a good thing Brie had already finished her whiskey, or she would have choked on it. Five hundred years! It took her a moment to compose herself. Either this guy looked great for his age, or he was totally crazy. And what did that make her? Because she wanted to know more.

"Okay. And are all of your regular clients angels?" She was determined to keep an open mind, despite her brain rebelling against the information.

Ezra shook his head. "Not really. There are not many angels in the human world anymore. There's more to this world than you are capable of imagining. I cater to the needs of those in that world. My clients are looking for special items, powerful magics, and protection. I have been in this world for a long time. I have the access, or the connections, to get just about anything in what could be called the magical world."

"So, of the people I've met the past few weeks, some of them are clearly dangerous, as you've warned. But not in the 'usual' way, right?" Brie figured now she could use more whiskey.

"I assume you mean Albert and Helena. You would be correct. Albert Hsu is a vampire. He was turned in the midst of the rubble of the Great San Francisco Earthquake. He's a real piece of work. But he's trying to kick the whole killing humans thing, so he comes to me for pints of human blood, sourced fresh and willingly. Doesn't make him any less dangerous though. He's relapsed before and is still fairly new to the whole thing. Vampires have to be invited into private residences, so if you're afraid, you can hide in my apartment. He won't be able to get in."

He got up and picked up a crystal decanter still over half full of whiskey. Crossing to the couch, he refilled Brie's offered glass and his own before settling again in his chair.

"Now Helena is much older. She's a baobhan sith, which is sort of like a vampire and a fae. She's completely dangerous. However, she made an agreement with the city guardians that she wouldn't hunt for sport here. Each week, she comes to me for the name and address of a willing victim. It's always someone who is already dying and just wants to get the dying over with. It keeps Helena under control; otherwise, she would tear the hearts out of men and drink their blood as much as she pleased."

Brie shuddered. "That's pretty gruesome. I don't have to be around when she's here, right? I really don't want to be her next meal," Brie said, sipping from her glass. "And she didn't seem to care for me much."

"She usually comes in on Sundays." He got up and moved to sit next to her on the couch. He grabbed her free hand and held it between his own. "She won't lay a hand on you. I promise you that, Bridget. Working for me means you're under my protection." Ezra leaned forward and held her gaze as he squeezed her hand, a binding promise behind his words.

She nodded once, then sat back, brought her feet up onto the couch, and crisscrossed her legs, begrudgingly pulling away from Ezra's touch. It was too distracting right now. "So, who are the city guardians?"

Ezra shrugged. "Just some old spirits, some older than others, and representatives of different factions. Nothing happens in New Britain without their knowledge, but they typically don't interfere unless there is a potential risk to the inhabitants."

"Ah, gotcha. Like a magical city council." The thought made her smile just a little at the absurdity.

Ezra sighed; then, his face turned serious. "Bridget, let me be frank. Magic is entirely real. The simple magics you perform for your religious purposes are cheap, pale imitations of what real magic is and can be. In this city alone, there are real witches, like Lily, demons like Apollo, and a whole host of good, evil, and gray creatures. They all come here at one point or another looking for something. Not all of them are kind to humans, either."

"Lily is psychic, isn't she?" Brie asked, cutting off whatever else Ezra was going to say in his little speech. The whiskey in her hand was already half gone.

"She's a seer, among her many talents. Her gift is not always clear, though."

"She saw me." *The first day we met Lily knew my name.*

Ezra's face softened just a little. "She saw you. But she also saw things surrounding you that have no association with you whatsoever. She missed the mark on that one a little."

It was as if the amber liquid in her glass had suddenly become the most fascinating thing she'd ever seen. "And when you say witch, I take it you don't mean like me?"

"No, not like you. Lily is a witch in the classical sense. She comes from a long line of witches that once served a powerful being called the Morrigan." Ezra's voice took on a somber timbre, wistful almost. He turned away from her, angling himself toward the fire.

"Who's the Mor—" Ezra cut her off before she could finish asking.

"It's not important," he snapped. The softness from his face was gone now; the neutral mask had returned. Though they sat physically close together, he now seemed much more distant.

"Sorry. So you said Apollo was a demon?" Brie tried to keep her tone conversational, though the content of their conversation was far beyond unbelievable. If only she could keep control of her reactions, act nonchalant, maybe she could keep herself from totally freaking out.

Ezra's face shifted ever so slightly into one of mild annoyance rather than one of pure ice. "Apollo is an incubus, a... uh... hm... well, a sex demon. He was once an angel like me, but let's just say he had some issues with authority and was punished." He fell silent, looking bemused as he stared deeply into his glass.

Several seconds passed without a word between them. Ezra's gaze now fixed on the fire still crackling merrily in the grate while Brie looked down into her lap, the glass of whiskey clutched tightly in both hands. Processing everything he had shared so far would take longer than one night. As they sat in silence, Brie was at war with herself, debating whether she should just get up, leave, and never come back or stick around to see what more she could learn from Ezra about his world. She believed him, despite reason telling her it wasn't possible.

"It's a lot to take in, Bridget. I would completely understand if you want to quit. I can't make you forget what you now know. You are under no obligation to stay working for me. I will pay you for double the amount you have worked, and we can part ways without issue."

An out. Ezra willingly divulged secrets of an entire magical world existing around her, and he was still giving her a chance to run away. Without looking up at him, afraid she might lose her nerve if she did, she tossed back the last of the whiskey, then settled her gaze back into her lap. "Will I be safe working here?"

"What?" She heard him move next to her, his knees angling into view. Still, she kept her eyes trained on her lap.

"Will I be safe if I continue to work here? Will you make sure nothing bad happens to me?" With some difficulty, she finally managed to look up at him, to look him dead in the eyes without blinking. Ezra stared back, his face turning serious. He was much closer now, his knees just barely touching her thigh.

He took her hand again and placed it over his heart, holding it there. "Bridget, as long as you work for me, nothing will harm you. I swear it." It sounded like he was swearing an oath.

"Then I will stay. But I reserve the right to bail if it gets too weird, okay?" She didn't pull away; he kept their hands pressed against his chest.

"Of course. You will always have that right." He nodded, then stood, dropping her hand. Brie mimicked his movements, disappointed by the loss of his touch.

She fiddled with her hands, unsure what to do with them since neither of them moved toward the door. "I'm going to need some time to think about this. It's a lot, and honestly, it's super overwhelming," she finally said.

"I know. Take the next few days to think about it. If you don't come in next week, I will have my answer. I won't blame you for your decision, Bridget. Before I forget, here." He reached into his shirt pocket and pulled out a thick, folded envelope and handed it to her.

She took the offered envelope and opened it to pull out a check. Her eyes bulged as she stared at the number in total shock.

"I realize there is paperwork to fill out for a job that I should have already had you fill out. I have it if you want to take it home and return to me when you're done. Taxes have already been withheld. I like to keep my books balanced to avoid a tax audit. We can get you set up with direct deposit if you like."

It took her several seconds to realize he had said anything. "Ezra, this is way too much. It's like double my first paycheck. I'm only working part-time. Hell, this would be too much if I was working full-time. There's no way you can afford this!" What was she saying? This much money could get her groceries for a month. *This is Whole Foods money.*

Ezra waved her off. "That's your pay. It's non-negotiable under your performance review, which is excellent, by the way. After the work you've put in, I think this is fair. Business is far more lucrative than you can even imagine."

She stared at the check for a moment longer, still in shock. "Now, it's late, and your brother is probably already wondering where you are." Ezra led them to the office door, not looking back at her.

"How did you know I had a brother? I don't think I've mentioned him before," she asked with a hint of suspicion.

One shoulder lifted in a shrug, but he didn't say anything. He stepped aside to let her pass through the door first, a hand guiding her near the small of her back without actually touching. Just close enough to feel his warmth. She craned her neck to look back at him, trying to see if there was more to glean from his face than from the statement alone. He stared back, unflinching, his face betraying nothing as they moved into the shop proper.

At first, neither of them noticed the man standing at the counter.

A clearing throat brought their attention to the newcomer. The man was tall, gaunt like he had once been dead but had come back to life, his gray hair tied back at the nape of his neck. He was wrapped in a large fur overcoat despite the warmth outside. Rings with uncut precious gems glittered on his fingers in abundance. All that was secondary to his eyes, so blue and hard that they could very well have been made of ice. The way he glared at them made Brie squirm as if those ice-blue eyes could freeze her soul.

Ezra stopped just over the threshold and pulled Brie back toward his body with a firm grip on her arm, the other arm wrapped around her waist in a protective stance. The man before them smiled; it was as if the very air around them became thinner and colder.

"How good it is to see you again, Ezra," the man said in a rough voice.

CHAPTER 6

Brie felt Ezra's grip on her arm tighten, drawing her gaze away from the old man in front of them to up at Ezra. "Moloc," he said by way of greeting, jaw tight. "What are you doing here? We're closed."

The old man, Moloc, tutted at Ezra. "Such manners. After all I have done for you over the centuries. This is how you greet me. I thought your mother taught you better."

Everything within Brie screamed that this guy was the most dangerous thing to walk through the shop door yet. He radiated evil and danger. It was easily one of the worst times for her to be defiant; maybe she would have stayed silent if it wasn't for the weight of Ezra's arm around her waist.

"We're closed. You need to leave now." Her voice sounded braver than she felt. Once again, Ezra's hand tightened, almost to the point of being painful. He released her waist, pushed her behind him so he could block part of her body with his shoulder, and reached his hand out to keep touching her.

"Bridget, don't," he said through gritted teeth, not once taking his eyes off Moloc. Nevertheless, Moloc's attention now drew to Brie; those ice-shard eyes of his were focused solely on her face.

"Hm, interesting. I sense nothing from you, girl. A common human, Ezra? A pity. Your last consort was of such considerable power; this one hardly merits a comparison." Moloc's tone was demeaning. Ezra visibly cringed at his words. Brie wasn't sure whether she should take offense or not. Not that she cared what the literal embodiment of evil thought of her.

"She's my employee and under my protection. Whatever it is you wish to discuss with me can wait until she is home safe." Ezra didn't move from his position, half shielding her, which Brie found herself grateful for. Just having Moloc's eyes on her filled her with overwhelming fear.

Ezra's hand slid down her arm to grip her hand as he pulled her toward the door they had just walked through. He leaned close to her ear and whispered. "Think of home, Bridget. Picture your front door. Don't stop thinking about it until you cross the threshold."

"What about you? That guy is totally evil." She was afraid for him. Brie turned her head and looked into his face to see the tension he held there.

"Don't worry about me. Everything will be fine, I promise. Now, picture your door." Ezra nudged her forward toward the Storage Room door. With one finger, he pushed the six button, then took the hand he was holding and placed it on the doorknob before snatching his hand away quickly.

Brie pushed the image of Moloc standing behind them out, though she swore she could feel his icy stare on the back of her neck, closed her eyes, and thought only of the front door of her apartment. She turned the knob.

The door swung open, and with Ezra's hand on the small of her back urging her forward, she took a step over the threshold. Eyes open, she could see that one foot was in the entrance of her apartment, while one foot remained in the shop.

She struggled to keep herself from panicking, but she managed to calm herself enough to keep her concentration. She turned in the doorway. Ezra stood just behind her with a pleading look in his eyes. Behind him, still standing at the counter, Moloc smiled, sending the sensation of ice down her spine.

"Go," Ezra whispered and lightly pushed her the rest of the way through the door. She stumbled into her apartment. The door slammed shut on its own; Brie was left bewildered and shaking in her living room. Unable to stop herself, she turned and opened the front door, the one that had just a moment ago led to the shop. But now, beyond the door, was the same drab hallway that was always there. Brie felt just a little disappointed, and scared.

From their hallway, Wes appeared in an under-shirt and boxers. "Brie, you're late. I was starting to get worried. I left you like five messages and a million texts. Is everything okay?" Wes immediately went into big brother mode as he crossed the room to wrap her in a hug. Something about her face must have tipped him off that something was wrong beyond being late coming home.

Brie let herself be held for just a moment, then pulled away. As much as she wanted to tell Wes every-thing, there was no way he would believe her. And right now, Brie wanted to be alone with her thoughts. "I'm fine, just a busy day. Sorry I made you worry. Ezra and I got to talking, and I lost track of time. I think I'll head to bed." She started toward her room.

"But—" Wes began; Brie waved him off.

"Later, Wes. I'm drained." She stopped short of the hallway. "I love you."

"Love you, too, Brie," he responded, his eyes still full of worry.

Only once she was in the safety of her own room did Brie dare to fully breathe.

Brie set Sundays aside for her own coursework and grading. Since it was still close to the beginning of the term, she was mainly answering student emails and staring at her dissertation, getting nowhere.

Wes spent the morning interrogating her about what had happened the night before. Brie kept to her resolution not to tell Wes much of what Ezra had divulged. It was too much, and there was no doubt in her mind that her brother would insist she see the campus psychiatrist and quit her job. So, she shrugged him off and told him she had just gotten caught up in her work and talking to Ezra. Wes clearly didn't believe her, but he didn't push further. He let her be when she disappeared into her room to work.

At some point in the day, she should go to the shop to pick up her paperwork since she didn't get it the day before. That was her excuse, anyway. She really just wanted to check on Ezra after the previous night. The way Moloc looked at her was still etched in her mind, and she suppressed a shudder. When her back started to ache from hunching over her laptop, she decided a break was needed, and it was as good a time as any to go to the shop. Maybe she would figure out on the way over if she was quitting.

Brie didn't bother to change out of her leggings and oversized shirt with the Ramones on it, which she was sure belonged to Wes. The weather was dry and warm; even though it was mid-September, the summer planned to keep hold for as long as possible.

Instead of hesitating at the shop door like she had the other day, Brie found herself nearly running through the door to see if Ezra was inside. The bell tinkled her entrance.

Ezra stood at the counter, but he wasn't alone. His focus was on a small man sitting on the counter. The man's cheeks were ruddy; his long hair and mustache were a matching grey. He wore clothing that was a little threadbare and patched in places, loose but clean. Judging by Ezra's face, he was annoyed but attentive. Brie inched closer to the two and understood Ezra's annoyance immediately. The customer was asking rapid-fire questions in a language Brie didn't understand. Ezra looked as if he had grown tired of answering a long while ago.

Ezra's eyes met Brie's briefly, and without saying anything, he held up four fingers, then nodded toward the door behind him. Brie took the hint, swept across the room and behind the counter, then punched the number four button and slipped inside the break room. The man on the counter didn't even notice her presence; instead, he kept up his constant chatter.

The crow teacup sat on the counter upside down. Brie walked to it and flipped it right side up; it filled immediately with a deep burgundy liquid. "I don't think that's tea, little cup," Brie said, looking at the liquid inside. She took a swig anyway and was surprised to find it was a fruity, dry red wine. It was exactly what she needed right now. Curling up on the wicker couch, she lounged with her teacup of wine and waited for Ezra to finish up front.

Thirty minutes passed before the break room door opened and an incredibly disgruntled Ezra entered. Brie sat with her feet tucked beneath her, scrolling through her phone while sipping her second cup of wine. Ezra marched over to the couch where Brie sat, snatched the teacup from her hands, and downed the rest of the contents.

"That's not tea." Ezra made a face. "Good vintage, though." He thrust the teacup back into her hands and sat down heavily next to her.

"So I guess you had a fun time with that customer?" Brie asked, watching the teacup refill in her hands. She took a sip, then passed the cup over to Ezra, who took a large gulp and passed it back.

He ran a hand through his hair before responding. "Kuknya comes in every Sunday to ask a million questions about various charms he will never buy, then, after wasting at least an hour of my time, he'll buy an ordinary Matryoshka doll. Then he leaves and shows up again the next week to do it all over again."

"And what is Kuknya?" Brie asked with curiosity in her voice after taking another sip of wine.

"Domowik. There used to be a Polish family that lived around here. They came before the Iron Curtain, and he came with them. But the family is long gone;

last one died in the nineties and Kuknya just sticks around, bothering me when he gets lonely." Ezra took the proffered teacup without looking and drained it. Brie nodded with a bit of a grin, finally feeling more relaxed, just being in Ezra's company, talking about magical creatures like it was normal.

"What's a domowik?" Her attention was on the teacup presently refilling in her hand.

Ezra flung his head back to rest against the couch. "A type of house spirit. They are usually tied to a particular family and look after them in exchange for offerings. But without a family left to care for, Kuknya just sulks around their old home. I don't know what else he does, but he now has a considerable collection of those nesting dolls. And he's extremely exhausting."

Brie handed over the full cup, figuring Ezra needed it far more than she did. They sat in silence for several long minutes. Tucking herself into the side of the couch, Brie lounged and looked over at her boss. His head was still tilted back, his eyes now closed. He looked peaceful, his whole body limp as he sat there. She couldn't stop herself from thinking about how handsome he looked while relaxed. The couch was small enough that their legs touched just a little. All of her focus was concentrated on that one spot.

She felt her cheeks heat up; she quickly banished the thought from her head. Wes's words from the other day about sleeping with her boss suddenly rang in her ears. That was it with the wine then. Time to focus on something else, or her mind might stray again. Though she wanted to know what happened with Moloc after she left, she also didn't want to break the peace Ezra was experiencing. The man looked tense most of the week; she didn't want to ruin his one moment of relaxation, so she asked another question.

"So... do you have wings or something like that? Since you are an angel, fallen or otherwise." Since this man was already gorgeous, she would imagine wings would make him irresistible.

Ezra lifted his head a fraction and cracked open one eye, directed at her. "I do," he said slowly.

"Can I see them?"

Ezra surprised her by chuckling softly before dropping his head back and closing his eyes. "No." They lapsed back into silence. In a matter of minutes, Ezra's breathing became deep and even. Brie looked up from her phone, which she had been scrolling through absentmindedly, letting the last of the wine silence her mind.

"Did you fall asleep?" she whispered to Ezra, dropping her phone into her lap.

"Mhmmmf. Resting my eyes," was his mumbled, half-formed reply.

"What about the shop? Do you want me to watch the counter while you nap? I'm not dressed for work, but if you don't mind..." Her feet landed on the floor and she stood.

Finally, Ezra lifted his head and opened both eyes to look at her. "I put up the 'Be Back Soon' sign. I usually do after Kuknya leaves so that I can have a few minutes to myself. But as you can probably guess, I had a rough night, so really, I could not care less about any customers today."

Brie didn't move, still standing, unsure whether she should go just to give him some space. "Sit down, Brie. It's your day off." He leaned forward enough to grab her hand and tug her back onto the couch. Brie let him, enjoying the way his hand clenched around hers.

Without thinking, Brie asked, "So, I have to ask, does this big business you claim to have come from Moloc?" She didn't need to look up to know she had said the wrong thing. Ezra sat up rigid; the peaceful lounge he had just been enjoying was gone completely. He was all hard edges and cold eyes.

"I don't particularly like doing business with Moloc, but yes, he provides a large source of my inventory. Now, I must get back to the shop. I will see you on Wednesday, Bridget." His voice was stern. Brie knew she was being dismissed for the day. He paused at the door, turning his head only enough for Brie to see the side of his face. "If you decide to stay, that is." His voice was softer, almost pleading. He didn't wait for a response; the door clicked shut behind him.

She sighed, grabbed the upside-down teacup and saucer, and set it on the counter before leaving the room. Unlocking the front door of the shop, she walked out into the bright afternoon.

It was starting to feel like one step forward, two steps back with Ezra. He certainly was a volatile man. *Volatile, handsome, and full of secrets.* Her first month was under her belt with classes and at the shop. Even if the money hadn't been ridiculously good, Brie knew it was her boss that would keep her coming back.

CHAPTER 7

Words and numbers blurred together on the screen. Brie dug into her bag and pulled out her reading glasses, chunky black frames with a greenish color on the inside. Slipping them over her eyes, they did little to help the blur. Between grading her class's most recent essays and, presently, the ledger book, she was surprised she hadn't gone blind.

Abandoning her glasses, she closed her eyes and rested her head on the counter next to the keyboard. A sigh escaped her lips. When she got to the shop earlier, bags under her eyes from a long night and day of actually working on her dissertation, hair thrown up in a messy bun that was already falling out, Ezra had said nothing. Instead, once she was situated behind the counter, he handed her a piece of paper with a list of orders and the amount owed before disappearing through the Storage Room door without a goodbye. He left the door slightly ajar so Brie could easily pop back and grab orders off the shelf near the door on the platform.

The previous Wednesday, Ezra had begun letting her handle customers so he could continue his work in the back. She started to recognize most of the regulars by what they were. A large number of lesser fae and sprites visited for charms, which turned out to be a bit of a specialty at the shop. Many witches, some even from Lily's coven, came in for rare ingredients or magical tools. A few seedier characters, like a couple of imps and hobs, came in occasionally for suspiciously shaped packages. But the ones she had met her first week were the most interesting, if a little terrifying.

While things improved at the shop now that she was privy to the inner workings and clientele, things at home had become grating. Wes had spent a good part of the entire previous week trying to convince her to quit the shop.

"I don't like it, Brie. What if your boss is like some maniac? What do you really know about him and his 'customers'?" He had used air quotes, going over the same thing just before she left for work that day. Brie had shrugged and reminded him that the money was really good, and the work was easy. It was a mystery to her as to why Wes was so against the place. He hadn't been to the shop, didn't know Ezra, and Brie hadn't supplied him with much information about her daily activities there. She still had not told him anything about the magical nature of the place or that her boss was actually an angel. Plus, her curiosity about the magical world was too intense to quit now.

The bell tinkled, drawing Brie out of her head. She looked up to see the vampire, Albert. In a blink, he was standing before the counter, something Brie was confident she would never get used to. He sneered down at her on the stool, something she knew she would get used to.

"Where's Ezra? I have come for my parcel," he drawled with his typical condescending tone. He looked at Brie as if she were something less than human and could barely bring himself to speak to her.

Brie glared back at him. "Ezra's busy. I'll just go get your order for you." Backing up toward the door, she never took her eyes off Albert's sneering face for a second. Ezra said he was dangerous, and Brie was taking that seriously, never giving him her back.

Slipping through the Storage Room door, she heard distant banging. Wherever Ezra was in the Storage Room, it was pretty far back. Brie consulted the note he left for her and turned to rummage around the shelf next to the door. The small package for Albert was easy to find as it was sitting front and center, just at eye level. Ezra must have arranged the shelf by upcoming orders.

With the package firmly in hand, she walked back to the front of the shop, not bothering to even call out for Ezra, confident she could handle the vampire.

Albert was still at the counter, drumming his slightly sharpened nails on the aged wood. "Took you long enough. I swear you humans waste so much time. I—" Whatever he was going to say next was cut off by the tinkle of the bell.

A breeze of floral and spicy herbs swept into the shop as Lily walked in, smiling widely in her dirt-covered overalls. Moving farther into the shop, she first called out a hello to Brie, then her eyes moved over to Albert, and her wide smile suddenly turned shy as her cheeks reddened.

"Hi Bertie, it's been a while since I've seen you here. We usually cross paths around the same time each week. Was starting to think you were avoiding me." Her voice sounded breathy. *Surely Lily doesn't have a crush on Albert*, thought Brie.

Brie was nearly floored when Albert returned Lily's smile, and if a vampire could blush, Albert's face would certainly light up a room. "Miss Lily, what a pleasant surprise. Yes, it... well... it has been a few weeks. I do apologize. I've had appointments that forced me to come in earlier. Not that I was avoiding you, Miss Lily. I would never..." Albert must have realized he was rambling and finally stemmed the flood of words at Lily's girlish giggle.

"It's okay, Bertie. You're a busy man. I understand. Are you planning on coming to my family's Samhain celebration next month? I would love it if you came."

Lily nervously tucked stray hairs behind her ears, trying not to look hopeful.

Albert took a step closer to Lily, looking at her with a fondness Brie had never seen before. The whole scene was freaking Brie out on so many levels, but she could only gawk at them from behind the counter.

"I wouldn't miss it for the world, Miss Lily. The best part is getting to watch you dance... I mean... the dance. The dance that all the witches dance, which you also dance in. That one. I should... I should go. It was lovely to see you, Miss Lily, as always." Then he quickly, and with no grace, kissed her on the cheek, grabbed the package Brie had placed on the counter, tossed his payment in its place, and disappeared out the door.

Lily stood rooted to the spot, a wide-eyed shock on her face as her hand came up to cradle the freckled cheek Albert kissed. "Well, that was some of the most awkward flirting I've ever seen, and I live on a college campus," Brie said with a grin.

Lily seemed to return to herself and cast her eyes down in embarrassment, cheeks flaming. "I don't know what you mean. Bertie was just being friendly and sweet; he's just a nice man."

Brie snorted loudly. "He has been nothing but rude and menacing to me in the weeks I've been here."

The witch walked up to the counter and leaned over it. "Oh, that's just because he doesn't really know you. Once he gets more comfortable around you, he's really a sweet guy. He always has a smile and a kind word for me."

Brie laughed. "That's because he likes you. And here I thought you were supposed to be some great seer."

Lily perked up. "I sometimes forget you know about all of this now. And I wouldn't say I'm a great seer. I just have the gift, and it doesn't always work the way I want. Things get much more clouded when it involves myself. Bertie and I are just friends. He always asks about my plants."

"Because he likes you! I doubt that bloodsucker really cares all that much about plants," Brie said with exasperation. "Is that a thing, anyway? Vampires and witches getting together?"

At her words, Lily's whole face was a red beacon, but she quickly changed the subject. "Anyway, Samhain is coming up next month. I know it seems like ages away, but my family hosts this big party every year on our farm. There's food, drinks, dancing, and a bonfire, of course. Oh, and my gran is breaking out the runes for some divination. Now she has a real gift. You'll come, right?"

The last time Brie celebrated any holiday with a group, she spent the whole evening alone, slowly drinking herself into a massive hangover. However, there was something endearing about Lily and her energy. There really wasn't a way for Brie to say no. "Could I bring someone? It's just that my brother and I usually celebrate together, and I don't want to leave him home alone."

"Yeah, absolutely!" Lily said brightly. Then she leaned closer to Brie, her voice dropping to a conspiratorial whisper. "Ezra will be coming as well. I made him promise last year, and I'm charging you with making sure he has fun. He always sulks at parties."

Brie stared back. "I'm just his employee. I doubt he would appreciate me pushing him to have fun."

"He won't mind. Trust me, I've seen it. Plus, you have a month to get all cozy with him."

"I'm not trying to cozy up with him," Brie protested half-heartedly.

Lily winked and grinned, then straightened back up. "So I should probably get my order and get out of here. I have some harvesting to do before moonset."

Brie took that as her cue to slip into the Storage Room. Just as she made it through the door, she ran straight into Ezra's chest as he was reaching for the doorknob. She stumbled backward; Ezra caught her with a hand on the small of her back, saving her from falling.

"Sorry, I was just getting Lily's order," she mumbled, looking up into Ezra's face. He looked down at her and said nothing for a long moment. There was something unreadable about the way he looked at her; it made Brie squirm.

He held her for longer than was necessary. Then, as if snapping out of a trance, Ezra removed his hand from her back, nodded, and turned toward the shelf where Lily's order sat, front and center at his eye level. "Do you always arrange the shelf for whichever regular is coming in?" Brie asked to break the silence, following him into the Storage Room.

Ezra turned, holding a plant with magenta leaves. "The Storage Room does it for me. It's too large to organize its whole self, so it takes pride in having at least this shelf organized for convenience."

Brie frowned. "You talk like the Storage Room is alive." The thought alone unnerved her, considering she was standing inside said Storage Room.

Ezra shrugged as he headed back toward the door. "It's not exactly alive in the traditional sense, but that doesn't mean it does not have awareness. And it tries to be helpful when it can."

"You could have just said it was a magic room." Brie put her hands on her hips as Ezra headed to the door. He stepped through and held it open for her, the plant held in his other hand. Brie hurried through after him.

"Fine, it's a magic room," he said as he shut the door behind them, a hint of a smile on his plush lips.

Lily gasped as Ezra set the plant on the counter. She leaned close to the leaves and began to stroke one as she cooed at the plant like it was a baby or a cute animal. "It's even more pretty than I thought! Whatever supplier you have, Ezra, keep using them! My garden is going to be the envy of the whole ass coven."

"I have no doubt about that. I already put it on your tab," Ezra said.

Lily hefted her newest purchase before looking directly at Ezra. "I was just telling Brie about Samhain at the farm next month and how you're bringing her. She needs to be with her own kind on the holidays."

"But I'm not like you, Lily. I'm just a... um... hedge-witch." For some reason, that made Brie feel a sense of failure. Growing up, she had never felt bad about the paganism Maddy raised her with, but now, knowing a little about the wider world of magic, Brie couldn't help the feeling of inadequacy.

Lily took one hand off the potted plant and waved it dismissively. "You're one of us, Brie. Anyway, I gotta go. See you both next week."

Ezra, who had been silent at Lily's declaration, finally found his voice. "What do you mean I'm taking her? I wasn't planning on go—"

"Bye!" Lily called brightly, purposely cutting Ezra off as she walked out the door.

Ezra huffed in annoyance as the bell tinkled Lily's departure.

"How big is her tab? She's always in here?" Brie asked to lighten the mood.

Ezra ran a hand through his hair, messing it just so. "I honestly have no idea. I stopped actually keeping a tab with her after the second time she came into my shop. I couldn't take money from a six-year-old with two missing teeth."

Brie laughed. "She's been coming here that long?"

Ezra nodded, glancing down at where Brie sat. "All her life, and her mother before her, and her gran. She was less bratty as a kid, though." Brie watched as a genuine smile lit up his face. It was the most beautiful thing she had ever seen.

"Ah, you big softie. I bet you also gave her candy when she came in, and you probably had a sheet of stickers to give her, too," Brie teased.

Ezra glared at her. "Even as a kid, she didn't like much candy. It was actually strawberries and no stickers. I gave her small dream charms. No kid should have to deal with nightmares."

After a few seconds of silence, in which Brie could only stare at him, even as he didn't look at her, he cast Brie a parting look, then headed for the Storage Room. He paused before walking through the door. "Just yell if you need anything. I'll be working closer to the front for a while."

"What are you doing back there, anyway?" Brie asked.

He heaved a sigh. "Inventory. It has been... uh... a while since it was last done."

Brie cocked an eyebrow. "Define 'a while.'"

"Like seventy years, give or take. Just after the Second World War." He sounded sheepish in his response, one hand running through his hair, mussing it up again.

"Then I'd say it's way overdue. Get your ass back to work, slacker." Brie laughed.

"I'm still the boss here, you know," Ezra said with that small grin of his as he slipped through the door. He left Brie standing at the counter, chuckling to herself with a warm glow radiating through her.

CHAPTER 8

Ten years ago

Brie was sixteen, working with Maddy on some homemade spells.

"You've taken to herb work so well, ma petite, but you're still confusing your crystals," Maddy chided, though a smile covered her matronly face.

Crystals had always been Wes's specialty; Brie preferring the greener things. But Maddy insisted on giving them both a well-rounded education in pagan traditions and spell work.

"I'm just not that into crystals. Can't I just focus on plants?" Brie asked, turning a piece of quartz over in her hand, feeling the crystal grow warm from her body heat.

Maddy's warm hand covered hers to still her movements. "Of course, cher. But it's good to be full-bodied in your knowledge. Wes won't be around forever to help you pick crystals."

The younger girl snorted. "What are you talking about? Nanny goat will always be around to harp on me about picking the wrong ones or to chuck them at my head."

Her foster mother smiled. "I have told that boy headshots are not allowed. But I know you throw them right back. I swear, it's like the two of you have been siblings all your life."

Something warm filled Brie's chest, that feeling of home and belonging she had felt since arriving at Maddy's three years before. Her heart soared just a few weeks ago when Maddy announced, on her sixteenth birthday, that she was working on the paperwork to formally adopt them both. She wanted to have it done before Wes turned eighteen.

Brie had never felt so happy in her life. Even working with crystals.

A look passed over her foster mother's face suddenly, one that Brie couldn't read. Maddy let go of her hand quickly.

"Cher, I want to teach you something, and it's important that you remember. It will keep you safe." There was a hint of urgency in her voice, but she kept it suppressed.

Brie just nodded. "Repeat these words: *ikh bin mir aun ir zent ir. Ikh bafray dikh,*" Maddy said the words slowly and with precise sounds. She made Brie repeat the phrase over and over again until she could say it flawlessly.

"What does it mean?" Brie asked, curious.

Maddy didn't answer at first. Then she said, "It's something that will sever bad energy. You'll know when you need to use it one day. Just use it with intent, ma petite. Promise me that."

Brie nodded. "Okay." She didn't really understand why it was important or how she would know to use it. Maddy just patted her cheek and smiled, though wariness remained in her eyes until Wes entered the room loudly and interrupted them.

CHAPTER 9

The Storage Room door slammed shut behind her. Brie stalked over to the shelf and pulled a small wooden box marked for Apollo from where it sat right at her eye level. "Ezra!" she yelled in the direction from where a symphony of bangs and clangs originated. She tapped her foot impatiently as she balanced the box in one hand.

A minute later, Ezra came careening from around a shelf, eyes wide. "Are you okay?" His voice sounded breathless.

"I'm just great." She stomped up to him and shoved the box into his chest. "You deal with him. If I go back out there, things are going to get real violent. He's laying it on extra-thick tonight."

Ezra looked down at the box and then back to Brie with a smirk. "I already gave you full permission to kick his ass. I would very much like to see that, actually. Don't worry; I'll take care of it."

"Are angels even allowed to say ass?" she grumbled, crossing her arms, still very much annoyed.

Ezra leaned down to her level, his face only a few inches from hers, his grin now smug. "I just did." He straightened and walked out of the Storage Room. Brie didn't move. Her cheeks flushed, and heat flooded her core. Ezra's grin changed his whole face into something light and incredibly attractive. She had started to see him smile more as the weeks went on. The difference it made to his face constantly had her warm all over while in the shop.

Suddenly, something fell with a loud thud to her left, causing Brie to jump. Turning in the direction of the sound, she saw a book, small and bound in leather, lying on the ground. The shelf it must have fallen from looked stable enough, and from what Brie could see, was full of mismatched items, most not even books. Stooping down to pick up the book, she ran her fingers over the gold embossed title and the small torch image etched underneath. It looked exactly like the one Ezra wore on nearly all of his shirts like a company logo.

She thumbed through the pages, skimming a line here and there. It was an old book; Brie was familiar with the author, but not this particular title.

The Storage Room door opened, and Ezra stepped through the threshold. "I don't know what he said to you, but he wasn't even implying anything. He directly said, 'Let's skip dinner and fuck.' He's gone and he won't be in next week. So, you don't have to worry about committing any murders. What's that?" He nodded to the book in her hands.

Brie held it up for him to see. "It just fell off one of the shelves. I was just putting it back."

Ezra walked closer to her and took the book from her hand, fingers brushing against hers. He studied the cover for a second. "*Letters From The Earth,* by Mark Twain. It's one of my favorites. It's based on me, sort of. Sam was a good friend, and he had such a curious mind. The Storage Room must want you to read it."

"It just fell off the shelf. Wait. Hang on. You knew Mark Twain?" she asked, incredulous.

Ezra laughed a little, and Brie suddenly felt utterly enamored with the sound. "Yeah, I did. Sam was great. Back in the day, we used to hang around Nikola's lab all the time. He would share some of the things he was working on. I remember Sam had a bad habit of touching everything in the lab. Absolutely drove Nikola crazy." He let out a wistful sigh, remembering friends now long gone. "You should read the book though; nothing just falls in the Storage Room without reason. It tends to think it knows best. Bit of a med-dler." The last bit was directed outward like he was addressing the Storage Room.

"You mean Nikola Tesla, right?" Brie could hardly picture him with the two legendary men.

"The same." He nodded.

He offered the book back to her, and Brie took it, clutching it close to her chest. "So, this is about you?"

Ezra shrugged, walking past her to head back into the depths of the Storage Room. "I was an inspiration, but Sam had his own story to tell. Now, back to work, Bridget. And read the book. At the very least, it'll make the Storage Room happy." Then he turned out of sight, and Brie made her way back into the shop, the book tucked under her arm.

"Hey, Brie. Whatcha reading?" A familiar voice called out to her a few feet from where she sat in the student center. Brie sighed heavily and bookmarked her place before closing *Letters From the Earth* to look up as Craig approached.

"Just something a friend is letting me borrow. I'll be handing back your latest paper tomorrow if that's what you were going to ask." She hoped that was all he wanted, and he would be on his way. Brie knew that wasn't her luck.

"Ah, no, I figured that. But actually, I wanted to see if you were busy this week. I know you said you work, but are you free any day this week to go over the paper you assigned? Some of my friends are getting together at one of the coffee places to get work done." Persistence was his strong suit.

Her fingers clenched tight around the book in her hands. "I really don't see why you can't just come to my office hours for that." Brie didn't want him to come to her office hours, but they existed for a reason.

"It's totally fine. We've totally done it with Dr. Fry before; it's totally chill. Just for an hour—it would be a big help. Just say yes. Coffee is on me." Brie could see there was no deterring him. Though she knew she should just insist on using office hours, she thought that maybe she should be encouraging someone who actually participated in her class; that's what Dr. Fry would tell her. Hopefully, he would realize she just wasn't into him, get over his infatuation with her, and this would just be a good old-fashioned study session.

"One hour. I'm free before six this weekend, just not Sunday." She would not give up her one weekend day for an undergrad, and at least she had an out, so she wouldn't have to stay long. "And I'm not giving hints about the midterm," she said with finality.

Craig grinned widely. *It's nothing like Ezra's smile*, Brie noted. Whereas Ezra's grin enhanced his face, bright eyes crinkling at the corners when it really covered his face, Craig's grin twisted his face into something like that of a mischievous child's. Brie was already regretting her decision.

"Great! How about I pick you up at your place at three tomorrow? We can walk together."

Brie furrowed her brow. "It's not a date. So how about four, and I'll meet you wherever." She definitely didn't want this guy to know where she lived.

"Deal! Meet you at The Java Donkey tomorrow at four. See you around, Brie." Once he was out of sight, Brie groaned loudly. She really didn't want to indulge Craig, but this was strictly going to be a study session and help with a paper; that was part of her job. She only hoped now that he would see how uninterested she was, drop it, and just focus on his work. But his track record indicated that this would probably only encourage him.

A few hours later as Brie walked up to the shop, she nearly fell through the threshold when the door was wrenched open before her fingers fully settled on the doorknob. Helena pushed her way out, knocking Brie's shoulder painfully. The auburn-haired beauty was covered by a dark coat, her face buried deep in the hood. The sun had just begun to set, so Brie presumed that Helena was hiding herself from any sunlight.

Helena snarled down at her; she had a good several inches on Brie. "Watch your step, human. Just because you are Ezra's pet doesn't mean you are not still just food." Then she was gone, off into the slowly dimming light.

Brie continued into the shop, trying not to let Helena's words frighten her, yet they still did. "If you didn't insist on always being fifteen minutes early, you would have missed her entirely," Ezra said from behind the counter as she entered.

"She's going to try to eat me one of these days, isn't she?" Brie asked, half as a joke, but also seriously asking.

Her boss shrugged. "Probably, but you're under my protection so long as you work here, and she really doesn't want to deal with the trouble."

"Oh good. Here I was worried," Brie responded sarcastically, flinging her bag down on the floor next to the stool.

"Should I get the teacup to help with this mood?" Ezra arched an eyebrow.

"How do you do it, Ezra? How do you just take all this in stride, dealing with monsters coming in every day, just letting them go back out into the city?" Brie looked up at him in earnest. Ever since Moloc came into the shop, she had been thinking about it, but seeing Helena look down on her like she was a snack brought it to the forefront of Brie's mind.

For a long moment, Ezra said nothing. Instead, he stared straight ahead in thought. Brie kept her gaze on him the whole time he mulled over what he was going to say. "There's more to this world than you know, Brie. What happens here in my place is but a small fraction of it all. There are monsters, but there are also wonders." He turned toward her. Brie could see something there, glinting in his eyes. *Is it sadness or something more?* "I believe that humans and magic can coexist, and both should have free will. That's why I fell. I wanted to be part of that world. That's why I help them all, even the monsters, because I believe in something greater than myself."

She could only stare at him as he lost himself to his own memory, his own yearning. His eyes may have been on her, but he didn't see Brie. His goal was admirable, and she respected him all the more for it.

Without thinking, she placed a hand on his arm and gave it a comforting squeeze. His eyes moved to where she touched him, but the faraway look remained.

The bell's tinkle broke whatever spell of memory Ezra was under. A tourist wandered in off the street. Brie gave Ezra one last lingering look before turning her attention to ushering the tourist out quickly. Ezra followed her movement with eyes that were still not quite seeing the present.

Once the tourist was back on the street, grumbling as Brie all but pushed them out the door, she turned back to the counter. Ezra was gone, and the Storage Room door was shut.

The Java Donkey was the embodiment of a college coffee house. There were scuffed tables and oversized chairs that were getting a little threadbare.

A few couches were pushed up against the walls and completely taken over by groups of people huddled around laptops. Behind the coffee bar, the baristas buzzed around, preparing drinks for the line of people waiting. The whole place smelled like espresso and cinnamon. For a Saturday afternoon, it was pretty packed with people.

As she walked through the door, her eye caught the waving arm of Craig at one of the tables. Hands clutching the strap of her ever-present messenger bag, she walked over toward the table, already wishing it was time for work.

Craig stood up and pulled out the empty chair for her before taking his seat next to her. She felt trapped. Across from her sat a blond girl who was in her class; a light-brown-haired guy that Brie didn't recognize was off to her other side.

"Brie, you know Mariah. And this is my boy, Emory. He's my roommate." Craig indicated each in turn; Brie received a small smile from Mariah and a head nod from Emory. "Let me go get you a coffee, Brie. Be right back." Then he was off to the coffee bar without even asking Brie if she wanted coffee, which she didn't. There had been no chance to ask for tea.

"So Brie, you TA for Dr. Fry, right?" Emory asked, trying to keep silence from the table. Brie folded her hands in her lap to keep from fiddling with the strap of her bag, which was still slung across her shoulders.

"Um, yeah. It's my second year with her." Brie was doing her level best to keep from pulling her phone out of her pocket to look at the time.

"What's that like? I've heard she's kind of a hardass in class. Is she like that with her grad students?" Mariah asked, leaning forward to rest her elbows on the table. Brie liked Mariah. She participated in class with insightful responses that demonstrated that she had done the reading. She even utilized office hours for genuine questions, which few people did.

Brie shrugged; she knew it was an open secret that most of the undergraduates dreaded Dr. Fry's classes. "She can be. I mean, she's my advisor, so if you think she's hard on undergrads..." Brie shook her head. "But really, she's brilliant. I'm lucky to work under her." Brie really felt that way. While tough in her critiquing of Brie's thesis, Dr. Fry was also fair and nurturing in her academic pursuits. She pushed Brie almost to her breaking point, but never beyond, and after her complaining subsided, she was always thankful for Dr. Fry.

The other two just nodded. Brie knew she wasn't changing hearts and minds about Dr. Fry with her statement. She said nothing further; the table lapsed into awkward silence. Emory shifted uncomfortably, then turned his attention to Mariah and started a conversation.

Brie tuned them out immediately. Maybe it was rude, but she didn't care. She didn't want to be here hanging with Craig and his friends. Brie contemplated making a break for it before Craig returned, eyeballing the distance from their table to the door. Then, just as she had decided to bolt, Craig reappeared with two steaming cups of coffee in mismatched cups.

He placed one in front of Brie, set the other in front of himself, then pulled out a few sugar packets and little containers of creamer from his pocket. "They have great coffee here, probably the best on campus." He started pouring packet after packet of sugar into the brown liquid and then three containers of creamer. *What is the point of getting coffee if you can't taste it?*

She took a tentative sip and made a face as the coffee slid down her throat.

"Good, right?" Craig looked over at her with eager eyes, like he was personally responsible for brewing the coffee.

"I'm sure this is good coffee, but I'm not a fan." She set the cup down gently so as not to slosh the hot liquid.

Craig looked a little crestfallen at her reaction. "Oh, well, that's a bummer. It's definitely my favorite."

Brie wished she had water to wash the taste out of her mouth. "I'm not a fan of coffee in general," Brie finally responded.

Craig shrugged. "I thought grad students lived off coffee and Red Bull. All the ones I know do. Maybe you just need to drink coffee more to get a taste for it."

He then flung his arm around the back of Brie's chair. She rolled her eyes and tried to inch away from him.

"I'm good, actually." She crossed her arms defensively. The other two at the table remained silent, suddenly very interested at their own half-filled cups.

Craig removed his arm from behind her and put both hands up. "Hold up, I'm sorry. I was just joking. It's cool. Coffee is not for everyone. Can I get you something else? What do you like?"

Brie shook her head, keeping her arms locked tightly in front of her. "It's fine. Don't worry about it. I'll just drink this." She indicated the cup of coffee. "I have to go to work after this."

"Oh, where do you work?" Mariah asked brightly in an apparent move to steer the conversation away from the drink disaster. *At least she knows how to pick up on things,* Brie thought.

Her attention now off Craig, Brie loosened her arms a little and focused on Mariah instead. "This little antique shop downtown. I'm mostly doing inventory and digitizing the records."

Mariah scrunched up her nose. "Sounds boring."

It was difficult to hold back the laugh that threatened to spill out of her. "You could say that. But my boss lets me do my course work if I need to, and he's been good to me, so it's not a bad place to be. It has a certain charm." *And there are supernatural beings, a Storage*

Room that may or may not be alive, and, oh yeah, a hot boss who happens to be an angel. Total snooze fest,

"Doubt it's very busy. I mean, we're in a college city, and antiquing isn't one of the bigger hobbies here. Maybe I could drop in some time and keep you company." Craig's tone was friendly, but underneath his words was a layer of suggestion that Brie did not like.

"She already has to see you in class and right now in her free time. Why the hell would she want to see your ugly face while she's working, too?" Emory laughed at Craig. He yelped as he received a kick under the table from his friend. *Goddess, even Emory gets it.*

Brie took this exchange as her excuse to escape. "Well, I should head out. I need to head home before work, anyway." She turned her body slightly to go, but Craig placed his hand on her arm, stalling her. She flinched; he didn't seem to notice or care because he kept touching her.

"But you just got here. Why don't you stay? Text your boss and say you're sick. Come on; it's Saturday. You should be having fun." Craig's voice took on a whiny, pleading tone. It grated on Brie's nerves.

"I'm not ditching work tonight. You told me this was to work on your paper. I don't see any of your class stuff with you." She was now annoyed and fully prepared to shove Craig out of the way.

"Come on, man. Let her go to work. Not all of us can be trust fund babies like you," Emory said, throwing his friend a look that was a mix between a glare and a smirk. Brie decided she liked Emory. He could at least read the signs that she wasn't feeling this little outing.

Craig pouted for a second before letting go of her arm. As she stood, she adjusted the strap on her bag, realizing her hands had barely left it the whole time. "Well, um... thanks for the coffee, I guess. It was nice to see you again, Mariah, and nice to meet you, Emory. Bye." She turned to head for the door, but Craig caught her arm again. She looked down at where his hand gripped her upper arm, then back to his face. His touch made her skin crawl.

"Wait! Can I come by some time to see you at work?" His pleading cow eyes did nothing for her.

"Let go," Brie spat through gritted teeth, eyes narrowed, not liking his touch. He released her immediately.

"Sorry. Can I at least text you or something?" His voice kept up the pleading tone. To Brie, all it sounded like was childish whining.

"No," she said. Then she turned sharply and marched out the door, not once looking back at Craig.

It wasn't even five yet when she barged through the door of Spirit Antiques. The sound of the bell was more like a bash than a tinkle. Across the room, she saw Ezra startle where he stood hunched over the counter.

He took in the sight of her, his eyes traveling quickly over her body as if scanning for injury. Brie had tried to cover as much skin as possible without completely overheating before leaving for the coffee shop. The burgundy-colored dress had a modest Peter Pan collar, and because it stopped above the knee, she had thrown on opaque black tights. In her rage, though, she felt warm. Ezra finally ceased his scan on her face and kept it there as she stomped her way over to him and tossed her bag on the floor with little ceremony.

"Bridget, are you o—"

"Teacup, now!" she growled, cutting him off. Somewhere in the back of her mind, she knew better than to talk like that to her boss, but at the moment, she didn't care. Grumpy and hungry because she didn't bother to go home and eat before going to the shop, Brie was settling into a bad mood. Ezra could forgive her later when she bothered to apologize.

For his part, though, Ezra just nodded and disappeared into the break room before returning a moment later with the crow-covered teacup sitting upside down on its saucer. Without so much as a word, he handed it over to her, their fingers touching lightly during the transfer. Ezra moved his hand away quickly, as if he had received a shock. Brie didn't notice; she was completely focused on the cup, which she flipped over; it immediately filled with a deep amber liquid.

She drained the cup in one gulp, let the teacup refill itself, and then sipped at the second drink. "I'm technically not working yet, so it's not drinking on the job," she said, a hint of sarcasm in her voice.

"Bad day, I take it?" Ezra raised an eyebrow, taking the teacup from her hand after her next sip. He brought the cup up to his lips and took a drink, his eyes widening as he did so. "That's not wine," he coughed out.

Brie snatched the cup back and drained it a second time. "Nope, it's scotch. And yes, it was a bad day. I've been trying to put this guy off, and he just won't take the fucking hint. I tried to be nice about it and show him that I'm not interested, but he just won't stop. So the motherfucker lured me by telling me he needed help with a paper. And like an idiot, I thought that was the only thing he wanted." The teacup refilled again. "I don't even know why I'm telling you this. It's not like my petty human problems are that big of a deal compared to everything you have going on." She went to take another drink, but Ezra grabbed the cup and downed it before she could grab it back. He flipped the cup over and placed it on the saucer.

"I've known you for over a month now, and I can say that there is nothing subtle about you, Bridget. You are very direct." Ezra actually smirked at her. Brie decided to chalk the fluttering in her stomach up to the alcohol and not Ezra's smile.

She huffed and crossed her arms. "With you, maybe, but that's only because you have this whole comforting, nice angel vibe about you. I should be nice to my students."

"I have never been comforting or nice, Bridget." *Goddess above, did his voice just get huskier?*

With no force behind it, she swatted his arm. Her head was already feeling a little fuzzy. Too much alcohol, too quickly, with nothing in her stomach, a bad combo. "Psht, you have been both to me almost the whole time I've been here. Who gives a job to a total stranger without looking at a resume or references? You didn't even ask for my name! And I just went along with it, totally cool because you have chill angel vibes."

"Now it's chill angel vibes?" Ezra's smirk grew impossibly wide as he moved the teacup out of Brie's reach. He was enjoying teasing her. She made to grab for the teacup but managed only to bump into his arm. She didn't move back.

She craned her head to look him in the eye. "Yes, chill angel vibes. You've been great to me. I probably should have eaten something before going straight for the teacup. Is there anything in the back?" She didn't wait for a response as she started to head toward the door and punched the number four button on the panel. She had to put distance between them before doing something stupid. Food and water would help clear the cloud of alcohol and extreme desire.

"Should be some snacks. I will order something more substantial for you, though. Cheese pizza with pineapple, right?" Ezra was already pulling out a cell phone, which Brie had never seen him use, from his pocket. Her hand stopped on the doorknob. She looked back at him with wide, slightly glazed eyes. "Yeah, it's my favorite. How did you know?"

"Lily, obviously." He rolled his eyes. "She called me this morning to let me know. Though why she thought that was pertinent information that required a five-thirty phone call is beyond me." Brie smiled because, of course, Lily would think a favorite food was important. She and Lily were similar. Brie knew that already, and food was very important to Brie.

Something warm radiated through her that wasn't just the alcohol. The break room was as inviting as ever. Brie found packs of cookies and trail mix in one of the cabinets. On the counter stood a bowl of fruit that wasn't there last time. With a banana and a pack of trail mix in hand, Brie rejoined Ezra in the front of the shop.

Ezra still had the phone to his ear when she walked through the door; he looked very much annoyed. "They put me on hold. Is that typical?"

Brie shrugged, feeling a little less hazy now that she had started to eat. "It's Saturday, prime pizza day in a college town. Seriously, you've lived here long enough to know that."

Ezra tapped his foot. "Maybe, but I've never ordered pizza," he huffed. Brie shrugged and shook a bit of trail mix into her hand. She walked around the counter and began to wander around the shop. Even though she had been there for over a month already, Brie had not taken the time to peruse the front of the shop other than to chase tourists out. She suspected that most of the items in the front were just for show, to give the shop the look of an actual antique store.

Her fingers brushed over objects as she walked. It all looked a bit like junk to her. Pieces of old kitchen appliances, books with nondescript covers, faceless dolls, and intricate jewelry sat beside each other with seemingly no order.

An old typewriter caught her eye, sitting by itself on a rickety table in a corner. A blank sheet of fresh white paper sat in it, waiting to be marked. Brie placed one finger on a key, letting it rest there for a second, feeling the slight wear of the plastic beneath her finger before pushing it down with a satisfying snick. On the paper, though, instead of a typeface black 'f,' it typed out a word.

It said, "fuck."

"It only types out swear words, no matter what you type. It belonged to Hemingway. It used to type full expletive-laden sentences whenever anyone else used it, but the magic has faded some since his death." Ezra stood behind her left shoulder, too close, looking at the typewriter. His steps had been completely silent as usual. Brie had learned to stop jumping every time he appeared.

She turned toward him. "How did you end up with it? Friends with Hemingway, too?"

"Actually, we never crossed paths. Years ago, someone sold it to me for some pixie dust. He had won it in a card game against Hemingway." Ezra leaned over and pressed a few random keys on the typewriter. On the paper, it now said "asshole son of a whore." His laugh was quiet. "Old man had a sense of humor," he mumbled.

Straightening once again, he addressed Brie. "I would be careful about touching some of the stuff out here. Some of it gets a little too attached. I once had a sugar canister follow a tourist home. Had to call in some favors to fix that one." Something in Ezra's voice made her suspect he enjoyed talking about his shop's character. The regulars didn't poke around the shop; the tourists couldn't understand what sat on the shelves and did not get to stay long enough to find out. Maybe the front of the shop displays were just for Ezra.

"What made you decide to open Spirit?" Brie asked finally.

Ezra looked around at the shelves surrounding them, mulling over his answer. "I guess I just had too much stuff and needed a place to put it all. A uh... friend of mine once suggested I set up a stall for my stuff. I didn't take it seriously until sh— they were gone." Ezra's face twisted with emotion. Brie had the urge to reach out and smooth his features and apologize. The bell tinkling pulled their attention from each other. Ezra walked away, rounding the corner of the shelf.

The pizza delivery guy was already walking out the door when Brie left the typewriter behind and walked away from the shelves. She could still feel the effects of the scotch she had downed, but the smell of hot pizza had a powerful allure.

"Here. I'll be in the back." Ezra placed the pizza in her arms.

"Do you want some before you go?" she asked, lifting the box toward him.

"I'm not hungry. Yell if you need anything. Leave the teacup alone; it's enabled you enough today." His laugh was intoxicating to Brie.

Brie frowned at his retreating back. "The teacup was just being helpful!"

Ezra opened the Storage Room door and walked through but turned before shutting the door. "You're welcome, Bridget."

"Thank you!" she yelled before he shut the door. With no reservations left, she set the pizza on the counter and started devouring slice after slice. Her head buzzed a little, but her stomach was full; her bad mood was now mostly forgotten.

Pizza finished and alcohol starting to burn away, Brie settled into her usual spot in front of the computer after stashing the empty box in the break room. As she picked up where she left off in the ledger, the door opened, and Brie looked up into the face of her advisor, Dr. Fry. "Oh, hello, Brie. I didn't realize you worked for Ezra."

"Dr. Fry? What are you doing here?" Brie's eyes went from wide in surprise to narrowed in suspicion. "So, what are you?"

Rather than be offended, Dr. Fry smiled, her eyes behind her coke-bottle glasses glittering. "Always so direct. That's one of the reasons I picked you as my advisee, Brie."

CHAPTER 10

Dr. Fry stepped slowly toward Brie as if she was afraid the younger woman would bolt. Despite meeting more than a few dangerous creatures at the shop, Brie had never had the urge to run quite like she did after seeing her mentor walk in.

"You don't need to be afraid of me, Brie. You know that." Dr. Fry stepped closer, reading the panic in her eyes.

Brie nodded. "I'm not afraid. I just want to know what you are."

Dr. Fry said nothing until she had finally reached the counter, though she kept a little distance between herself and Brie. "I'm human, same as you."

One eyebrow raised, skepticism written all over Brie's face. "Then how do you know Ezra?"

Dr. Fry smiled again. "Old family friend, you might say. I've been keeping an eye on him for years, as a favor to his mother."

"His mother? How long have you been keeping an eye out for him? I mean, you know that he's... um...

that he's..." Brie bit her lip, unable to say it aloud to Dr. Fry. This was a clashing of her two worlds, and it left her deeply unsettled.

"That's he's an angel? Of course. As I said, I'm doing this for his mother. I've been watching over Ezra for close to three hundred years now. Seems like such a short time in the grand scheme of life, though," Dr. Fry said calmly, as if this were any normal conversation they would have.

Brie gave her professor a charged look. "I thought you said you were human."

Dr. Fry smiled. "I am. Fully and completely human in the technical sense. But my death has been postponed indefinitely until my services are no longer required."

Sucking in her bottom lip, Brie finally said, "I don't understand."

Dr. Fry reached one of her hands across the counter to touch Brie's. "Let's just say that while eternal life may seem like a blessing, sometimes it is also a punishment."

Brie looked to where Dr. Fry now reassuringly patted her hand in a motherly gesture. "So why are you spending it looking after Ezra? Or working at CCSU, for that matter?"

With a final pat on Brie's hand, Dr. Fry withdrew her hand. Her eyes turned sad behind the large glasses. "One day, I hope to tell you, but that isn't my story to tell. As for the university, when you have acquired several lifetimes' worth of knowledge, it would be selfish to hoard it all for yourself. And I enjoy teaching and my research."

"So that leaves me with more questions than answers." Brie crossed her arms, annoyed at her mentor's vague responses, though honestly, she should be used to vague answers by now.

"That's academia, my dear Brie. You best get used to it if you plan to finish your Ph.D.," Dr. Fry responded blandly.

Brie huffed. "I'll just go get Ezra then." Her professor nodded, her eyes glittering with some insight Brie was not privy to. She turned sharply on her heel and pushed the number two button before barging through the Storage Room door.

"Ezra?" she called out, not hearing the familiar banging. She waited thirty seconds. Ezra didn't appear, and no other sound could be heard in the Storage Room. She called again, louder this time. But all remained quiet, and Ezra did not appear.

"Okay, don't panic. Your advisor is out there waiting, totally being way old as fuck, and your boss has disappeared into the giant magic room. Everything is just brilliant," she muttered to herself.

Brie turned to what she had started to call the Pick-Up Shelf, hoping to find exactly what Dr. Fry needed sitting at eye level like everything else. But the usual spot was empty. Indeed, the whole row was empty; everything packed neatly on the shelf above or below where she was looking.

"Great, and now the Storage Room is broken. I have no idea what she's picking up. Umph—" Brie was suddenly hit in the back of the head by a small object. It didn't hurt exactly, but it surprised her enough that she staggered forward into the shelf. "Dammit! Geez, I'm sorry! I didn't mean to call you broken," she called out to nothing in particular. Maybe she would have felt silly for talking to a room, but somehow she knew the Storage Room appreciated the apology.

Brie looked down to see what the Storage Room had thrown at her. She stared at it, puzzled. It was an egg; instead of white, the shell was a swirl of black and midnight blue. As Brie picked it up between thumb and forefinger, she examined it for any cracks from where it had hit her or the floor; the shell was perfectly smooth. It seemed heavier than it should have been.

The longer she stared at the egg, the more the colors appeared to swirl and shift, and the whole thing began to grow heavier in her hand. Brie's arm began to shake from the effort of holding it, until her arm gave out, and suddenly the egg dropped to the floor. This time it did crack, and the shell's colors rose into smoke and filled Brie's vision.

She coughed and sputtered inside the cloud of blue and black, shutting her eyes as she waved her hands in front of her face to clear away the smoke. She heard the sharp intake of breath directly in front of her. Slowly, she opened her eyes, afraid of what she might find standing there.

Before her was Ezra, hunched over at the waist, hands on his knees. His dark hair covered his face as he took another deep breath. Finally, he lifted his head and saw Brie. "Brie, ah... thank you. I thought I was going to be in there a while." He took another breath, slowly straightening back up to his full, impressive height.

"What just happened?" Brie asked, hands up in surprise.

Ezra ran a hand through his hair, his go-to tick, looking sheepish. "It was so stupid. I was inventorying some Assyrian items that I haven't touched in probably over a century, and I picked up a lamassu clay tablet."

"That still doesn't explain the you in an egg part." She put her hands on her hips, waiting.

"I'm getting to that. I must have been distracted and did not read the tablet. The lamassu attached to that particular tablet clearly had a sense of humor because its idea of protection is to send people into eggs. Which I'm sure was fine for an ancient Assyrian family, but is inconvenient for me." At this last, he directed his voice over his shoulder, presumably toward where the tablet lay.

"Well, then it's a good thing the Storage Room chucked your egg prison at my head, or you would have been stuck forever." Brie wanted to smile, but her thoughts kept wandering back to the front of the shop where her mentor waited.

"Not forever. A few hours, maybe. The tablets were used for what you would call a magical panic room. So what did you say to offend the Storage Room?" His look instantly made her feel guilty, like whatever she had said to the Storage Room was also a personal insult to him.

Brie looked anywhere but at his face as she kicked the ground. "I called it broken," she said in a mumble. Her head snapped up and she looked at him defiantly. "To be fair, I went to get an order and the whole damn shelf was empty!"

"If the shelf is empty, they didn't order anything. The Storage Room is good at remembering orders. Come on then. Let's go see what they want." He gave her a look that signified that this should be the most obvious thing in the world.

He brushed past her toward the door. "Ezra, wait!" Brie called out before he was completely out of her reach. He turned to look at her, waiting, and she immediately started to fidget under his gaze. She cast her eyes to the floor. Brie could not exactly say why she had all these jumbled feelings; it wasn't as if Dr. Fry was going to suddenly drop her as a student. And Dr. Fry being immortal was hardly the weirdest thing since she started at the shop. *This really doesn't change anything. So why do I feel so panicked?*

Ezra must have recognized the war in her mind from just her face. One hand came to rest on Brie's upper arm with a comforting squeeze. The other he used to tilt her chin up to look at him. Brie immediately felt some of the tension in her stomach ease. His touch never seemed to fail to work magic on her body.

"Everything okay? Do you want to stay back here while I handle them? I know some of my customers can be intense. It's okay, Brie." His eyes were soft; Brie felt comfort radiate through her whole body from just that look alone. *Probably one of his angel powers*, Brie tried to reason. She didn't even register that he called her simply Brie again. Instead, her focus was on his touch, still on her chin and arm.

"It's not that." She didn't move, fearing he would let her go. "It's just... it's my advisor out there. I've been working under her for two years now, and I feel like I suddenly don't know anything, and that she might drop me as a student now that I know what she really is." These were irrational thoughts; Brie was fully aware of that, but something deep-seated within her told her everything was wrong. She wasn't a crier, so Brie twisted her hands together in front of her, frustrated at herself.

He moved his hand to fully cup her chin, forcing her to keep eye contact. "Bridget, I promise you that nothing bad will happen. Most of the creatures around here just want to carry on with their normal lives. So don't worry, okay, sweetheart? Now breathe."

She nodded, taking a deep breath to steady her mind. Her brain didn't let her think about the fact that Ezra had just called her sweetheart. One thing at a time.

Brie felt the warmth slowly leave her body as Ezra let go of her; she allowed him to lead them to the door and back into the front of the shop. Dr. Fry stood next to the counter, texting away on her cell phone as she waited. It surprised Brie to see her professor texting. The older woman, *much older*, Brie reminded herself, looked up as Ezra and Brie entered. Her smile fixed on Ezra as she slid the phone into one of the pockets in her sweater vest.

She received only a deep scowl in return. "Catherine, what are you doing here?" Ezra's voice held a sharp edge, which surprised Brie, especially since he had been so gentle only moments before.

Dr. Fry didn't seem to mind. "Nice to see you, too, Arakiel. I have a few messages to impart: one official and one unofficial. Should we have Brie leave the room?" Her advisor's sharp eyes moved to Brie, and if her words didn't make her feel like a child, the look Dr. Fry gave her certainly did. "No offense, dear. Both are personal." *As if that makes me feel better.*

Brie opened her mouth to argue, but Ezra stilled her with an upturned hand. "Whatever you need to say, Catherine, it can be said in front of Brie. I trust her."

Dr. Fry merely shrugged. "Official business, then. The Council is meeting next week, sooner than their usual Samhain gathering. Word has reached us that the warlock Moloc Vangren has entered our borders without permission, and actions must be taken to secure the creatures of New Britain. You are expected to be there next Wednesday, the same time as usual."

The grave look that Dr. Fry had adopted now completely vanished. "And the unofficial business is that you should call your mother. She worries about you, Arakiel. It's been such a long time. She misses you."

Ezra scoffed. "If she cares so much about me, why did she destroy the one thing that ever mattered to me? She should know not to send her little project to deliver messages. If she has something she wants to say, she can come here and say it." The anger flared off him. Until now, Brie had never seen him angry. There was more than just anger; there was sadness. It looked so wrong on his beautiful face.

The mournful look on Dr. Fry's face made Brie's heart hurt. She was sure there were tears in her mentor's eyes. She never expected that from the unflappable Dr. Fry. "Oh Arakiel, if you only knew—" she began.

"A pleasure as always, Catherine. Please leave now. And don't let this meeting affect your work with

Bridget. She's not your pawn." That last was said so harshly, commanding.

Dr. Fry gave one last sad look toward Ezra, then Brie. "I would never do anything to Brie, Arakiel. She's one of the brightest students I have ever advised." She kept her gaze on Brie, the spark igniting again in her eyes as she looked upon her student. "I will see you Wednesday, Arakiel, whether you like it or not."

She was gone in a moment; somehow, the air felt cold where she and Ezra had faced off. Beside Brie, Ezra closed his eyes and pinched the bridge of his nose in irritation.

Maybe she should give him space and time to cool down, but Brie had one pressing question. "She called you Arakiel. Apollo did, too. Why?" She thought this was the least intrusive question at the moment and hoped it was safe to ask.

Ezra sighed so deeply that Brie began to worry that she had once again overstepped with him. "Never mind. You don't pay me to intrude on your personal business. I'll just—"

"Bridget, it's okay." He cut her off with a sharp look. "Arakiel is the name my mother gave me back when names were still new. It means 'earth of god.' I was Arakiel until I needed a fresh start and to put the past behind me. So I became Ezra and have been ever since."

She knew she was staring at him, though it didn't stop her. Ezra had shared something personal with her; she didn't know what to say. After nearly a full minute of agonizing silence, she finally found her voice again. "I can understand that. When Maddy adopted us, me and Wes, I couldn't wait to change my last name to St. James for her. For so long, I hung onto a name my parents passed on, but when I was old enough to realize they were dead and never coming back, I couldn't wait to have a new identity as Maddy's daughter. So I totally get it."

Pausing, she couldn't bring herself to look at Ezra. Besides Wes, Brie rarely shared her personal life and feelings with anyone. "It's the life we make for ourselves that's more fulfilling than the one created for us," she said, still averting her gaze.

Ezra made a noise through his nose, and Brie finally looked up at him. His face was a mix of emotions, none she could easily read. "That reminds me of something a friend once said to me many centuries ago."

"You know what they say: great minds and all that." Brie beamed, hoping it would keep him on the pleasant side of his emotions.

His reciprocating smile held a twinge of sadness. "Yes, great minds. Well, I should get back to the Storage Room."

Once again, Brie was left feeling that she had made him uncomfortable. "Wait. Is there a way I can contact you if I need you when you're way in the back? Like texting, or something, so I don't have to scream for you, or for if you get stuck somewhere again."

Black hair fell over his forehead as he shook his head. "Cell phones don't work well in the Storage Room. But I think I have something we can use instead. Stay there." He slipped through the door and reappeared in seconds, holding what looked like two clam shells. He handed one over to Brie, who could only stare at the thing in her hand.

"Ezra is this a—" she started, a mischievous grin slowly spreading across her face.

"Don't say it, Bridget," Ezra responded, a warning in his voice. Brie didn't heed his warning at all.

"Shell phone?" The grin was wide and completely overtook her face as she tried to keep from laughing.

"I'm taking them back now," he said, reaching lazily toward the one in her hand. She pulled away, the shell phone safely in her cupped hands.

"Too late! I'll call you on the shell phone if I need anything." She laughed loudly as Ezra grumbled, hiding his own grin, and walked back into the Storage Room.

Brie opened the shell phone less than a minute after Ezra left the room. Inside, an ethereal glow appeared on each half of the shell. She held one end up to her ear like a regular phone, feeling a little silly as she did so. "Testing, testing from the shell phone," she said, not knowing how well the thing would pick up her voice.

"Please don't call them shell phones," Ezra groaned. His voice came through so clearly it was like he was standing right next to her.

Brie smiled. "I'm calling them shell phones, and there's nothing you can do about it."

"Get back to work, Bridget," he said. Brie could picture him frowning at his shell phone on the other end.

"Sure thing, boss man. Shell phone out!"

"Brie!"

She closed the clamshell, cutting off his loud groan. Brie laughed as she set the shell phone on the counter and pulled the ledger to her workstation.

CHAPTER 11

"If anyone you don't know comes in, get them out. If they don't leave, press three and go to my apartment. It has more than enough wards; you will be safe until I get back. Don't roll your eyes, Bridget," Ezra snapped as Brie sighed again. They had been over this three times already.

"I'll be fine, Ezra. If anything happens, I'll just ring your shell phone." She quirked an eyebrow at him, barely managing to keep the smile from her face.

It was Ezra's turn to roll his eyes. "I regret ever buying those damn things, let alone giving one to you."

"Don't you have a meeting to get to?" she snipped.

"One last thing." Ezra dug into the pocket of his jeans and pulled out a skeleton key dangling on a delicate silver chain, the bow of which was shaped like a small crow's skull. He handed it to her, withdrawing his hand slowly once it reached her fingertips. "I probably won't be back before closing. Lock up at exactly ten, then go straight home. This is your copy of the shop key. Keep it around your neck at least until after you cross your threshold."

"Yes, Mother." Brie placed the chain around her neck, then studied the key and chain. The delicate chain was definitely not one Ezra would wear. He must have picked it out for her. The chain itself was a work of art. She was mesmerized by it.

"Bridget." Ezra's voice was a warning. She dropped the key, and it made a small thump against her chest.

"Don't worry. I'll be fine. Bad things happen, hide in the apartment. Lock up, go home. Nothing to worry about." She looked up at him with a reassuring smile. He still didn't look entirely convinced but gave her a nod and half a smile, regardless.

"Be safe, Bridget," he said, giving her shoulder a lingering touch.

He left soon after, looking back at her through the glass in the door before moving out of sight of the shop. Brie felt a fluttering in her heart as she watched him disappear. She shook herself, unwilling to examine the feeling further.

"Don't worry. It just takes practice. Try again," Lily urged.

"It's not going to work, Lily. I don't have your kind of magic," Brie whined in return.

She flopped her head onto her arms where they rested on the counter. A single stock of asphodel buds sat before her. For the last hour, Lily had been trying to teach her to infuse magic into the buds to make them bloom, to no avail. Instead, Brie's eyes felt like sandpaper from staring too long and forgetting to blink. A headache was starting to form.

"Seriously, Brie, don't give up. Magic isn't something that you can learn in a day. You already have the will; I can totally tell. So keep at it." Lily's smile was encouraging and warm, which made it harder for Brie to sulk.

"So, do you have an order in?" Brie asked, straightening up and looking away from the asphodel buds. She needed a break from magic practice.

"Mm-hm, should be some fertilizer. There's this hag, in like Bulgaria, I think, that just has the perfect mixture for some of my perennials. I can't seem to replicate it on my own. Ezra gets it from her for a discount. She does some kind of old folk magic spell on it. Keeps my plant babies happy." Lily's smile always grew when talking about her garden.

Brie nodded before heading into the Storage Room. There on the shelf, just where it should be, was a lumpy bag labeled " ." The bag was large. Brie realized the shelf had expanded to fit so she could easily see and pick up the bag. Rather than being heavy like she expected, the bag weighed next to nothing.

When Brie returned to the front and placed the bag on the counter, it didn't even make a sound. Lily made no immediate move to grab it. "How are you doing with no Ezra around?"

Brie shrugged. "Not too bad. So far, it's been pretty quiet. I'm just dreading the time when Albert shows up."

"Oh, I doubt he'll be in tonight. He's one of the vampire representatives on the council. Bertie is very active in our community." Lily's whole face lit up as she talked about Albert. Brie still couldn't wrap her head around that attraction, but then again, Lily knew Albert way better than she did. Maybe under the sneering, deathly pale face was a heart of gold. Or something like that.

Brie was relieved to learn he wouldn't be coming in on the night Ezra was out of the shop, especially after Ezra had given Brie that whole spiel about being in the store alone.

"Want me to stick around for a while longer?" Lily asked. Brie looked first to Lily's bright face, then down at the still closed buds of asphodel and shook her head.

"Nah, I'll be fine. It'll give me time to practice without the stress of trying in front of someone. Plus, I'm sure you have stuff to do." Brie kept her voice light, even though she felt a niggling sensation in the back of her mind that wanted Lily to stay.

Across from her, Lily grabbed the bag of fertilizer, letting out a long breath. "You have no idea. Mom and granny have already started preparations for Samhain, and my sisters have already cleaned every surface at least twice. It's a month-long preparation for two days. I'm just stalling here to keep out of the crazy."

The pang of sadness that bloomed in Brie's chest was so sudden it nearly stole her breath. Lily had a loving family. She grew up knowing what she was, and clearly, she was happy, whereas Brie never knew her parents. She was in her teens when Maddy finally took her in and she had felt loved for the first time. There was also Wes—they grew up like real siblings, and she loved him dearly, but Brie had never been able to shake the feeling that her own parents never wanted her. Brie's face betrayed nothing of her internal storm. Instead, she smiled at Lily. "Well, you can't hide forever. I guess I'll see you next week. Ezra said it's been added to your tab, so don't worry about it."

Lily nodded with a smile bright as a noon day sun. "See you later! And if you need some company, just shoot me a text or something."

"What, your psychic powers can't just pick up when I need you?" Brie laughed.

"That's not how it works and you know it." Lily's responding laugh was loud and joyful.

She took two steps toward the door but turned back to the counter. "And Brie, he's been through some pretty bad stuff. You both have. But I can see the tangling together of your destinies happening clear as day."

"What does that even mean, Lily?" Brie furrowed her brow. Lily shrugged as if she couldn't fully explain.

"Maybe you should try kissing him and find out." The bell tinkled as Lily left the store. Brie stood there, stunned. She had thought of what it would be like to kiss Ezra many times. Maybe she had noticed the way he would watch her or touch her longer than was necessary. But he was still her boss; it wasn't like anything could happen.

Brie leaned over to grab one of her textbooks, determined to get some of her own coursework done while Ezra was out and to push kissing out of her mind. Head still bent down, rummaging through her overstuffed bag, she heard the bell tinkle again.

"Lily, I told you it's fine. I'm okay by—"

But when Brie straightened, it wasn't Lily standing there. It was Moloc. His face split into the cruel smile she remembered from the last time. Brie couldn't help the half step back she took. "Ah, Mistress Bridget. I had hoped I would find you here, without Ezra to bother us."

Another step back, though Brie couldn't tear her eyes from the sinister face before her. "Ezra is in the back. He'll be here any minute." *Goddess, I hope I sound braver than I feel.*

Moloc's cold eyes narrowed. "Don't lie to me, girl. I know very well he is at that meeting with the rest of those misguided fools who call themselves a council. At this moment, they are hidden away, discussing my return to this pathetic city."

Ice slushed through her veins. She should run now. Just push the number three button and hide away in Ezra's apartment. But fear kept Brie rooted to the spot; she could only look back at Moloc with wide eyes.

Moloc lifted one of his boney-fingered hands, palm open toward Brie. "Now, let's see what's inside." His voice dripped with menace, and his eyes held a determined sheen. An electric blue light shimmered around his hand; it looked almost beautiful.

Then there was pain.

It felt as if her head was splitting open and Moloc's fingers were rooting around in her brains. Her eyes slammed shut; she tried to scream, but no sound came out. Images of her life, and something more she didn't recognize, flashed through her mind, almost incomprehensible to her through the pain. Brie was vaguely aware of the tears streaming down her face, but only the raw pain mattered.

Just as suddenly as it came, the pain ceased. Moloc lowered his hand. Brie crumpled to the floor, conscious though her whole body screamed in agony. She was out of Moloc's line of sight now that she was on the floor behind the counter. Gathering what little strength she had left, she started to inch herself backward toward the Storage Room door, willing herself to move even while all she wanted was to rest.

Moloc's voice arrested her movement for a second, but after a quick recovery, she persisted. "Ah, just as I suspected. I knew it was only a matter of time before you found your way back to him. Ezra doesn't know what you are, does he?" He moved to look down at her over the counter.

Her back now against the door, Brie used the doorknob as leverage to hoist herself up. She felt a whole-body exhaustion and pain, the likes of which she had never experienced before, but somehow she pulled herself up. "I don't know what you're talking about," she spat.

The cruel smile once again spread across Moloc's features. "No? Well, how fortunate then. It will make things much easier this time."

Brie seized the moment to punch the number three button and yank open the Storage Room door. With a tug that seemed to take all of her remaining strength, she pulled the door closed behind her and heard a definitive click. Before she had even had a chance to look at her surroundings, the door shuddered under a loud bang and rattle, but then all was quiet.

Move, she told her body. It took longer than she wanted before it actually obeyed. She staggered away from the door, which, unlike its counterpart in the store, was a solid, heavy, dark wood. No more noises came through the door, and it remained firmly shut. Ezra's wards held.

Brie moved away from the entrance slowly, down a dimly lit hallway. Finally, the hallway opened into a large living room. Brie assumed it was a living room, though it looked more like a well-stocked forest shelter.

At first, Brie thought she was actually in a forest rather than indoors. The trees around her were so real; the faint wind that rustled her hair smelled of pine and decaying leaves. Then she saw the dark brown molding that clearly made up the walls. Bookshelves were scattered around the whole room, each stuffed full of a variety of books of every genre. The hard-wood floor was covered in Persian rugs of emerald, silver, brown, red, and orange, like the floor of a forest, but softer. On top of the rugs sat furniture that looked as if it had grown right out of the floor, with twisting branches forming a couch and chairs. Emerald cush-ions covered all the furniture for added comfort; blan-kets lay on the back of the couch and chairs.

Most striking of all was the arch of tree branches across the entire ceiling with patches of starlight between them. Ball-shaped paper lanterns hung from the tree branches above, giving off a gentle glow to light the room.

Enchanted was the first word that came to mind, like an enchanted forest. It was a shock to see Ezra's home, especially since it didn't seem to match his personality. There was something about it that made Brie feel instantly at ease. The terror from a moment ago was forgotten; she knew with absolute certainty that she was safe here.

Peering through the forest room, she spotted the kitchen. It was a large space, open to the living room but more in the shadows. Beyond that was another dim hallway that Brie assumed led to Ezra's bedroom and bathroom.

Do angels sleep? she wondered.

Now that the adrenaline rush had worn off, Brie started to feel the exhaustion in her body. Her head ached painfully, and her whole body seemed to be made of lead. With slow steps, she made her way to the deep couch. She had planned to sit, but the need for comfort was overwhelming, and she laid down, pulling the soft blanket from the back of the couch to drape over her body.

"I should call Ezra," she whispered to the room, even as her eyes grew heavy and the softness of the cushions cradled her body. Before she could even think to reach for the shell phone in her pocket, she was asleep.

Some time later, though Brie had no idea how long, she felt her body being lifted from the couch. Still too tired to fully awaken, she could feel arms wrapped around her and pressed against something hard on one side. Under normal circumstances, Brie would have thrashed and fought off the arms supporting her, but her strength was spent. She gave one pathetic attempt, managing to wiggle only slightly. The arms under her knees and back tightened a little.

"I've got you, sweetheart. Go back to sleep," a soft voice spoke to her. Somewhere in her mind, she recognized the voice and relaxed in his grip, never once bothering to open her eyes. Instead, she snuggled closer to the warm body that held her and listened to his heartbeat against her ear.

Ezra placed her gently on his bed. He tugged off her shoes and placed them on the floor before pulling the blankets over her sleeping form. With her very last ounce of consciousness, Brie felt the soft brush of his fingertips on her cheek and a gentle press of his lips on her forehead. Then everything was still and peaceful.

CHAPTER 12

S unshine cut through the large bedroom window, heavy dark drapes pushed aside. The first thing Brie noticed as she started to wake was the pounding in her head, like a hangover after a rager with Wes. With a loud groan, she rolled over on the bed, away from the sunlight, eyes remaining firmly shut.

The smell of the pillow where she buried her face was the first indication that she was not in her own room. Woodsmoke and vanilla filled her senses. Next was the bed itself, which was incredibly soft and much larger than her old, twin-sized mattress. It felt like she was lying on a cloud, wrapped up in blankets that were warm but not stifling.

Despite the extreme comfort, the foreign feeling of the room clawed at her mind, and she sat up in a sudden panic. Pain exploded in her head at the quick movement. Brie squeezed her eyes shut and gripped her head as a loud groan pushed its way out of her throat.

Once the immediate pain subsided a little, she opened her eyes and was greeted by the sight of Ezra sitting at the foot of the bed. "How are you feeling?" His voice was just above a whisper, probably in deference to her headache. He handed over a glass of water and two aspirin, which Brie took without question, popping the pills and draining the glass before answering.

"Like absolute hell. Where am I?" She let her gaze wander around the room.

Ezra took the empty glass from her. "You're in my room. You were asleep on the couch when I arrived home. I thought you would be more comfortable here."

"Then where did you sleep?" Some part of her secretly wished he had stayed in the bed with her. She chased that thought away quickly.

Ezra shrugged. "I didn't. Angels don't need to sleep, not really. But I have developed a bad habit, you might say." He paused and let the silence hang between them. Brie brought her knees up to her chest under the blankets and wrapped her arms around them.

"Bridget, what happened last night?" Concern clouded his beautiful face.

Brie sank her chin onto the tops of her knees and sighed deeply. If only she could forget the previous night altogether, but Moloc's cold eyes and cruel grin were forever etched in her mind. Whispers of the pain still echoed through her body. She willed herself not to cry.

There must have been tears forming despite her best efforts because, in the blink of an eye, Ezra was seated next to her on the bed with one arm wrapped around her shoulders. The gesture was all it took to open the floodgates, and tears rushed down her face unchecked. Her body sought to be comforted, so she angled herself to bury her face into Ezra's chest, her hands gripping his shirt like a lifeline. Her bent knees turned and rested against the side of his thigh. Ezra automatically adjusted his grip on her as he brought his other arm around her to rub soothing circles on her back. His chin rested on the top of her head as he held her while she cried.

"I thought he was going to kill me. It was like he looked into my head and whatever he saw was bad," she managed to choke out as a wave of fresh tears spilled out.

She couldn't see his face, but his chest rumbled when he spoke. "Moloc."

Brie nodded against him. The crying did nothing to help the pounding in her head, but there was no controlling the stream of tears now that they had started. For several minutes, she cried while he remained quiet. Ezra gently held her and continued to rub circles on her back. Brie allowed herself to slowly relax into the gesture and let the calm wash over her.

He said nothing as her tears started to subside, and the tension in her body started to slack just a little. "I don't usually cry. This is so dumb," she said, rubbing her eyes with the heels of her hands.

After one last shuddering sigh, Ezra moved her gently away from his body, keeping a hand on each of her biceps. Ezra's brilliant green eyes roved over her face. Bringing one long-fingered hand up to her face, he cupped her cheek and used his thumb to brush away the last of her tears. The same comforting sensation she had felt before in the Storage Room spread throughout her from just that touch, and Brie let out a deep sigh.

"You had a rough night. It's okay to feel overwhelmed," he said, keeping his hand on her cheek.

Finally, she found her voice again, her thoughts brimming with questions. "Ezra, why did Moloc come after me? What does he want with me?"

His hand lingered a moment longer on her cheek before he removed it and dropped his hands from her arms completely. "Bridget, I'm not entirely sure why Moloc targeted you. But I have a feeling it was just to get to me. There's something I need to tell you, Brie, about my history with Moloc." Ezra's voice sounded pained, like he would rather talk about anything else.

"Okay, tell me." She scooted away from him, scrubbing her face of any remaining tears. She stretched out on the bed, laying on her side so she could look at him as well as curl in on herself. Ezra leaned back against the pillows of the bed and brought his feet up to lie beside her. His hands clasped over his chest as he opened and closed his mouth, deciding where to start.

"I've known Moloc since before my Fall. When I left everything behind, it was because he told me about a better existence. One where humans could have the knowledge of the world and live peacefully with our kind. He led me to believe in something better, and like a fool, I swallowed every word because by then I had spent so much time among humans, I hoped to see something good, to be something good."

Ezra took a deep breath, and Brie remained motionless beside him, waiting for him to continue. "When I left the Above, I made a pact with Moloc, which should have mutually benefited us both. But he only used me for the divine power he could not have for himself. And for centuries, I let him lead me down a path farther away from the light. All that time, I convinced myself that I was doing good."

He gave her a piercing look, and his voice dropped just above a whisper. "I was not good, Bridget."

Brie's breath caught in her chest, struggling with the idea of what he meant. But Ezra pushed on, averting his gaze once more.

"For centuries, I followed Moloc blindly. I thought my actions were helping to bring peace and knowledge. My power was used to build empires. I didn't know, or didn't care, that it was at the cost of many lives and the subjugation of so many. So many lives were destroyed, and so much power was taken from them to feed Moloc. He was my mentor until the day I met the Morrigan."

Another pause as his eyes grew distant, staring up at the ceiling. "She was a goddess unlike any other, and I was completely captivated by her fury and might. But sometimes she could be gentle and funny. Oh gods, could she make me laugh. I would have followed her anywhere. But I was a different person then." He looked wistful. "I think I just wanted to be loved so desperately. It blinded me to her cruelty."

Brie felt like her heart was twisting in her chest. He had mentioned the Morrigan beforehand, and something told her that things didn't end well. Ezra did not look over at her. He was lost in his own memories now and did not see the thinly veiled look of defeat on Brie's face.

"What happened to her?" Brie found herself asking. Did she even want to know the answer?

Her voice seemed to bring Ezra's attention back to the present and his focus on her. The haze of memory was gone from his eyes; instead, they turned wistful as he looked at her.

"She died."

"How can a goddess die?" Brie hoped the question wouldn't shut him down. She wanted to know more. There was still so much about this world that she didn't know.

Next to her, Ezra ran a hand through his hair and closed his eyes. "She was bound into a mortal body and killed. Only someone exceptionally powerful could do that, like the kind of power my family has."

"And you think one of them did it? Why?" *Why would his family betray him like that?* Brie couldn't imagine.

Ezra shrugged, keeping his eyes closed. "I don't know. Maybe. They spent centuries trying to get me to come home. I wouldn't be surprised if they thought breaking my deepest connections with the mortal world would send me flying back to the Above. But she died in my arms, and I vowed never to go back. Moloc tried to get me to continue on with him. My time with Morgana had caused our arrangement to become estranged. But I couldn't be around him either. So I left everything behind. I started anew, though Moloc was never far behind because of our pact. I've been alone with my shop ever since."

Tentatively at first, Brie reached out and grabbed his hand where it now lay on the bed between them, giving it a gentle squeeze. Ezra's eyes snapped open and met her gaze. Mustering the courage to speak, Brie gave his hand another squeeze. "Well, now you have me."

A beat of charged silence passed as they just stared at each other. Ezra's eyes softened as he returned the squeeze. He rolled to face her, and with his other hand, he lightly touched her cheek. His voice was soft when he spoke. "Yes, I do. Brie, I—"

Whatever he was about to say was cut off by Brie's cell phone vibrating loudly on the bedside table, where she definitely didn't put it last night. Ezra sighed as he tore his eyes from her, picked up the phone, and handed it over.

"Wesley is worried about you. He called this morning while you were still sleeping. Talk to him. I'll go make some breakfast." Brie nodded, wondering at the moment they just shared, before accepting the call on her phone.

"Brie?! Is that you?! It's not the boss again, is it? I want to talk to Brie right now!" She could tell her brother was on the verge of a meltdown.

"Wes, calm down. It's me. I'm alright." She waited for Wes's lecture.

"You didn't call or text or even leave a note! I thought something had happened to you. And then when I finally got an answer from your phone, it was your boss saying you weren't feeling well and that you were staying the night." He was near screeching as he worked himself up into a frenzy.

Brie sighed; she felt so guilty making Wes worry. "I'm so sorry, Wes. I just felt super awful and pretty much passed out on Ezra's couch. I'll be home soon, though. Promise." Not exactly a lie, but she wished she could tell him the whole truth.

A loud huff came through the phone. "Brie, just be honest with me. Are you sleeping with the dude? Because I don't think it's a good idea. I can't tell you what to do; it's your choice. But just know I'm on team Don't Fuck Your Boss."

"What?! I'm..." Brie's eyes flicked to the door as if she could see if Ezra was behind it, then she lowered her voice. "I'm not sleeping with him. He's my boss, Wes. He just let me crash for the night because I was in rough shape. I'll be home soon to get some stuff for class." Ezra was a handsome man, very interesting, and great to talk to when he actually stayed around for longer than five seconds. But he was still her boss and was loaded with centuries of personal baggage.

"I'm just going to eat and then head out. See you soon." She hung up before Wes could start again.

As soon as the call ended, Ezra popped his head around the corner of the door. "Do you like chocolate chips in your pancakes?" he asked innocently.

Brie scrambled off the bed, shoving her phone into her back pocket. "Is there any other way to eat pancakes?!"

CHAPTER 13

" Brie, I'm begging you, please just quit. I can help you find another job; just don't go back to that place." Wes stood in the doorway of her room, one hand on the frame while the other gesticulated wildly in front of him. Inside her room, Brie was packing up her messenger bag with papers to grade. At Wes's words, she turned and crossed her arms tightly.

Since she had gotten home earlier that morning via the number six button on the Storage Room door, Wes had basically been following her around their apartment, begging her to quit. She felt guilty not telling her brother what really happened, so she gave him an edited version of the truth: that some homeless guy wandered in and was being threatening toward her. And since Ezra was out, she went and hid in his apartment and started to feel sick, but she didn't feel safe going home in the dark.

Brie figured that would be enough and Wes would probably insist on walking her home or something. Instead, her brother continued to badger her about quitting. She was touched that he cared so much about her safety, but Wes had no idea what really happened at the shop. As far as Wes knew, the regulars were just ordinary people, Moloc was just some homeless man, and last night should have been nothing to worry about. Wes's insistence that she quit was starting to grate on her nerves.

"Wes, I like my job. It pays really well, especially for how little I have to do. And I like Ezra. He's been nothing but great since I started." She didn't even bother to stifle the sigh. She was in too deep now and knew too much of that other world. To leave would probably be more dangerous because she wouldn't have Ezra's protection.

And she didn't want to leave Ezra. They were friends now, and even with the regulars he got along with, he still seemed so lonely. Brie didn't want to leave him, especially after that morning.

But Wes didn't need to know all that. So no matter how much it pained her to lie to her brother, Brie did it anyway.

Ezra was behind the counter when she walked into the shop later. Their eyes met across the room, but Brie stood rooted to the spot just inside the door.

"I distinctly remember saying you could have the day off, Brie." His voice was soft.

She shrugged. "I know, but I'm not going to let that old toad scare me out of this place. Besides, staying home means listening to Wes list all the reasons why I need to quit." Crossing the room, she dumped her bag in the usual spot and turned towards Ezra.

"You could still use the rest after last night. You'll get paid for the day, regardless; you know that." He looked down at her with concern, probably debating whether to just throw her through the number six door or not.

"I'm not a charity case, Ezra. I get paid to work, so here I am to work." She straightened her ponytail, working around the two pens already stuck behind the elastic, then shook out the rest of her ginger hair. Ezra's eyes followed the movement.

"I still think you should get some rest. Take a break from the ledger tonight, at least. There's plenty of safe stuff in the shop to explore, or you can just relax in the break room. Whatever you want." Ezra's voice was on the edge of pleading. She noticed his hands clenched into tight fists.

Brie snorted loudly. "Ezra, give it a rest. You're just as bad as Wes. I'm not a porcelain doll or anything. But I'll make you a deal. I won't do anything even remotely stressful if you tell me what happened at the council meeting last night." She gave his arm a bump with her shoulder.

At the heart of it, Brie wanted to know why Moloc was walking around freely when the magical city council clearly didn't want him in the city at all. *Do they know Moloc has been to the shop before?*

Ezra sighed heavily. "It wasn't that exciting, Brie. It was a lot of bureaucracy and idle chatter. None of the beings in the city are strong enough to do much about Moloc. Not even me. Even if I was able to, which I'm not, our pact prevents me from using my power against him. The best we can do is keep up our wards and protection magics." He stopped and stared off at one wall for a long time. When he spoke again, it was just above a whisper. "I will never be truly free of him."

"Did you use any of that protection magic on me?" Brie asked suddenly, pulling him out of the fall into his own mind again. Especially after last night, she had to know. Because if he had placed any protection magic on her before last night, then she wondered if she was underestimating how dangerous Moloc really was.

"No, but you have protection now, Brie. I was stupid not to place them on you before, but I swear you have protection magic now. Moloc shouldn't be able to find you outside of this shop, and I've tethered the protection magics of this place to you to strengthen that defense. I won't let him hurt you again." Ezra's eyes gleamed. There was an edge to his tone, like he was pledging an oath. He seemed to do that a lot with her.

Sucking in her bottom lip, Brie averted her eyes from the look he was giving her. That look made her cheeks feel flushed and her stomach flip. There was no way she could look at those beautiful emerald eyes of his while talking about Moloc. When had things gotten so charged between them? Lily's words haunted her: *kiss him and find out.*

"Did you tell the council about Moloc coming here the other week?" she asked, trying not to fidget, to not think about how much she wanted to wrap herself around him.

After a long moment of silence, Ezra responded, "No, I didn't tell them. I couldn't."

"Why the hell not?" Brie whipped her eyes back up to his face, trying not to yell and mostly succeeding, all thoughts of lust gone. If he knew Moloc was evil and a threat, why not tell the council of his comings and goings? "And are you going to tell them what he did last night?" It was a challenge, and she had no intention of backing down.

Ezra at least had the decency to look away. "No." His eyes roved everywhere but would not land on her.

"Why? I don't understand. You're just going to let him run free around the city doing goddess-knows-what to whomever he wants, and you don't care? You're going to just let him come after me." Anger and fear welled up inside her, and she didn't care if her tone was accusatory.

Moving just slightly so he could sit on the stool behind the counter, Ezra sat down heavily, hanging his head so he couldn't look at her. "I took an oath many centuries ago, a blood oath, to Moloc. And in our world, blood oaths are unbreakable save for death. And Moloc is impossible to kill, so we are forever bound."

A step toward him brought Brie between his knees. Head still lowered, he didn't move at all as she stood before him. With one hand, Brie cupped his downturned cheek, lifting it to look at her. His golden-brown skin was smooth and warm beneath her fingertips. An agonizing sadness looked back at her through his eyes, and Brie understood what Ezra meant when he said he wasn't strong enough.

"We'll get you out of this. Together," she promised, not blinking as she stared at him.

For a moment, a hint of a sad smile tugged at the edges of his mouth. "Okay, Brie, whatever you say." His tone was still defeated as he placed his hand over hers and removed it from his face. He didn't let go of her hand, though; instead, he kept her hand nestled in his, settled on his thigh.

"Exactly! Whatever I say. I like it when you're pliable." She smirked, looking only at him and not their hands, though it felt electric where their hands met.

His grin was slightly forced, but the tension was mostly gone. "Don't get used to it, sweetheart. I'm still a mean, grumpy, old man. Set in my ways and all that."

"We'll see about that." She smiled, glad that the air was lightening between them. It was only a temporary distraction. The threat of Moloc still hung over them. But seeing the hopelessness in Ezra's eyes made Brie determined to free him from that monster. It made her want to fight for him.

The tinkle of the bell made them tear their eyes from each other. Brie felt fear rising within her at the sound, the nagging worry that it was Moloc coming through the door.

But it wasn't. It was Apollo dressed in dark jeans with a dark brown leather jacket; his hair was expertly tussled to look like no effort was put into it when, in all actuality, an obscene amount of effort was put into his hair. And, of course, his trademark smug grin that immediately made Brie tense up.

"Hope I'm not interrupting anything." Apollo waggled his eyebrows at them, taking in their close proximity and joined hands.

Brie stepped away quickly, pulling her hand from Ezra's. She turned and glared at Apollo. "I'll just go get your order," she grumbled at him, walking to the Storage Room without looking back. The box for Apollo was incredibly small, perhaps the size of a ring box and wrapped up in brown paper and twine like every other package.

When she emerged from the Storage Room, Apollo was leaning over the counter, and he and Ezra were deep in a whispered conversation. She couldn't see Ezra's face, but Apollo's brow was furrowed, and Brie recognized worry in his eyes.

The minute he looked up and saw Brie, the worry melted from his face and that goddamned smirk returned in full force. "There she is, the Beauty of Spirit Antiques. We were just talking about you," Apollo crooned.

Ezra must have shot him a look because Apollo winked back at him. Brie took her spot next to Ezra at the counter, who turned to her and grimaced. "We were not talking about you. Don't listen to him."

"I never do," Brie replied, shooting a pointed glare Apollo's way.

Apollo clutched his heart in mock pain. "Whatever have I done to offend the lady so? You are too cruel to me, Mistress Brie."

"Not cruel enough, it seems. And you tried to glamour me into having sex with you on our first meeting! I think that's a big something you've done to offend me." She had to stop herself from slamming the little box on the counter. Instead, she set it down with just a little more force than was necessary.

"You should watch yourself, Apollo. This one will tear your head off. And I would gladly watch." Ezra genuinely laughed.

But the smirk didn't stray an inch from Apollo's face. If possible, it turned even more smug. "Ah, I see how it is." He looked between the two of them. "Well, if that's the case, I'm out. Let me know if you need a third sometime. I would love to have you both screaming my name." He blew a kiss to Brie and then to Ezra before grabbing his package and leaving.

"Can I punch him next time? Please?" She groaned.

"Only if you let me watch while you knock him out cold," Ezra responded with a small laugh.

"Deal!" Brie said brightly. She thrust out her hand, he took it, and they shook on it. But then they didn't let go. His green eyes roamed over her face and the moment was suddenly so intense that Brie barely let herself breathe.

Ezra stood abruptly from the chair, barely missing Brie as he did so. "Now, take it easy. I'm working near the door today, so run in if anything happens. Okay?"

"Mh hm, okay, Dad." Brie laughed, waving him off, turning quickly to hide her blushing face.

Brie sent up a prayer of thanks to the Goddess when Ezra told her at the beginning of her shift the following week that Helena was not going to be around for two weeks, and she was to hold back her orders. Not that she saw much of the woman, but even the occasional run-in was too much.

"Business will start picking up since it's October. Everyone wants to be all set for Samhain. Lily will practically move in, so expect to see her outside of her usual days. If it's anything like last year, Granny Everett has them all working round the clock to set up. Sometimes Lily would stop in just to take a short nap in my office." Brie laughed at Ezra's description. No doubt he kept pillows and blankets in there for her use.

"I'll give you a call on the shell phone when she comes in, then. Or if I need anything. And I'm putting her up in the break room for a nap. It's cozier. Now get to work; I'll be fine." She decided to beat him to the punch on his worrying.

For the last week, it was the same spiel every shift. If she needed anything, call him. If she felt afraid, call him. Obviously, if Moloc came in, call him. Then he would move on to rationalizing why he shouldn't work in the back and just accompany her at the front of the shop. They probably spent a solid half hour each shift arguing about his staying before Brie eventually got tired of it and physically pushed him through the Storage Room door and slammed it behind him. Even the Storage Room was on her side, locking the door a few times once Ezra was inside so he couldn't get out.

Ezra gave her a dubious look, but only put up a slight resistance before slipping through the Storage Room door, leaving Brie alone in the shop.

For a while, she stayed at the counter doing school work and grading papers. Midterms were coming up soon, and she knew she should be thinking about that. It wasn't the most exciting thing, but it allowed her to relax. After last night, she needed to relax.

Usually, Brie was a deep sleeper, rarely interrupted with dreams. But now, dreams plagued her every night. Some were pleasant, like the one where she was lounging in a house that looked as if it grew straight from trees. It reminded her of Ezra's home.

But then there were the horrific dreams. Brie wouldn't exactly call them nightmares, though they frightened her. She would find herself on a battlefield covered in bodies and soaked with blood. But instead of feeling afraid or sickened, Brie delighted in the sight of it, in the whole scene of destruction before her. More than that, though, was the feeling of blood and gore gushing into her boots, still warm, and the stink of the dead splayed out as far as the eye could see. It was all so vivid, and that's what frightened her the most. It felt more like a memory.

Most confusing of all were the flashes of dark hair, bright eyes, and her fingers running over the pearly white wings of another. They were familiar and not, but the sensation filled her whole being with an excitement so different from the other dream.

Both types of dreams were overwhelming and alarming. When she woke up, it was with a racing heart and a body soaked in sweat. As much as she wanted to lie her head on the counter and rest for just a moment, she was determined to keep herself awake in case she dreamed again. She stood at the counter, worried that if she sat, she would slump on the stool and drift off.

Brie felt herself nodding off all the same until the tinkle of the bell and a gust of cool wind blew through the shop, jarring her back to her senses. Her first thought was a tourist had wandered in since it had been slow in the shop all day. What she was not prepared for was to see Craig walking in, a boyish, shy smile on his lips.

Shoulders slumping heavily, Brie didn't bother to stifle her loud sigh. It did nothing to deter Craig from approaching her at the counter. "Hi, Brie!" he said, too brightly for Brie's liking.

Rather than return his greeting, she said, "How did you find out where I work?" There was a rigid coldness to her voice, but she doubted he would notice.

He didn't. Instead he gave her a guilty smile. "You never said which place you worked, so I... uh, I asked your friend, Wes. I've seen you two hanging out around campus, so I figured he would know. He said you would love a visitor since it's so miserable here. I can see what he meant." He looked around the shop, taking in the stuffed shelves and lack of customers.

She was going to murder her brother when she got home. After the obnoxious coffee shop incident, she had ranted and raved to Wes about him, so it was a huge breach of trust for him to send Craig over to her work. And then he had the gall to insult her shop!

"Wes is my brother, and he was wrong. I love this place. It's better than teaching a bunch of uninspiring undergraduates." Despite the evil warlock asshole trying to kill her, that is. And sure, maybe she was being harsh, but she hoped the dig would at least be noticed by him.

The smile on Craig's face faltered by only a fraction, but he powered through. Clearly, no was not in the guy's vocabulary. "Oh, I didn't know he was your brother. You two don't look anything alike. I'm sure it's pretty tiring holding two jobs, though, plus being a grad student. Anyway, this place looks pretty dead, so I thought I would keep you company. I brought snacks." He held up a plastic bag Brie hadn't noticed he was holding.

Wes, that conniving asshole, probably told him to bribe me with food, the one thing she could hardly resist. She was definitely going to murder him when she got home and dump his body where no one would ever find it again. "Yeah, he's adopted. Anyway, I really don't want visitors while I'm working." She hoped her glare would be enough to send him on his way.

The smile on Craig's face dropped suddenly, and the color drained from his face. For a moment, Brie thought her glare had finally worked. Then she watched as Craig's eyes traveled up, looking at something behind her. She didn't need to turn around to know Ezra was there, even if she didn't hear him walk up. *Sneaky bastard.*

"She has someone to keep her company, thanks." His arm snaked around her waist, pulling her to his chest. "Can we help you find anything?" His deep voice was edged with menace. It took all of Brie's will-power not to smirk at the effect it had on Craig.

"I... uh... j-just came to see B-Br-Brie," he stammered. To Brie, he seemed like a scared child. She secretly hoped he would run out screaming; that would be a great sight.

"Well, you've seen her. So either buy something or get out." This time, Ezra's voice was a growl. His hand tightened on her waist; it was enough to set her whole body aflame.

Brie angled herself toward him and slipped her arm around him, moving closer. Maybe it would lead Craig to assume there was something more there and leave, but also she just wanted to keep touching him. "Sorry, Craig. I have work to do. Thanks for dropping by. Never do it again." She dismissed him with a wave of her hand.

Several seconds passed with Craig just staring at them, fear all over his face. His eyes never left the imposing man. "She said go, kid. And don't come back to my store." It came out as a growl, something she had never heard from him. The sound had her clenching her thighs; the protective alpha male thing turned her on more than she thought it would.

As if snapping out of a trance, Craig ran from the shop without a backward glance. He was already halfway down the street before the door finished shutting. "Thanks. That guy has been bothering me all semester, and he doesn't know how to take a hint or a blatant no." Brie looked up at Ezra with a smile on her face.

He looked down at her with a smirk of his own. "Any time, sweetheart. I'm happy to help get rid of any unwanted suitors." They were still attached at the waist, his hand resting over hers. It took a while for Brie to realize this and several more beats before she quickly detangled herself from him, a splash of pink on her cheeks. Gaze averted from his face, she took a step away, trying to act casual, like they hadn't been wrapped around each other seconds ago. But oh, she missed his warmth already.

"So did you magic him to leave, or does your imposing figure just naturally scare all the boys away?" she joked.

"I would say fear is a much more powerful magic than you realize." He laughed. "But maybe I did use a little magic to make him want to get away." Brie laughed loudly.

"How did you even know he was here? I didn't even get a chance to call you."

Ezra said nothing but pointed up, and Brie followed his finger with her eyes. Above the Storage Room door was what looked like a snaking spyglass with a blinking eye magnified on the end. It was positioned to look toward the counter.

"I installed some security measures, just in case you can't reach me for whatever reason." The laugh was now gone completely from his voice.

"It's kinda creepy." The eye blinked again, and Brie shuddered. "Actually, it's really fucking creepy."

"Don't worry; it's not a real eye. Well, I mean, it didn't belong to anyone. It's only enchanted. It belonged to the pirate Charles Vane, but he didn't really need it after he was hanged." Ezra's face was grim, but Brie could see something still sparkling in his eye.

"That really doesn't make it better, you know," Brie countered, crossing her arms, trying desperately not to laugh.

"Maybe not, but this way, I can keep an eye on things," Ezra said with a straight face, a mask of complete stillness on his features.

Brie raised an eyebrow. "Was that supposed to be a pun?"

Ezra didn't give in to the smirk that Brie was holding back. "Possibly. I'm trying it out."

"How about you don't? It doesn't suit you. That was truly awful." She groaned. Then she burst out laughing, no longer able to keep up the illusion of annoyance.

In return, Ezra grinned, his smile beaming. "Duly noted. No more puns, double entendres, or jokes of any kind."

"Good. I'm going to get some tea and pretend that the creepy eye of Charles Vane doesn't exist. There isn't one in the break room, is there?" She looked only a little worried.

Ezra shook his head. "The break room is eye-free."

"Keep it that way." She laughed as she hit the number four button and slipped into the break room, the door clicking shut behind her.

CHAPTER 14

As Samhain approached, so too did midterms. Brie spent all of her free time studying for her own midterms, as well as crafting the midterm for her class. It was the first time Dr. Fry had had her write the exam rather than just proctor and grade it.

It was incredibly nerve-wracking. Brie was trying to find a good balance between difficult questions and some easier ones so as not to completely tank everyone's grades. So far, she had been through three versions, one that ended up being all no-brainer questions that anyone who showed up to class would know. Version two was so hard that she would have hated herself for even administering it. The current version was a little better, mostly multiple-choice, but she was trying to work in several explanatory questions and maybe an essay.

The shop wasn't allowing her much time to work, either. With Samhain just a week away, the shop had become overwhelmingly busy. Regulars appeared several times during the week. New customers rushed in, frantically asking for things Brie had never heard of or to pick up orders. Brie barely had time to sit anymore. Even Ezra had abandoned most of his work in the Storage Room to assist customers with specialty items, the two of them dancing around each other, arms and fingers brushing as they grabbed packages.

Lily practically lived in the shop, just as Ezra had said she would. Every day she came in with a mile-long list from her granny with new things to obtain for the Samhain party her family was hosting. Her usual lovely smile and bright eyes were replaced by a frantic wide-eyed look and set lips. Her hair, usually arranged in a curly wild halo around her head, was now wrapped into box braids and pulled back from her face. Her sleeves were always rolled to the elbow despite the cooling temperatures. The fragrant wind that always seemed to accompany her took on notes of spices and crisp apples.

"I can barely move from all the lifting and carrying granny has me doing. I swear it wasn't this bad last year," she whined to Brie for what seemed like the hundredth time that week, her head cradled on her arms across the counter. Brie just patted her friend's head in sympathy.

"Do you need any extra hands? I would be happy to help in any way," Brie offered. She would find the time to help Lily, even if there was little time left that wasn't devoted to school or work.

Lily lifted her head and waved her off. "Don't worry about it. You don't really have the extra time, anyway. Besides, I already know this is going to be our best year yet; I've seen it. Sort of. It'll all be worth it come this weekend. And after Samhain, I'm going to sleep for two days straight." The two women shared a laugh, happy just to enjoy each other's company for a few minutes.

"Lily, are you going to take the pomegranates or continue distracting my assistant?" Ezra walked out of the Storage Room with a large box filled with brilliant ruby pomegranates.

"Just a minute, you old grouch," Lily said to Ezra, then turned her attention back to Brie. "So next weekend, you're coming, right? I already told Ezra that he's taking you." She grabbed Brie's hands in hers, warm, calloused hands rubbing against Brie's softer fingers.

"I never agreed to anything!" Ezra protested but was quickly shushed by Lily.

"Nobody asked you. You were told. You're going to take Brie and show her a good time if she wants to go." She leveled an unblinking glare toward Ezra, who quickly averted his gaze and huffed loudly.

Brie laughed at her friends. "Yeah, I'll be there. Wouldn't miss it. Is it still okay for me to bring my brother? It's just, we've never not celebrated Samhain together, and it would feel weird not having him there."

Lily's smile grew wide. "Of course! Wes is absolutely welcome. The more, the merrier. And trust me, this party is huge. And don't worry—we'll make sure he doesn't get freaked by any magic happening."

It took Brie a moment to realize what Lily meant. Somehow she hadn't even thought about the fact that Wes knew nothing about magic, real magic anyway. The supernatural had become such a part of her daily life that she had forgotten that a crucial person in her life was completely unaware of it. Lily's words were reassuring, and she didn't want to exclude her brother on a major holiday.

"Great! And once Wes has a few drinks in him, he won't notice anything, anyway. So, Ezra, what time are we meeting to head to the farm?" Brie turned her attention to Ezra, who stood sulking at her side. He still held the box of pomegranates though the counter was directly in front of him. The weight of it didn't seem to bother him, though, which Brie attributed to supernatural strength.

He sighed deeply. "Seven. I will pick you up at seven and drive us over."

Lily squealed in delight. "Awesome! I can't wait. This is going to be the best Samhain ever! Brie, you're going to love it. And Ez, you're going to have a good time even if it kills you. No time for argument; I gotta go, anyway." Without pausing, she grabbed the box from Ezra, hefting it like it weighed nothing. With one last wave and a flash of her bright smile, she was gone. Only a trace of that apple and spice scent remained.

"Do we still have to move that carriage out?" Brie asked once Lily was gone.

"Yes, but we'll take it out the side door in the Storage Room," Ezra said, holding the Storage Room door open for her.

"There's a side door?" Brie looked at him as she passed by him and into the back room.

"Temporarily," Ezra said, following behind her with his hand on the small of her back, letting the door shut behind them.

On the morning of Samhain, Brie rose at the crack of dawn with a racing heart and tears staining her face. What she thought was going to be a few bad nights of sleep had turned into several weeks of vivid dreams and all-too-real-nightmares.

Her dreams felt so familiar, like she was reliving a memory, like she was actually there. Sensations that she wouldn't normally have in a dream were prevalent in these. And the coppery taste of blood was always in her mouth.

Then there was the battlefield. It was almost always a battlefield. Bodies piled high, rivers of blood flowing to cover her bare feet; the stench of decay and shit flooded her senses. Brie stood in the middle of it all, her mind split between the feelings of anguish and delight.

But the image that caused the tears was one she remembered the least. There was pain, lots of pain. Her whole body felt heavy, and at the tips of her fingers, she felt cool, downy feathers attached to a pair of wings. There was a small comfort in touching those wings. As the pain intensified, almost to the point that Brie thought she was surely dying, she awoke.

It must have been Moloc, she thought to herself. When she was younger, before Maddy, Brie had frequent nightmares, similar to the ones she was again experiencing since Moloc reached inside her mind. He did something to her, but Brie didn't know exactly what. Nor did she know how to make the dreams stop. All the herbs and charms she knew were to help with sleep, not to stop dreaming. Even a dream weave didn't work.

With a heavy sigh, she rose from her bed to get ready for the day. Ezra said he would pick them up at seven that evening, which left most of the day to prepare. There were cookies to bake, snickerdoodle, Maddy's favorite, and she and Wes were going to purify the apartment in welcome of the holiday.

On Wes's insistence, Brie also needed to put together a sachet or two of mugwort for protection. Not that it would do any good, she knew, but it would make Wes feel better.

For all Wes knew, they were going to a normal coven's Samhain celebration. He still didn't know about that other world. According to Lily, all manner of creatures showed up, not just witches. It was a "nondenominational, free-for-all party" as Lily put it. Although her friend assured her that Wes wouldn't notice anything, Brie couldn't help but worry about how he would react if he did see something magical, which seemed likely. Wes freaked easily.

She should have sat down with him sooner and explained at least the basics so he wouldn't panic or anything. But he would think she was crazy, double down on pushing her to quit the shop, and probably make her go see the campus psychiatrist. There was no chance he would just believe her word, no matter how much he loved her.

Springing it all on Wes in one night might be cruel, but it was better than the alternative. Still, Brie couldn't stop the awful feeling in her stomach that she was being a bad sister, that she wasn't giving Wes the attention she used to.

"He can handle it," she decided, dressing quickly and heading to the kitchen to begin baking before Wes woke.

"Have you got Maddy's picture for the altar? Will they even have one?" Wes asked as he pulled on his shoes.

"Yes, I have it in my bag. And I already told you like three times that Lily said there was a communal altar for anyone to use." Brie tried to keep the annoyance out of her voice as she paced back and forth in their living room, waiting for Ezra. Wes sat on the couch, bouncing his knees with nervous energy.

"And you have the mugwort, right?" he implored again.

For all the good that will do against real magical creatures. "In my bag and in my pocket." She patted the left pocket of her flowing, long-sleeved, black dress, where a small sachet of the herb sat.

Brie seldom wore anything particularly embellished, instead going for a more practical look. But for tonight, she decided on a festive yet elegant look. Her wild ginger hair was loose around her shoulders. Gone were the myriad of pens and pencils she kept in her hair. Instead, atop her head sat a crown of yellow and red leaves with a few blooms of asphodel woven in, courtesy of the plant Lily had given her. Golden earrings shaped like small stalks of wheat dangled from her ears, a present from Maddy to wear during Samhain when she was eighteen. She even went as far as putting on additional makeup, a few brushes of gold over her eyelids. Since it was Samhain, she felt like she should welcome the witch's new year with some style. The fact that she would be seeing her handsome boss outside of the shop had nothing to do with her clothing choice. Not that she expected anything to happen between them. He was her boss, after all. Over the last several weeks, they had been opening up to each other, and it seemed like they were always touching in little ways.

"We can always just stay home and do our own thing like usual," Wes tried one last time. It was a mystery to Brie why he was so anxious about going. Wes wasn't the most sociable person, yet he still liked a good party; this was pretty over the top for him.

Brie gave him a look as she ceased her pacing. "Wes, you don't have to go. But I would like to, and I already promised Lily I would be there. She's so sweet, Wes. You're going to love her. Plus, there's going to be tons of food."

Wes perked up at the mention of food. A healthy appetite was a shared trait between them. "You know my weakness, witch. I'm going, but I don't have to talk to your boss, right? I'm not a fan."

"You don't even know him," she responded.

Wes crossed his arms with a huff. "I know all I need to know."

Brie threw up her hands dramatically. Wes was stubborn, and since he decided to hate Ezra, that was what he was going to do. Nothing Brie said was going to change his mind.

At exactly seven, a knock sounded at the door. Brie nearly jumped out of her skin since she was so focused on pacing. On the couch, Wes looked disgruntled and tucked his arms tighter against his body.

Brie answered the door to find Ezra dressed in dark jeans, a black Henley shirt, and a black coat. He filled their doorway like a shadow.

"Ready to go?" he asked Brie, his gaze on her alone. He didn't acknowledge Wes as he stood from the couch. For a second too long, Brie stood there holding the door open, looking at Ezra, appraising his appearance. When her brain caught up, she moved away and turned back into the apartment.

"Yeah, just let me grab my bag. Oh, Ezra, this is my brother Wesley. Wes, my boss Ezra." She stooped to pick up her bag from the floor. In doing so, she missed the glare that Wes shot Ezra, and the look of distrust narrowed at Wes from Ezra.

"Cool, ready to go. Shall we?" Brie straightened, shouldering her bag full of cookies, mementos of Maddy, and a few extra herbs. With a nod from Ezra, he led them out of the apartment building and down to the street. Next to their building was a small parking lot, usually filled with old Honda Civics and a few newer Priuses. But tonight there was a new addition that definitely didn't fit with the rest.

A sleek, new, black Cadillac Escalade was parked very crookedly over two spots. There was no question about whose car it was.

"Wow, Ezra, you park like a real asshole." Brie laughed, heading toward the car. Ezra unlocked the doors with the fob, grumbling at her statement. Behind them, Wes said nothing. Instead, he turned his glare to the offending car as if the poor parking job was a personal offense.

Ezra opened the passenger door and helped Brie up into the tall SUV. Behind them, Wes snorted. They climbed in. Brie noted that the interior was spotless. There was even the new car smell lingering in the air. She was willing to bet that Ezra never drove it.

"Do you have the directions? Lily didn't give them to me since she volunteered you weeks ago," Brie asked, hoping his car had navigation since her maps app would drain her phone's battery like crazy, and she worried she might need it later.

"I've been to the Everett farm enough times. I don't need directions," Ezra said, starting up the car and slowly backing up.

In the passenger seat, Brie tried to keep her gaze on the road instead of making side glances at Ezra. It was a difficult task considering this was the first time she had seen him outside of the shop, and somehow it just felt different around him. In the backseat, she heard Wes sigh loudly.

"So Wes, Brie tells me you study geology. Do you have a favorite rock?" Ezra tried awkwardly. It took everything within Brie to suppress a groan. *Why is he so painfully awkward now?*

Wes scoffed. "Really, man, that's the best you can come up with? What's my favorite rock? My focus is mineralogy, for one, and two, at the moment, I'm pretty fond of black tourmaline."

"Is that because of its magnetic susceptibilities or that it is often used for banishing?" Ezra retorted. Brie could see the small smirk on his face, though he didn't take his eyes off the road.

Brie turned in her seat as far as the seat belt would allow, looking at her brother behind her, not able to clearly see his face in the darkening light. She could easily tell he was grumpy. He probably thought Ezra didn't know anything about crystal magic.

"A little of both, but definitely the second," he grumbled.

The rest of the thirty-minute drive was spent in silence. Wes pouted in the back, and Brie nervously fidgeted with her hands in the front. Ezra seemed content to just focus on the road, though now and then, Brie caught him casting side-eyed glances her way.

Finally, Ezra turned off the main road and onto a dirt drive that disappeared into the woods. It would have been pitch black were it not for a line of milk jugs that had been cut to hold candles that lit up both sides of the drive leading back to the farm. After a couple of minutes, they pulled into a makeshift parking area that was already full of cars. Apparently, the magical community mainly used human transport.

Ezra parked in the first open spot he could find, and the three disembarked. Once her bag was secured over her shoulder, Brie turned to Wes.

"Listen, I'm going to need you to be cool, okay? We haven't been to a Samhain celebration in a long time, and you know, things can be weird for us loner types. So promise me you won't freak out." She placed a hand on his shoulder and looked at him intensely.

Wes's eyes softened, and he laid his hand over hers. "Don't worry, Little Witch; it'll be fine. I can handle being around a bunch of strangers for one night. It's what Maddy would have wanted for us anyway, right?"

She nodded her head. "Right." A pang of sadness shot through her at the thought of another Samhain without Maddy.

"The party is this way, unless you want to spend the night with the vehicles," Ezra said, indicating a smaller path lined with jars filled with candles to light the way.

Brie and Wes broke apart, and the three of them began down the path. As they walked, the sounds of a party in full swing reached their ears. They turned around a copse of trees and suddenly an open field lay before them, filled with all manner of people. At the outer edges of the field were several tables piled with food, some of which was clearly brought by others, probably to honor a family member. Glowing orbs of warm light hovered over the tables to provide illumination, seemingly unattached to anything.

At the northern point of the field, a large altar was set up, already piled with photographs, portraits, trinkets, food, and mementos of the dead. There was a small group already situated there, talking amongst themselves, occasionally pointing to one picture or another.

At the center of the circle, a large bonfire crackled merrily as a few children tossed apple pieces into it before running back into the crowd, giggling. A group of people was already dancing around the flames in loose formation, voices rising with delight.

Brie looked into the crowd and managed to see the familiar faces of those who came into the shop. There were so many more that she didn't know, nor had she seen anyone like them. Several people in the crowd had wings of various shapes and textures. Some had brown or dark feathers, while another had what looked like green parchment wings. Then there were many with tails that drifted behind them or remained wrapped around their waists. Plenty of the revelers had hooves of some kind, though it was hard to see much in the dim light. Ezra's hand pressed lightly into the small of her back, urging her forward. A tingle shot up her spine from his touch.

Before they could venture very far, Lily appeared suddenly in front of them, a brilliant smile on her lovely face. The box braids were gone. Instead, her hair was back to her normal halo of hair, now decorated with asphodel. A burnt orange dress hugged her curves and brought out the gold tones in her dark skin. She looked every bit a fae queen.

"You made it! Oh, you're Wes! It's so great to meet you finally. I know it's your job to look out for your sister, but tonight we are looking out for you. Come on. Let's get your stuff to the altar, and there's so much food." Lily's whole greeting came out in one big rush of words, her excitement infectious.

Lily immediately latched a hand onto Wes's arm and pulled him into the crowd. For his part, Wes was so bewildered by the flurry of energy from Lily that he let himself be led away; Brie and Ezra left to trail after them.

"I don't know what's going to frighten him off first: the attendees or Lily's eagerness." Ezra leaned close to whisper to Brie as they walked.

Brie tried to stifle a laugh. "Be nice. she's just excited. You know she came into the store three times yesterday, and two of those times were to pick up something she had already picked up last week. It's all her hard work paying off. Let her have this."

"I'm nice to exactly one person, and that's Lily," Ezra retorted with a straight face.

"You're nice to me," Brie responded, eyes softening in his direction.

"I tolerate you, at best." Ezra kept his voice even but couldn't hide the tiny smirk on his face. Brie hit his chest with the back of her hand in a playful swipe, causing Ezra's smirk to widen into a full-on grin.

Ahead of them, Wes looked over his shoulder at Brie with bewildered panic in his eyes as Lily still led him by the arm, talking animatedly with her free hand. Brie gave him a shrug and a smile, and Wes tentatively turned his attention back to Lily.

Once they reached the altar, which was even more stuffed full of mementos of the dead than could be seen from afar, Brie found an open space and placed the picture of Maddy down. The photo had been taken just after she took in Brie and Wes. Her still youthful face held a wide smile bracketed by laugh lines, her bright blue eyes shining with stars. Brie loved that picture of her because it reminded her that no matter what Maddy had been through in her own life, she still had enough kindness left in her to change everything for two lost kids.

She placed some of the snickerdoodles next to the photo and Wes plunked down a piece of citrine, Maddy's favorite crystal due to its properties for joy and optimism.

Lily and Ezra let the two siblings have their moment together. Before he left, Ezra again placed his hand on the small of her back and leaned down to whisper, "Take all the time you need."

After a few minutes of reflection and whispered words of love and thanks to Maddy, Brie and Wes turned back to the party, wiping away a few rogue tears. It was easy to miss her bright smile as she danced around the fire on the holidays. But it also made them appreciate the time they had had with her.

This time Lily grabbed hold of Brie. "My granny is doing divination tonight. She's one of the best diviners around, but she only brings out the runes for the holidays. Come on!" Lily pulled her away from the altar and toward a table with a small group of people standing around it, one of which was Albert Hsu.

"What about Ezra and Wes?" Brie asked, still letting Lily lead her away.

Lily waved her hand dismissively. "They will be fine. Ezra knows everyone here, and Wes will stick with him even though he doesn't like him simply because he doesn't know anyone else."

"Oh, and did you 'see' that?" Brie joked.

"I don't need the sight to clearly see that Wes is not a sociable person. And the glares he keeps shooting Ezra pretty much confirmed his feelings," Lily stated.

They drew up to the table where an old woman with fly-away white hair sat wrapped up in a white shawl. On the table before her sat a smooth stone bowl presently filled with an array of carved bone runes.

Her aged and crackling voice finished a reading for a young woman with cloven feet and a head of bushy auburn hair.

Albert turned to look at Lily as the two women stood watching. Eyeing him with a sideways glance, Brie saw the vampire visibly relax, like he was a taut string now given slack.

"Miss Lily, it's a pleasure to finally see you. I hope I didn't lead you to believe I would not attend by arriving so late." Albert, the asshole vampire who never had a kind word for anyone, was nearly stuttering and could barely keep eye contact.

Lily let go of Brie and immediately placed a hand on Albert's forearm. "I would never think that, Bertie. I didn't doubt for a minute you would come. Are... are you enjoying yourself? I saved the blood from one of the pigs for you. I didn't want you to go hungry or anything."

A blush covered her entire face and Lily's grip on Albert's arm tightened. Lily went a darker shade of red when Albert put his hand over hers and left it there.

"You are so thoughtful, Miss Lily. You did not have to do that for me." He could finally look at her; it was as if the two could see nothing but each other. Brie started to feel increasingly uncomfortable standing next to them, so she tried to direct her attention elsewhere as she slowly inched away from the pair.

"Of course I did, silly. I wanted you to be happy and enjoy yourself." Brie could practically see the heart eyes Lily was throwing Albert's way.

"Miss Lily, I—"

"Hey, I'm going to get a reading from your granny. Bye," Brie interrupted, moving quickly away from the pair of hopeless love birds before she vomited all over their gooey feelings. The two barely noticed her departure.

The bowl before Lily's granny was now empty, the runes held in a velvet bag in one of the old woman's bony hands.

"Come here, child, and let me read your runes." She beckoned Brie in that cracking voice. An empty chair sat across from the old woman; Brie sat down lightly and put her hands on the table.

The old woman jiggled the bag in her hand; Brie heard the click click click of the bones hitting each other lightly.

"Pick four and hand them to me," Granny directed, extending her arm so that the bag of runes was before Brie.

"Do I need to focus on a question or something?" Brie wasn't super familiar with runes, but with most of the divination she had come across, focusing on a question was vital.

The old woman scoffed. "Just pick the bones, girl."

Without further hesitation, Brie plunged her hand into the bag and felt around, letting a few bones just brush her fingers before finding four that seemed exceptionally appealing in her hand. One by one, she laid them in the elder's palm.

The old woman tossed the runes into the bowl and cast her eyes downward. "Let me see. There is eiwaz, thurisaz, oh. Oh!" the old woman exclaimed suddenly. Her eyes widened as she stared down at the runes.

"Give me your hand, girl. I need to read your palm," she demanded.

"What?" Brie asked, confused by the woman's sudden outburst.

"Your palm, girl, show me your palm." Instead of waiting, the old woman reached across the table and pulled Brie's right hand into her own. Brie said nothing as she watched the woman lean over her palm and trace the lines of her hand.

After what felt like an eternity, the old woman looked up so suddenly that Brie worried she would hurt her neck. Granny stared at Brie, unblinking for two heartbeats.

"It is you. Our Lady! She has returned!" Her voice crescendoed into a jubilant yell, which drew the attention of all in the vicinity. Everyone around them and many farther away moved closer to hear what was going on.

In an instant, Lily was there, standing next to her granny, Albert directly behind her. "Granny, what's wrong?"

The old woman lifted her hand to point directly at Brie, who still sat, stunned. "She has returned to us. Our Lady, the Morrigan. She has returned to her faithful servants after all these centuries."

Lily's granny kept Brie's hand in a vice grip, her palm still facing up. She tried to pull her hand back, but the old woman placed her other hand over Brie's outstretched one, trapping it with surprising strength.

"Granny, are you sure?" Lily asked, now at her granny's side, her eyes trained on Brie, barely containing her excitement. Her granny removed one hand from Brie, took Lily's hand, and brought it down over Brie's trapped one.

"See for yourself, my Lilybell. Tell me what you see," she cackled.

"Don't move, Brie. And don't be afraid." Lily gave her a reassuring smile as she slipped her fingers over Brie's palm.

Brie watched as Lily's eyes grew glassy and distant. Whatever she was seeing was something none of the rest of them could see. Then the light returned to Lily's face, and she was smiling.

"The Morrigan has returned! Oh, Brie! I knew it! Before, it wasn't clear, everything was cloudy and confusing, but now I can see it so clearly. Granny always said you would return in our lifetime, but I didn't believe her." Lily gripped Brie's hand tightly, awe in her eyes. But though Brie wanted to smile back at her friend, for the first time since she had met the witch, Lily's infectious personality didn't work on her.

Instead, her eyes darted around the field. Just moments ago, everyone was off in groups around the fire, the table around the old woman only had a small crowd. But now, it seemed like all the revelers in the field had stopped to stare at her. Even the music seemed to have stopped.

Brie felt nervous, maybe even dread. She didn't understand what the witches meant when they proclaimed her to be the Morrigan returned. She was Bridget and had always just been Brie, a girl whose parents had died. A nobody girl who fought and scraped her way to a better life. What did it mean to those around her for her to be the Morrigan? Not that she would suddenly feel changed just because a couple of witches announced she was some long dead goddess. More than anything, she felt disbelief.

"Lily, I don't understand. I'm not... I can't be the Morrigan. She's dead. Ezra told me." Brie hoped that Lily would reassure her. That no, Brie was right, the Morrigan was dead, and that it was a bit of Samhain fun.

Lily gave her hand a reassuring squeeze. "It'll take some time, Brie. Your memories are probably just awakening. Soon your powers will, too. But we are here to help you. Just like my ancestors did in the old days."

Brie snatched her hand out of Lily's grip. "I need a drink." She covered her face with her hand and rested her elbows on the table. Beside her, Lily laughed loudly.

"Yeah, I bet. Come on. Tonight we celebrate the cycle of life and death with our Lady Returned!"

Brie took one last look at Lily's granny, sitting at her table looking full of life and mirth, before Lily dragged her off into the crowd. The music struck up again, as did the chatter. But as they pushed their way through the crowd, so many hands reached out toward Brie in praise. It made her uneasy; she mostly felt it was all a joke, maybe a tradition Lily's family did each year. *It is absurd to think otherwise*, she thought as she drew her bottom lip between her teeth.

The rest of the night was a blur of drinks, large plates of food thrust into her hands, and people of all types touching her hands and arms in excited tones. Lily led her around the party, proclaiming to all of her coven members that Brie was the Morrigan reincarnated, as if they didn't hear it the first time. More than a few burst into tears and grabbed for Brie's hands.

Alcohol took the edge off a little, but did nothing to make Brie believe or feel more comfortable with the idea that she could be a reincarnated anything.

More than a little tipsy, Brie managed to get away from Lily long enough to look for Wes and Ezra, neither of whom she had seen since Lily had carted her away to see her granny. She wanted to know what they thought of Lily's declaration.

Stumbling down a path lit with jars holding candles, she meandered away from the party by herself. The farther she walked, the less she heard of the riotous festivities behind her, but she didn't feel an ounce of fear in the near-complete darkness. It felt comforting, actually.

At last, she reached the end of the path; spread before her was a collection of pop-up tents settled in front of a large farmhouse. Lily had mentioned before that anyone could stay overnight. This must be what she meant.

A few dim candles lit the large wrap-around porch of the farmhouse. Brie could see four figures sitting in rocking chairs. Approaching the house, she could make out the voices of Wes and Ezra, but she didn't know the other two.

"Brie, come up and join us!" Wes called out to her when she reached the bottom step of the porch. She looked up at the four people sitting there. Ezra and Wes sat off to her left; a middle-aged man and an extremely old man sat off to her right. From their appearance, they had to be Lily's relations, probably father and grandfather.

All four men had large glasses clutched in their hands, taking liberal gulps. "We've been hiding out with Mr. Everett and granddad Everett. And granddad has been making incredibly strong drinks all night." This from Ezra, his speech slightly distorted, like drunken slurring, but not quite.

"Are you drunk?" she asked, knowing full well she was nowhere near sober herself.

"Yes," Ezra and Wes said in unison, then turned and chuckled at each other. Well, at least they were getting along now.

"There's plenty more if you want some, missy. These boys let it go straight to their heads, but you look like a hardy one. Let me get you a glass." Granddad Everett rose from his chair on surprisingly steady legs, and with a flash of a toothy smile that reminded her of Lily, he walked into the house.

Brie made her way to the top of the porch and surveyed the scene before her. Wes and Ezra had matching loose grins that could only come from extreme inebriation; to the right, Mr. Everett had his chin resting on his chest, clearly down for the count.

In a sudden movement that caught Brie off guard, Ezra was standing before her, holding her hands in his. Despite being tired of people grabbing her tonight, Brie didn't mind his touch. A slight blush rose unbidden to her cheeks.

"Isn't she so pretty, Wes? The most beautiful woman I have ever seen," Ezra gushed, turning first to address her brother and then to look back at Brie. His eyes were glazed from drinking, but they still roved over her face and down to their joined hands.

Behind him, Wes laughed. "You've been saying that all night. You're just mad because I get to see her every day, and you only get her four days out of the week. She's a brat, anyway. You'd get sick of her being around all the time."

Ezra laughed. "It is not fair he gets you all the time." His hands moved up to cup her cheeks. "You could come to the shop every day and just sit there and be you. I would pay you, too, just to sit there and be perfect."

Now Brie's cheeks were an inferno. Ezra could probably feel the heat burning her face, but she couldn't look away from him even as she heard Wes laughing again in the background.

"Ezra, can angels even get drunk?" she asked, though the evidence was right in front of her.

"Angels can do just about anything, sweetheart." Ezra actually winked, or at least tried to; it came off as more of a blink. His hands still rested on either side of her flushed face. The world seemed to narrow to only the two of them. Yes, they were both intoxicated, but alcohol had ways of diminishing inhibitions, so maybe he meant everything he said. It would explain why he always found ways to touch her, why he tried to look at her all the time.

One of his thumbs moved to caress her lips, and Brie closed her eyes to let the feeling sink in. "Can I kiss you?" he asked in a whisper, leaning close to her face. Brie's eyes shot open to stare back into his brilliant green ones. She nodded. Ezra wasted no time in pressing his lips to hers.

It was a soft, tender kiss. Nothing rushed or heated. His lips were so incredibly soft and pliable against hers. Her hands moved to his chest, feeling the warmth under her fingertips.

Somewhere in the back of her mind, a warning went off that this was wrong. He was her boss; they had an audience, which contained her brother, and she had something important to tell him. But as he kept kissing her slowly, all of her thoughts dissipated.

A sudden whooshing sound and a small gust of wind followed by Wes's gasp caused her to open her eyes and pull away from the kiss. Searching Ezra's face, her attention was grabbed from her periphery. Originating from Ezra's back, there was now a set of pure white wings framing his body. He smiled at her as he took one of her hands and brought it up to touch the wings on his back.

Her fingers brushed against the softest thing she had ever felt; he shivered at her touch. His wings were huge, nearly taking up all the space they had on their part of the porch and just barely brushing the ground.

The sound of his wings springing forth did nothing to wake Mr. Everett. Granddad Everett emerged from the house, set Brie's drink on a small table, and took his spot, not bothering to comment on Ezra's display. This wasn't out of the ordinary for him.

"You once asked to see them," Ezra whispered to her, letting her continue to stroke his wings.

"Ezra, they're gorgeous. I don't understand why you hide them." She ran her fingers over the feathers again. Ezra responded with a small shudder.

He caught the hand on his wing and brought it up to his lips, where he placed a kiss on her knuckle. "It's just easier to hide them, to hide what I am," he said evenly, the drunken slur already starting to diminish.

For a moment, they stared at each other. Ezra's eyes were the softest she had ever seen them, and he looked at her with such adoration it made her heart hurt.

"Ugh, do you two have to do that right here? There's, you know, tents right there. And shouldn't your shirt be shredded anyway since you just popped out some wings. Would save her some work," Wes said behind them with a laugh. If she was honest, Brie had completely forgotten he was there. All she could see was the winged man before her. Wes didn't appear bothered by the appearance of Ezra's wings, either, but she would have to think about that later.

"Magic, Wesley, it's called magic," Ezra chuckled.

Brie's head snapped to Wes and then back to Ezra. "Ezra, there's something I need to tell you. Can we take a walk?"

Ezra nodded; she grabbed his hand and pulled him to the steps of the porch. "We won't be long, Wes," she said over her shoulder.

"I trust you, Little Witch," he said with a half-smile. Brie nearly missed the last step at his words. Last time she had seen them, Wes had been adamantly against Ezra. What had changed while she was off at the celebration? She led Ezra down the lit path, determined to talk to Wes after she finished with Ezra.

Once the porch lights were in the distance, Brie tugged on Ezra's hand to stop him. Even in the dim light, she could tell the effects of the alcohol still lingered. Her news was too important, though, for him to be even slightly impaired.

"Ezra, something happened tonight. I don't want you to freak out, okay?" She looked at him, hoping her news wouldn't make things weird between them, especially now that he'd kissed her, which she had secretly wished for, but wouldn't let herself think about.

He faced her fully, a crooked smile on his face as he slid a hand up to cup her cheek again. "I won't freak out. Not when it comes to you. From the minute you stepped into my shop, I felt so drawn to you. There's something magical about you, Bridget. Did you use one of your hedgewitch spells on me?" he teased, ducking his head to kiss her again.

His plush lips on hers were intoxicating. She couldn't stop herself from pushing onto her toes to deepen the kiss, then wrapping her arms around his neck. His hands came to rest around her waist, stabilizing her balance. Brie very much wished they could stay like this all night and could forget about everything else.

Their lazy kiss grew more heated. When she felt the tip of his tongue at the seam of her lips, begging entrance, she gladly opened for him. Ezra wasted no time in devouring her, tasting every bit of her. A moan came unbidden from her; she could do nothing to stop it. A small laugh came from Ezra even as he somehow deepened their kiss.

Brie was on fire, her whole body burning with desire, all other thoughts forgotten for this one perfect moment. She pulled him still closer, pushing herself up against him. Ezra took the hint and snaked one hand down to cup her bottom, giving it a squeeze. This time he was the one to moan loudly, and she swallowed it down.

Brie let one hand twine in his hair; it was soft as sin. Why hadn't they done this sooner?

His lips pulled away, and she let out a small whine. He didn't make her wait long, kissing first her jaw, then trailing kisses down the side of her neck. At the juncture of her neck and shoulder, he stopped and sucked. If not for the hand on her backside holding her up, Brie's knees would have given out from the sheer bliss. Her breath came out ragged and fast.

Under her dress, her nipples hardened; with each movement against his chest, she felt a bolt going straight down to her core.

When they finally broke away for air, they were both left panting heavily, staring into each other's eyes. Brie felt lightheaded and satisfied. In the few short months she had been at the shop, being around Ezra had been the best part. He made her feel safe and seen, like he actually cared about what she had to say, even if she was being sarcastic. If only she could fall headfirst into that feeling and just enjoy herself, but Ezra deserved to know what was happening, even if she didn't quite understand it all herself, or what it meant for her.

Placing her hands on his chest, she stepped back just enough to look up into his face without straining her neck. He was so much taller than she was. "Ezra, this would probably be easier if you were sober, but I can't wait that long."

"Let me fix that, if it will make it better. I don't actually have to be drunk," he responded with a smile. Brie watched as the glazed look of alcohol disappeared from his eyes. She could see how his muscles, a moment ago loose and relaxed, now tightened and tensed. Clarity returned to his eyes. This was the Ezra she was used to. His broad smile settled into his familiar smirk. His eyes still sparkled, pupils blown wide with hunger.

"One of the perks of being an angel, I suppose," Brie said, with mock annoyance, to which Ezra nodded slightly.

"Inebriation is something of a choice to enjoy or not. But what do you need to tell me, sweetheart?" He looked at her with concern now, as if sensing the gravity of the situation.

In her head, Brie cursed herself for preemptively ruining the night with Ezra. But it would be so much worse if he found out from someone else. Her grip around his neck tightened. "Ezra, Lily's granny read my runes, and well... what she saw was something weird, something about, I guess, my past. Sort of."

Ezra quirked an eyebrow. "I don't understand. Did she see something wrong? Something with Maddy?" His hands gripped her waist, a comfort that gave Brie the strength to continue.

"No, nothing with Maddy. I don't know if wrong is the right word. It's just... well, ever since Moloc came into the shop, I've been having these dreams again. I used to have them as a kid, of someone else's life. I think they're just flashes, but so vivid and real. But they are not dreams, Ezra. They're memories. At least, that's what Lily said. Memories of my past life as... as... the Morrigan."

She looked down at the ground, afraid to meet his gaze, afraid of what she might see there. She stood in silence, only hearing the sounds of night creatures. There was no sound or movement from Ezra.

When she finally dared to look up, his face was white, eyes wide with shock. "Brie, what are you saying?" The hands on her waist gripped tighter. It felt more like he was trying to anchor himself than her.

Brie sighed heavily. It was so difficult to say. "The coven thinks I'm the reincarnation of the Morrigan. I don't understand how it's possible, but Lily has promised to help me figure it out. I'm not saying I believe it, because I don't, but I thought you should at least know before Lily says anything to you."

Ezra's eyes bored into hers, then they narrowed. He stepped away from her. "I have to go." He spun on his heel and started away quickly.

"Ezra, please! Don't walk away from me. I need your help to understand all this. Please!" She was begging; tears pricked at the corners of her eyes. This was not how she expected him to react. Not that she was entirely sure what he would do, but she never expected him to walk away.

Ezra stopped but didn't turn to face her. "I can't do this right now, Bridget."

Brie wanted to chase after him, but with a mighty flap of his wings, the same wings she had been admiring up-close moments ago, he took to the air, was out of her reach, and off into the darkness.

Minutes passed, and still, Brie stood on the dimly lit path alone, letting the tears flow freely down her face. The sound of scuffing shoes had her wiping her face quickly as Wes approached.

"I was worried you two weren't coming back. Had to make the executive decision to see if it was worth accidentally breaking up something I didn't want to see. Where's Ezra?" Wes asked, grinning.

Brie looked up toward the sky where Ezra had disappeared. "Gone. Wes, I need to tell you something. Well, more than one something. A lot of somethings, actually."

It took nearly all her willpower to tear her eyes from the sky and turn to face Wes. When she locked eyes with her brother, though, she saw something unexpected. Rather than drunken inquisitiveness, a look she had seen many times on his face, she saw clear understanding.

She must not have been successful at hiding her tears, because the next second, Wes had wrapped her in a tight hug, holding her close.

"It's okay, Brie. I know. You don't have to tell me anything." His voice was soothing. Normally, Brie would drop her concerns and just let the warmth from his embrace calm her, but the implications of his words had her drawing back suddenly.

"What do you mean, you know?" It sounded like an accusation. Did she mean for it to sound that way?

Wes shrugged, so nonchalantly. "You took me to a party full of creatures, with an angel, and I didn't flip out. That should have been your first clue. But Brie, I know what you are. I've always known, even if you didn't."

"Okay, first, you didn't say anything! We came to this party, and you didn't say anything! Goddess, I've been beating myself up for months because I felt I was lying to you, but no, you already know!" She was working herself up into a rage. She kept herself in check, barely.

"Little Witch, it's not like that. You don't have to beat yourself up. You can always trust me. I don't know why you didn't say anything." Wes had switched to his soothing voice, the one he always used when she was upset. It only added to her rage.

"Maybe it's because any normal person would think I was crazy. I thought my big brother would worry about my mental state and make me go get help. But I guess not. Because you know everything." She threw her hands into the air. She wanted to rage, to scream, to curl up and cry for days. But none of that would change anything. Wes knew about magic, real magic, and not once did he say anything to her. Even when she vented her trepidation about the shop, he must have read the signs of its nature. But he said nothing. One of the only people in the world she trusted with everything, and he lied.

"So tell me how you know about the Morrigan?" Her voice hardened as ice filled her veins. Wes knew and didn't say anything.

Sensing her rising anger, Wes held up his hands like he was approaching a frightened animal. "Brie, let me explain. We've been watching out for her for centuries. Waiting until she returned. I just never thought it would be me that would find her, find you."

Brie's confusion cut through her rage for a moment. "What do you mean? What are you, Wes?" She wanted to shout, to scream at him, but still, she held herself back.

"Little Witch—" his soft voice began, but she cut him off.

"Don't 'Little Witch' me, Wesley!" she snapped.

Wes sighed. "Brie, I promise you I am human. Totally and completely, nothing special there. But I'm from a long line of guardians who were once in the service of the Lady Morgana or the Morrigan. Lady Morgana was a goddess of war, and she commanded her own warriors, my ancestors."

He paused, searching for a way to continue. Waiting to see if Brie would even allow him to continue.

"Go on," Brie said through gritted teeth, her arms now crossed tightly over her chest, keeping her distance from her brother.

"My family served as her champion for centuries. And when she died, we continued our duty by waiting for her inevitable return. It was our duty to watch over her and aid in her protection, and fight for her when the time came. And the time has finally come."

"So you've known this whole time? Since we were kids with Maddy?" Tears started flowing down her face again, but this time out of anger and heartache.

Wes sighed deeply, closing his eyes for a moment. "I knew from the moment I met you, Brie, that you were the Morrigan. But from the time I was really young, I was taught my duty. My family didn't live long enough to see it through, but I did what I could to keep you safe until you came into your own. Although, I couldn't even get you to quit the antique store, even though I knew what it really was. I didn't want to risk your safety before you came into your powers. I guess I'm just a piss-poor guardian."

Her heart softened for only a moment. Wes, her loving brother, her favorite person, had always been overprotective. Brie had always been carefree and a little reckless, trying to drive her brother crazy as much as she could. But then the softness turned to ice. It didn't matter now. The big brother she loved so dearly had been lying to her for years. Even if he was just a regular human, he still had a connection to the magical world and had said nothing to her.

"What... what about Maddy? Did she know, too?" She didn't want to hear it, but she had to know if the one person who loved her more than anything, the only mother she had ever known, had also lied to her.

His averted gaze, and the silence confirmed it for her. Brie nearly choked on her sobs.

"I need to be alone. I can't handle this." Brie took a step back from Wes. He took one closer, holding out his arms as if to draw her back into his embrace.

"Brie, I'm so sorry, but you couldn't know. Not then, anyway. Please. Let's just go home, and we can talk." Another step toward her, slow like he didn't want to startle her.

Brie took another two steps away, tears flowing freely down her cheeks. "No, I said I need to be alone. Just go away, Wes!" she finally yelled as he started to step toward her again. She turned and ran down the path back to the Samhain celebration.

Brie vaguely registered Wes calling out her name. She just needed to get away from him, from all of it. Everything about her life was a lie, and everyone around her was in on the secret but her. All she wanted now was to fly away from the lies, but she just couldn't run away fast enough. With that thought, she started lifting into the air; the ground shrinking below her feet as she soared off into the night.

Her mind felt intact, but her body tingled with change. Turning her head slightly, she saw that there were black feathered wings where her arms should be. Where her feet once were, there was now a pair of crow's feet. The instinct to fly took over, and Brie flew the rest of the way to the Samhain celebration circle, her crow wings gliding in the air.

In her mind, she was panicked. Her body felt compacted and tightly bundled, but the air on her face was familiar and soothing.

Her sharpened eyesight spotted Lily, somehow easy to pick out even in the dark. She was situated on the ground next to a head of shining black hair; that's what Brie decided to land on. Albert gave a startled cry as Brie landed on him. Before he could take a swipe at her, Lily stilled his arm with a hand on his shoulder.

"Bertie, stop. Brie, is that you?" Lily asked, concern and curiosity on her face as she peered at the crow that was Brie.

Brie opened her mouth to speak, but only a caw came out. It was all Lily needed to confirm her suspicions.

"She's stuck, Bertie. She must have transformed for the first time. Hold on, Brie, we can fix this." Lily held her hand toward Brie while her other hand reached for Albert. Somehow, in the back of Brie's panicked mind, she knew Lily was drawing on Albert's energy as she laced their fingers together. Lily shut her eyes and began to mumble something Brie couldn't understand.

A warmth flowed through Brie's entire being, and her body felt like it was unpacking itself. The next moment she was sitting slumped on the ground next to Lily and Albert as tears streamed down her face in heavy waves.

Her vision blurred. Distantly, she felt a hand on her shoulder, then blackness swallowed her up. Her last shred of resolve and sanity melted. She was unconscious.

CHAPTER 15

Eight years ago

Flowers were woven into her bright hair, the sprinkle of leaves matching the forest green dress she wore. It was Beltane and her eighteenth birthday.

She, Wes, and Maddy had spent all day decorating the house in flowers and hawthorn, then delivered more flowers to neighbors. When they finished, the three of them had their own little birthday celebration for Brie as a family. Now, they were in an open field on some land one of the coven members owned, celebrating with their fellows.

The sun had just set, and the bonfire was being lit, sacred wood added to catch the sparks. This year, Brie had talked herself into jumping over the flames. Every year previous, she chickened out, but this was the year. Wes had driven in from school to be there, mostly for Beltane, he insisted, but Brie knew it was for her birthday. He promised to jump with her tonight.

Maddy stood near the food tables talking with the coven leader, a middle-aged woman with silvering hair and a youthful face named Celeste. It was like that at nearly every holiday. Maddy and Celeste barely left each other's side. Brie and Wes had encouraged her many times to just go for it with the coven leader, but Maddy always demurred.

But this year, Brie wasn't going to try to push the relationship between her mother and Celeste. No, this year, her eye was turned toward Tegan McClint. He was two years older, had been in the coven his whole life, and was back visiting for Beltane. She had always thought him cute, but college had turned him handsome.

Throughout the evening, he had stopped to flirt with her several times before Wes would pull her away. Beltane was a fertility festival, after all. It would be a shame to spend it alone.

As if summoned by her thoughts, Tegan came up to her. He stopped at her side, barely brushing up against her bare arm. "Looks like the dancing is starting. Would you like to join me?" He gave her a sideways glance, pink colored his cheeks.

Brie felt her own cheeks heat but smiled brightly. "I would love to." Tegan returned her smile, slid his arm around her waist, and ushered them toward the bonfire, where several couples and singles began a clockwork dance around the flames.

Around and around they spun, the flames dancing along with them. At one point, Brie saw Wes shaking his head in disapproval as she passed by him. It only made her laugh and smile more at Tegan.

She didn't think of Wes's face as she let Tegan lead her away from the fire to a secluded spot where he started to kiss her. She didn't let her mind wander as he laid her down on the soft grass, away from prying eyes. She focused on his eyes as they quickly removed each other's clothes. She smiled to herself as they writhed together under the stars in young lust.

CHAPTER 16

For the next month, Brie didn't see Ezra. When she went in to work, there was a note saying he was in the back. On Saturdays, a neat little envelope with her pay appeared at her workstation on the counter.

He was hiding from her; that much was clear. If Brie was honest with herself, she was a little glad she didn't have to face him after Samhain. She expected to see him after the first week. But then one week became two, then two became three, and still, he never appeared while she was in the shop. A few times, she contemplated calling him on the shell phone, knowing at the very least he would answer, thinking it was an emergency. Brie decided against using it, but she didn't know why—maybe just to give him space. He would come around eventually, or so she hoped.

It was a Wednesday evening in early December. The fall semester would be ending soon, so Brie had been taking advantage of the quiet in the shop to study and grade practice exams for Friday's review. When Lily arrived, however, it was time for magic studies.

After the revelation on Samhain, Lily had taken it upon herself to train Brie in magic. Not that Brie had any control yet. Until that night, she hadn't produced any magic. In the last month, all of her attempts were entirely contingent upon emotional responses like turning into a crow after her fight with Wes. Lily explained that the crow was one of the forms the Morrigan took; it was also one of her symbols. Somewhere in the back of Brie's mind, tucked under the memories that didn't belong to her, which had started to emerge more frequently in her dreams, the knowledge all fit perfectly. Her affinity for crows suddenly made sense. It wasn't her choice. It was something belonging to the Morrigan.

Brie was unable to take on the crow form again. A week after the holiday, she had nearly passed out, red in the face, from a lack of oxygen as she puffed up her face and concentrated on becoming a crow at Lily's instruction. It yielded no results other than a feeling of light-headedness. To her credit, Lily was a patient teacher who seemed to have an endless supply of optimism. It was really starting to annoy Brie.

"You've gotten so much better with the blooms. Just a few weeks ago, all you did was stare at them, but look at you now; it's like you barely even think about it and 'pop': asphodel blossoms everywhere!" Lily clapped her hands together in excitement.

Brie wanted to share in the excitement. After all, she was able to make things bloom now with barely a thought, but it did little to cheer her up.

Ever observant, Lily didn't miss the look on Brie's face. "You two still haven't spoken?" she asked.

Brie sighed heavily as she shook her head. "I haven't even seen him. He just hides in the back all day. He hates me, Lily," she mumbled forlornly.

Lily gave her a one-armed hug. "He doesn't hate you. It's just a little overwhelming when the girl you're crushing on turns out to be your reincarnated ex." A smile spread over her face as she waited for Brie to laugh. But Brie didn't. Couldn't.

Brie crossed her arms on the counter and slammed her head down on the fleshy part of her arms instead. "Goddess, that makes it worse! I knew I shouldn't have told you about the kissing part."

Lily gave her head a reassuring pat. "I'm your friend. You are obligated to tell me about the kissing parts, Brie. And anyway, it was obvious from the way he acted around you. But more to the point, just give him time. He'll come around and realize you are an amazing catch, reincarnated goddess or no. And when he does, you'll be able to wow him with all kinds of new magics! And if he doesn't come around, I'll kick his ass!"

But the only response from Brie was a loud, long groan as she began to pluck at the asphodel blossoms in front of her without looking at them.

Without warning, she suddenly popped her head back up and stared directly at Lily. "Enough humiliating me. Let's talk about how things are going with you and Albert Hsu now that you are 'official.'" She used air quotes to emphasize her sarcasm.

Instantly, Lily went completely pink and averted her gaze. "Things with Bertie are good. We've found a good flow that works for our schedules since, you know, he keeps night hours. But he's great. I still don't know where I got the courage to kiss him on Samhain, but I'm really glad I did."

"Obviously, the courage came from alcohol; that much is clear. And this would be so much more adorable if I didn't know you were talking about Albert. He's still an ass to me, just never when you're around because that's when the rest of the world ceases to exist," Brie whined. It was so true. Lily and Albert were such an odd match, but somehow deeply infatuated with each other.

It was also true that despite his newfound bliss, Albert Hsu still sneered at her whenever he was in the shop without Lily. If anything, it had gotten worse since Samhain. Brie had a suspicion it was due to her new status as a reincarnated goddess and Lily's involvement in helping Brie achieve her new potential. But whatever the reason, Brie wasn't interested in being Albert's friend. If he made Lily happy, though, that was all that mattered.

Lily gave her arm a squeeze. "He'll get over it. Even if I have to make him." She gave Brie an exaggerated wink, which caused the ginger girl to finally laugh. "Well, I have to get going; I have some herb harvesting to do before moonrise. Then Bertie and I are going out."

"Fun," Brie mumbled, only a little envious of her friend's newfound happiness.

Just after ten, Brie shut down the computer, shoved her work into her bag, then pulled on her winter coat. A glance out the window revealed small flakes of snow caught in the glow of the street lamp. Pulling her coat tighter around her shoulders, dreading the short walk home in the cold, she shouldered her bag. She slipped the shell phone into her outer coat pocket for easy reach, just in case.

With one last glance at the closed Storage Room door, she stepped out into the frigid night air and locked the shop door behind her. Walking with her head slightly bent down to shield her face from the brisk wind, she nearly broke into a sprint to get home quickly.

She was so focused on the warmth of her apartment waiting for her that she ran full force into someone on the sidewalk. The collision caused her to stumble backward and lose her footing. She was on her back, looking up at the night sky and a familiar face.

Ice-blue eyes descended on her, and a smile with no hint of mirth glared down at her. Brie felt her whole body grow colder, and she wanted to scream as she looked up into the face of the warlock Moloc Vangren. Scrambling, she shoved her hand into her pocket to grip the shell phone. Moloc's eyes turned mocking at her attempt.

"Ah ah, I wouldn't do that, dear Bridget. Or should I call you Morgana? Calling on your precious angel would only complicate matters. Besides, I'm not here to hurt you, my dear. I have a proposition for you." His chilling smile showed more teeth than seemed possible as he stretched out his hand to Brie.

Ignoring the offered hand, Brie slowly stood on her own, removing her hand from her pocket. "There's nothing you can say that will make me accept anything from you," she spat, perhaps with more bravery than she actually felt.

The smile on Moloc's face didn't waver an inch. "Now, now, my dear, there has been enough strife between us for more than one lifetime. Assuming you remember, of course. I'm sure we can reach an amicable agreement and bury the hatchet, as they say, once and for all."

Brie's mind screamed for her to run, go back to the shop, go home, just get away. Ezra had put protections on her and the shop, but she was sure Moloc would get to her before she took more than a step. Like it or not, she would have to put Ezra's protections to the test tonight. So instead, she crossed her arms over her chest and widened her stance. She would need to keep him in a good mood, enough to let her go. With false bravado, she said, "What do you want?"

The cruel smile grew impossibly wide, like at any moment Moloc would unhinge his jaw and swallow her whole. Brie suppressed a shiver as best she could. "Good, I'm glad you are so reasonable now, Morgana. As you know, long before he belonged to you, Arakiel was my creature. We have a deal, and he is not holding up his end of the bargain. Return him to me, and I will assist you in returning you to your full power. I can help loosen the bonds that tie you to that mortal body. All I ask is that you release him and disappear from his life for good."

Brie stood there, stunned for a moment. "Are you appealing to me or the Morrigan? Because she's not in control. I am. And I'm happy with this mortal body, thanks." She balled her hands into fists and continued angrily, "As for Ezra, he's his own man. He doesn't belong to you or me. So just leave him alone!"

Dropping all pretense of a smile, Moloc bared his teeth in a snarl and grabbed her arm roughly. His grip was like iron despite his aged appearance. "You insolent little girl! He has more power than you could possibly imagine. You are nothing compared to him, just a silly child playing with magic you don't understand. And one day soon, I will delight in watching your fragile mortal body die once again."

A spark within Brie ignited; she felt it flow through her body like warm water with a vicious undertow swirling below her skin. Her eyes took on a golden glow, and she saw Moloc's face shift from frightening malice to what looked like fear. His fingers loosened on her arm; she struck with a swiftness she had never possessed before.

Her fingers in turn wrapped around Moloc's retreating wrist, and she squeezed until she felt bones cracking from a strength that wasn't her own. The feeling pleased her, and a small smile spread across her face. There was nothing kind in the smile. Then she spoke in a voice that was nothing like her own. It was deeper, a husky feminine voice, somehow ancient, yet not. "I will soon wash the bloodstained clothes you wear, Moloc Vangren. It is then you will know that death is close behind. And I will delight in your death, just as you once delighted in mine."

The warmth within her traveled down her arm to the fingers gripping Moloc. He began to howl in pain.

When Brie finally gained the control to release him, there was charred black flesh where her hand had held him; glancing up, she saw the arm was burned red.

Moloc glared one final time, a look that desperately wanted to kill, before he turned on the spot and disappeared into thin air.

The warmth of the magic now gone, Brie felt her whole body droop with an all-encompassing weariness. She was tired and freaked out, not just by Moloc, but by herself. Something inside of her had taken control, and Brie was scared. Would the Morrigan try to take over, to become her? What would happen to her own consciousness, the part that made her Brie, if that happened? So many questions raced through her mind.

The rest of the walk home was slow going. Brie forced one foot in front of the other just to get there. When she finally made it to her room, it was all she could do to not just faceplant on her bed and sleep. Briefly, she thought about calling Ezra to let him know what had happened. Then the thought passed; the shell phone remained untouched in her coat pocket on the floor.

Soon after she crawled into bed, she heard Wes arrive home. It was late for him, but she didn't care. Things had been weird between them since Samhain. So when he knocked on her door and called out to her, she pretended to be asleep.

When actual sleep did come to her, her dreams were full of blood-soaked battlefields and bowed heads of heroes at her feet. Her rest was not peaceful that night.

CHAPTER 17

"And remember, there's no class next week, but there will be extended office hours, and you can always email me with questions about the final exam. I will not answer questions at 4 am, though, so you'll have to wait until a reasonable hour." There were a few chuckles as the class packed their bags and headed out. Brie quickly gathered her own things. She had a meeting with Dr. Fry in ten minutes.

As she headed for the door, she noticed Craig holding back from the others. Ever since Ezra had scared him out of the shop, Craig had left her alone, shooting her the occasional longing glance now and then. It looked like that was about to change.

"Hey Brie, I had a quest—" She wasn't in the mood.

She continued past him. "Sorry, I have to get to a meeting. Just email me if you have a question about the exam." She barely looked over her shoulder as she left the room.

Maybe she walked a little faster than she really needed to since Dr. Fry's office was just next door, a three-minute walk if she walked slowly. But if it got her away from another uncomfortable encounter, which she seemed to be having a lot of lately, then that was fine by her.

Dr. Fry's door was wide open when Brie arrived, so she went ahead and popped her head around the door frame. "Hi, it's me. Is this still a good time?" she asked, gripping the straps of her bag.

Her mentor was behind her desk, glancing down at her mobile phone held between both hands. She looked up at Brie's words and set the phone off to the side, face down.

"Of course. Have a seat. Please close the door behind you. I've had enough seniors trying to sneak in after office hours to ask a million questions." She motioned to one of the two chairs in front of her desk.

Brie removed her bag as she pushed the door closed behind her and dropped into the nearest chair. Dr. Fry clasped her hands together and leaned toward her desk, staring at Brie, waiting for her to begin. But Brie said nothing; her gaze roamed Dr. Fry's desk.

"Everything okay in your class? The kids aren't giving you a hard time? Sometimes they get so panicked over every little detail they think could be on the exam. No matter how many times you tell them it's not comprehensive, you'll still get the gaggle of worry warts who will come in asking about material covered in week two." She furrowed her brow when she got no reaction from Brie.

"But that's not it. Is your thesis going well? You haven't suddenly changed your mind on topics?" Dr. Fry looked genuinely worried. She probably thought Brie was on the brink of a breakdown and ready to quit altogether.

Finally, Brie shook her head. "Nope, sticking with the same topic, but I'll get back to you on whether it's going okay." She let out a dry laugh, trying not to think about her thesis and how little attention she had been giving it lately. Her personal life seemed to cloud everything else.

Dr. Fry leaned back in her chair, her eyes softening in understanding. "So this is not an academic matter." Not a question. "This has to do with Arakiel. I've hardly seen him, and when I have, he's looked quite off-kilter. Miserable even. Well, more than usual anyway."

"Well, then you've seen him more than I have. Ever since Samhain, he's been avoiding me, and I know it shouldn't bother me, but it does. And I worry about him, especially when he's working in the Storage Room and doesn't tell me where. That place has a mind of its own and can be a real dick sometimes." She sighed and slumped her shoulders.

It all came tumbling out before she could stop herself. She and Dr. Fry had never had a close enough relationship for Brie to feel she could open up about her personal life. But things had changed a lot in the last few months, and Brie strongly felt that the best person to talk to about it all was Dr. Fry.

Her professor leaned back in her office chair as she brought a finger to rest against her chin thoughtfully. "He has always had a flair for the dramatic. And he's stubborn, just like his parents. Did something happen during Samhain?"

It was an innocent enough question, but it was the one area Brie did not want to open up with Dr. Fry about. She averted her gaze and fidgeted with her fingers in her lap. "I'd rather not talk about that," she mumbled.

When her eyes moved up to look at her professor, she saw understanding. "Ah, I see. Brie, I'm sure you know that for Arakiel, it's not easy for him to form attachments. And to form a new one with you only for it to be revealed that you are the reincarnation of his lost love, well... it would break even the strongest of us."

Brie let out a choked gasp. "You know? How? Have you known this whole time?" She started to feel that same bubbling anger that always seemed to be within reach lately.

Dr. Fry must have sensed it because she was quick with her response. "No, I only found out after Samhain, from Apollo, of course. He's such a gossip. Really, the whole magical community is a bunch of gossips. But

I didn't want to overstep, so I waited until you were ready to talk."

"Fucking Apollo," Brie grumbled. "Hang on. How do you know Apollo?"

Her mentor looked at her, coke-bottle glasses shining in the light. "The community in this city is pretty tight-knit. We've known each other for quite some time. He's also the self-proclaimed king of the gossips, so just keep that in mind."

"Why does that not surprise me?" Brie said, then sighed, turning back to her own problem. "So what should I do? It's been a month, and he won't even be in the same room with me. This can't go on forever, right?"

The loud snort that came from Dr. Fry was unexpected. "It's really quite lucky you don't know his parents. You wouldn't be so optimistic."

"If he's an angel, wouldn't that make his parents like ... gods? Or god? Or whatever?" Brie had more questions piling up and felt like she was getting fewer answers. She came to Dr. Fry hoping to sort through her situation with Ezra, and instead, she wanted to know more about his past and his family. Maybe their shared past, if Dr. Fry knew anything. A groan threatened to burst from her, and she could feel a headache forming. Why didn't she ask him these questions when they were still on speaking terms?

Across the desk, Dr. Fry smiled knowingly. "It would. Sort of. His mother is one of the many out there, and his father is one that is no longer worshiped. He still hangs around, though, getting into trouble most likely. One of his schemes landed me in this state, but that's for another time." She let out a small laugh as she was drawn into a memory, her eyes no longer focused on the young woman before her.

Brie shifted uncomfortably in her seat, once again fiddling with her fingers. Dr. Fry turned her attention back to the present, looking at Brie. At that moment, Brie saw the wisdom of ages staring back at her. It was always there, only now Brie understood what it meant.

"Brie, talk to him. If he won't come to you, go to him. He will hide from you for eternity if you let him rather than face the issue. That's not just Arakiel; that's all men as a general rule. He has infinite time to sulk, too." Dr. Fry pointed her finger for emphasis.

"That's it? That's your great advice?" Brie asked, one eyebrow raised, a sinking feeling and annoyance taking hold.

Dr. Fry threw her head back and laughed. "Brie, I'm your graduate advisor, not your therapist. There's nothing that a little communication won't fix. Now, I suggest you take what little time you have before the onslaught of undergraduate emails hits to clear things up with Arakiel and get your head back into your academics and not on brooding boys."

She smiled at this, and Brie shakily returned the grin. Communication was something Maddy always stressed, too. It just wasn't one of Brie's stronger attributes. It was for Wes, but talking about feelings and what bothered her never came easily to Brie. But she was determined to try. Not just with Ezra, but with her brother as well.

"Thanks, Dr. Fry. I guess," she said, shifting in her seat.

The older woman gave her a knowing look over the top of her glasses. "Good. Now that the personal stuff is taken care of, let's talk about this final." Brie spent the rest of the hour discussing the final exam she had put together for her class.

The bag sat open on her bed as Brie contemplated whether to bring her laptop to the shop. On the one hand, she knew there would be emails throughout the evening, probably already there now. But on the other hand, she had her email on her phone, and she really needed to talk to Ezra. Heaving a sigh, she closed the bag and set it next to her desk where her laptop remained. If she didn't have her computer to distract her, maybe she would actually follow through with the talking part.

A knock came on her bedroom door frame. She looked up to see Wes standing at the open door. They had barely spoken since Samhain, which broke Brie's heart, but every time she thought about talking through things with him, she felt a stab of betrayal again. He knew what she was the whole time and said nothing. Wes was supposed to be the one person in the whole world she could trust without question. He was her family.

"Hey," he said hesitantly.

"Hey," she replied tersely.

Rubbing the back of his neck nervously, he said, "Can we talk?"

"I'm heading to work soon. Can we make this quick?" She crossed her arms, though it hurt her to be so cold to her brother. But she wasn't the one who was keeping huge secrets. Well, that wasn't entirely true, but not huge secrets that involved her life.

Wes stood at the door a moment, crossing and uncrossing his arms like he was unsure what to do with them. They just stared at each other across the room, neither taking the lead to start the conversation they needed to have.

Then Wes cleared his throat. "Listen, Brie; I wanted to apologize again for what happened on Samhain. And for not telling you sooner. I mean, it's your life; you should know just as much as everyone else. And it's kind of a big deal to find out you're the reincarnation of some all-powerful goddess. You should have found out from me, or Maddy, not from some stranger at a party. I did this all wrong, Brie. I'm sorry. I warned you I was a terrible guardian." He heaved a sigh after his rush of words, and his shoulders slumped as he waited for his sister's response.

Brie knew she couldn't stay mad at Wes. He never outright lied to her. It wasn't like it was a topic she would casually bring up and ask her brother about.

Without a second thought, she stood up, crossed the room, and wrapped her arms around Wes in a tight hug.

"It's okay, Wes. It was a weird night, and I was upset, but I think I understand. And you're not a terrible guardian; you were just trying to look out for me. I still love you. But if there's anything else about me or any past life I should know, you tell me now, okay?" She crushed him against her for emphasis.

Wes nodded against her cheek and squeezed her tightly.

Brie was the first to pull away. There was something she still had to know. "Why do you think Maddy didn't tell me? Why would she keep something like that from me?"

"I think she wanted to protect you until you were ready. I don't really know. When I realized what you were, I had a tough time even bringing it up with her. But she asked me to keep it between us. And that she would tell you when the time was right." Wes shrugged and gave her a look like he knew it wasn't a satisfactory answer. But they would never know the real reason Maddy kept the secret from Brie. Or why she never said anything when she was dying.

They stood together in silence for several minutes. "Let's do pizza and movies tomorrow after you get off work. I think we both need it. And if you have any more questions I can answer, I will." Wes took her hand and gave it a squeeze as he pulled out of the embrace.

Brie let out a heavy breath. "Yeah, I would like that."

Well, she thought, *one problem solved*. But that was the easy conversation, anyway. She would always forgive Wes. The awkward conversation still loomed ahead of her, and she found herself full of dread for her shift.

It was going to be a long night.

CHAPTER 18

When Brie entered the shop, it was completely empty. She wasn't surprised to find Ezra's note sitting on the counter, as was the new norm. Shedding her coat and scarf, Brie contemplated the ledger book and computer, deciding whether to start work to delay talking to Ezra, or just find him immediately.

It was a quick, though not easy, decision to make. If she started working now, she would put off talking to Ezra all night. Leaving her work untouched, she placed the service bell on the counter with the sign and entered the Storage Room. Besides grabbing orders from the shelf by the door, Brie had not spent much time in the Storage Room, preferring to give Ezra as much space as possible. It also meant she could avoid having things thrown at her.

So when she stepped past the order shelf and headed down into the rows upon rows of shelves, the whole of the Storage Room seemed to let out a sigh of relief, like it knew what was coming. She couldn't hear Ezra working, which left her with no way of knowing where he was in the cavernous room. But as it turned out, that didn't matter. The Storage Room provided for her.

A small colorful carpet zoomed around a corner and stopped next to Brie. It hovered about two feet off the ground, unmoving. Brie took the hint, awkwardly boarded, and sat down in the middle of the carpet. Once she was safely seated, the carpet took off again, zipping down row after row, taking corners too sharply, not enough to throw Brie off, but enough that she had to right herself several times.

A few minutes later, she heard the sound of Ezra banging away on something. A moment later, she saw him. The carpet didn't slow until it was nearly on top of him, stopping only a few inches from his leg. Brie clambered off with little grace, and the carpet banked and zoomed off again.

Standing before Ezra, the first time she had seen him in a month, she drank in the sight of him. He wore a black jumpsuit that looked well worn, with engine grease smeared on his hands and forehead like he had wiped his brow. *Is it possible he got more handsome?* Brie thought. Just seeing him made her feel like she could finally breathe again after a month of holding her breath. Ezra said nothing at her arrival. For half a second, he met her eyes and then averted his gaze quickly.

"I don't have time to talk. There's still a lot to do," he said gruffly, keeping his eyes trained on the floor.

"You can take a break," Brie responded matter-of-factly. She wasn't going to give him an out.

Ezra's eyes snapped up, but he still wouldn't look at her. Instead he looked past her shoulder. "No, I can't. Go do your job, Bridget."

"Or what? You'll fire me? We both know you won't," she shot back immediately. It wasn't how she intended to start this conversation, but she knew without a doubt that Ezra would never fire her.

She knew she had him when he opened his mouth to respond, but then closed it quickly. "You're taking a break so we can talk." She crossed her arms with finality.

He looked as if he would argue, but she cut him off. "I've given you space, Ezra. A whole month of space. I'm not going to allow you to avoid me anymore."

Ezra nodded slowly in response, though he didn't look enthused. His entire body was rigid, and his scowl felt like a dagger in her heart. They stood facing each other, silent. Brie had prepared herself for more of a fight to get him to talk. Now she was left scrambling about how to begin.

"Do you want to find somewhere to sit down?" he asked suddenly, finally looking at her directly.

"Sure." She turned to look for a place to settle.

And just like that, a small deep loveseat pushed itself out of the nearest shelf, moving as if it had feet of its own. It came up to Brie and Ezra before setting itself down, waiting for them to sit.

The Storage Room had a way of providing and seemed particularly eager to do so today. *Poor thing*, Brie found herself thinking. It probably didn't like the tension any more than she did.

The loveseat was cozy, but intimate. There was no way they would have much space between them. Clearly, the Storage Room was determined to get them to work things out in close proximity.

It was Ezra's turn to address the Storage Room. "You are being pushy again," he grumbled.

In response, there was a small squeak from the loveseat, and a little bit of space disappeared. Brie rolled her eyes and just took a seat before it got any smaller, forcing her sit on Ezra's lap. Reluctantly, Ezra took a seat but remained on the edge of the cushion. Space was so limited now that their legs pressed against each other, anyway. If the pained look on his face was an indication, he couldn't stand even that little bit of contact.

"So, do you plan to just avoid me forever?" Brie finally asked to cut the silence.

Ezra looked straight ahead. "Only one of us will live forever. I only have to wait one human lifespan." It came out as a petulant mumble.

Brie threw her head against the back of the love-seat and sighed deeply. "Doesn't it get exhausting being so extra all the time?" She pinched the bridge of her nose and closed her eyes, already exasperated with this conversation.

"Extra what?" Ezra asked, turning slightly toward her but not looking at her. His knee crowded her space, and she wanted so badly to lean into his touch. But they weren't there yet. Maybe they never would be again.

"Never mind. It's a generational thing. Point being, you are so dramatic. We could just talk about this like adults, maybe with like an adult beverage or something, and figure things out." Brie could use something to get her through this already awkward conversation.

"If I recall, alcohol contributed to the situation," Ezra mumbled, arms crossing over his chest. Goddess, he was acting like such a child.

"Maybe, but alcohol just lowers your inhibitions, so you still wanted to kiss me. And there's still the whole reincarnation thing that has nothing to do with alcohol," Brie countered.

"Brie, I don't think it's a good id—" Brie cut him off.

"Moloc found me again. Outside of the shop the other day. He wanted something from me that I won't give him." She started to trail off, looking away from Ezra. She decided not to tell him about Moloc's proposition. Not yet, anyway.

Ezra jumped up and glared down at her, finally giving her his full attention. "Why didn't you tell me?" he demanded.

She shrugged, letting his flare of anger roll over her. "Well, you weren't exactly talking to me. You wouldn't even be in the same room with me. So I didn't think you would answer your phone."

"I would have answered the phone if you called. That's what it's for," Ezra countered.

Another shrug. "I didn't trust you to answer." He had the good sense to look ashamed.

"I would always answer for you," he muttered, just barely loud enough for her to hear.

Her eyes snapped up to his. "Well, I'm fine. Obviously, I took care of him. Gave him a good zap." She pushed out her hands like she really was zapping someone.

"A good zap?" Ezra asked, still on edge even as he eased back onto the loveseat.

Brie shrugged. "I'm still trying to understand my new powers. They just kind of happen, mostly when I'm having like strong emotional reactions."

Ezra heaved a heavy sigh as he ran a hand through his hair. "I think a drink is a good idea, after all. Let's take this out of the Storage Room. It's being meddlesome enough as is," he said as he stood up.

He paused to wait for Brie to stand, then whistled loudly. Another carpet, this one patterned in reds and yellows and slightly larger, came careening around a corner and stopped in front of them. Without saying a word to each other, they climbed aboard. They didn't even look at each other the entire ride to the front of the Storage Room. A ride that took considerably longer than the first ride, Brie noted. *Meddlesome thing, indeed.*

Once back in the shop proper, Ezra walked to the front door, flipped the sign to "Closed," and locked the door.

"Aren't you worried about people missing their orders?" Brie asked as he passed where she stood at the counter.

Ezra shrugged one shoulder. "They'll just pick it up tomorrow." He then pushed the three button on the panel and opened the door. He held it open for Brie, who took one step, then stopped and gave him a quizzical look.

"Your apartment? I thought we would go to the office?"

"My place has better alcohol, and the couches are more comfortable. I figure this is going to be a long talk," he said, then indicated that she should go first through the door.

Brie raised an eyebrow but said nothing as she walked through the door into the darkened hallway of Ezra's apartment. As soon as she entered the living room, Brie threw herself down on the couch, kicked off her shoes, then tucked her feet up under her.

"Please, make yourself comfortable," Ezra deadpanned as he walked to the kitchen and pulled out two glasses, followed by a bottle of wine. He returned to the living room with just the glasses, filled with a deep red wine, and handed one to Brie before taking a seat on the opposite end of the couch.

Brie took a tentative sip, and her eyes widened in delight as the flavor hit her tongue. "This is delicious! Pinot noir is my favorite." She took another, more generous sip.

Out of the corner of her eye, she saw Ezra smile into his glass.

"What's so funny?" Brie asked, angling her body toward him.

"Hm, it's just curious. You're supposed to be the reincarnation of Morgana, but she hated pinot noir. Actually, she hated wine in general."

Taking a large gulp of her wine again, Brie responded, "That's not how reincarnation works, Ezra. I have my own likes and dislikes, my own personality. I'm just *lucky* enough to also have someone else's memories in my head and magical powers." The word lucky was dripping with sarcasm.

"Lily talked to you about reincarnation, but it's not like she's been through it before. I know you are your own person, obviously. You're nothing like her. I told you once that she used to make me laugh, but I don't think she ever intended to be funny. I just found it funny." Ezra paused, looking anywhere but at Brie, finding his drink the most interesting thing of all. It was going to be a long talk if he wouldn't even look at her again.

"She was intense, probably too intense. But then again, she was the mistress of war, and it was the most important thing to her, defined her. Morgana was the opposite of everything I knew from my life before, and I clung to her as an escape. There was nothing gentle or kind about her," Ezra continued, and Brie sat quietly, not daring to even move in case he ceased talking altogether.

Then his eyes snapped up to meet hers. "But you're not like that at all, Bridget. You are smart and sarcastic, but you are also kind and inquisitive. And so strong. You are her polar opposite in so many ways. And—" he stopped, averting his eyes again.

In her head, Brie was screaming out of frustration, wanting him to continue. But she kept quiet somehow, letting him decide when to continue.

He didn't for several long seconds. Instead, Ezra just sat there staring into his half-empty glass of wine, lost in his thoughts. Brie said nothing and just sipped her wine, though it was killing her to do so.

After what felt like an eternity to Brie, Ezra finally spoke again. "Brie, there's no sense lying to you or myself. I desire you, obviously, or I wouldn't have behaved the way I did on Samhain. You bring light to my shop every single time you are here. You're direct, and you don't take shit from anyone. I admire how much you know your worth. And by the gods, you are beautiful, and kind, and a real pain in my ass, and I enjoy that." He paused, and she waited for the *but* that was definitely coming. "But I'm your boss for one, and then there is the whole you being the reincarnation of my former lover part that complicates everything."

He looked at her with wide and honest eyes. Brie set her wine on the table and scooted her body closer to him, just shy of actually touching him.

"Ezra—" she started but didn't know how to continue.

"Brie," he whispered back, almost reverently.

Brie gave him a small smile. "Ezra, obviously I'm into you, too. I'm not saying I should be your girlfriend or lover, or whatever. It's weird enough with the rein-carnation thing. But I'm not her, and I don't think you want me to be her." She paused to gather the courage to continue. Ezra didn't interrupt. He just sat patiently, watching her. "And if we do happen to enjoy spending time together... I don't know. Maybe we'll just see where things go?" It came off as more of a question than she had intended, but it was out there now.

There was silence from Ezra. He looked at her, then down at his wine. Brie watched him, trying not to look too hopeful even though her stomach was doing flips. If he said no, she would just have to quit. There was no way she could keep working with that distance between them.

He set his wine down on the table and sighed. Brie tried to keep her breathing even as she waited for the worst: for him to tell her to leave.

So when Ezra leaned forward and pressed his lips to hers, she didn't respond immediately. She was too shocked to register what was happening. Her brain finally caught up just as Ezra started to pull away; she surged forward and deepened the kiss.

Ezra's hands circled her waist and drew her closer to him, pulling her onto his lap. Brie responded by running her fingers through his hair, letting one hand rest on his shoulder and the other gripping the back of his head. Both lost themselves to the passion of their kiss. Brie took control this time, slipping her tongue into his mouth without resistance.

She shifted slightly and Ezra let out a loud moan. It was then that she felt it, the growing bulge pressed between her thighs. A smirk formed on her lips, still pressed against his. Now she planned to be wicked. A lazy roll of her hips had him moaning louder, and the bulge beneath her grew larger still. She did it again, and her moan filled the room. She ached to have him there against her most intimate spot.

One of Ezra's hands moved slowly up from her waist to grab her breast. Brie arched her back, pushing her chest forward into his hand even as she once again rolled her hips. His thumb swiped against her hardened nipple, and Brie nearly screamed with ecstasy. No one had ever set her body aflame like that, just from kissing and light touches.

Ezra pulled away first, only enough to rest his forehead against Brie's and to drop his hands back to her waist. "This is a bad idea," he murmured, closing his eyes, trying to breathe deeply.

"I know, but you're immortal. You're allowed to have a few bad ideas." She smiled, her eyes closed, her heart still beating staccato in her chest. "Are you sure this is what you want?" She tried not to sound uncertain, but she didn't want him to feel like she was forcing him into anything if he was uncomfortable.

Brie kept her eyes closed even as he murmured, "Of course."

She made a contented humming noise and opened her eyes. She leaned forward and kissed him again. When she pulled away, sooner than she wanted, Ezra tried to chase her lips with his own, but she put her hands on his chest and pushed him back.

He stared at her, pupils so wide they nearly swallowed his emerald irises. It would be so easy to keep kissing him, to shed their clothes piece by piece and join their bodies together right there on the couch. Too easy.

A small grin formed on her lips. "I'm not going to let you fuck me tonight, Ezra." He shuddered beneath her at the sound of his name, then confusion clouded his face.

"What?" His eyes darted around her face, unsure if he heard correctly.

He was still half-hard beneath her, so Brie decided to have mercy on the poor man and swung herself off to sit on the couch next to him. Still close enough to lean against him, but with enough distance to cool their desire.

"You iced me out for a month. Just because you're hot and we've made up doesn't mean I'm just going to jump into bed with you. You have to earn it." She leaned over and planted a kiss behind his ear, delighting in his responding shudder and moan.

His hand moved to rest on her upper thigh, squeezing. "Sweetheart, this is cruel. Please–" His voice broke into pleading as she kissed him again. But every time he tried to pull her closer, she moved just out of reach.

"Just kissing tonight. I don't want our first time together to be make-up sex," she said as she caressed his arm. Then she allowed him to pull her back to straddle his lap again. Brie leaned in close to his ear.

"Because when I finally fuck you, Ezra, I'm all in, and I need to know you will be, too,"

He turned his head and met her eyes, then leaned in and kissed her tenderly.

CHAPTER 19

I t was well past midnight before they finally separated, reluctantly, with kiss-swollen lips and purpling marks on their skin.

"I should probably get home. Wes will start to worry if I'm too late," Brie said, though she didn't make any effort to pull away from Ezra. At least this time, she had remembered to text her brother that she was not coming home right away. Wes had responded only with "make good choices" and an eggplant emoji. Brie sent back a middle finger and shoved her phone back into her pocket.

Ezra brushed his nose against hers. "I know. I should set up a more permanent portal to your apartment. Just in case Moloc tries to repeat your last encounter."

"It's fine, Ezra. It's not that far of a walk, and I can take care of myself." She pulled away just enough to get a full view of his face.

Ezra kept his arms locked around her to keep her from pulling away farther, one hand stroking up and down her spine in lazy laps. "Sweetheart, I know what you are capable of, but for my sanity, please let me do this. I won't use it unless there's an extreme need. It will just be so you can get to the shop and back without putting you in a position where Moloc can get to you again."

It would have been easy for Brie to melt into his soothing touch and agree to anything, but just because they were all over each other for hours didn't mean she was ready to acquiesce to everything he wanted.

"I still walk to classes and go to school. I still have to grocery shop and live outside of my apartment and the shop. Are you going to put portals to everywhere I go?" she asked, an accusatory tilt to her voice, though she didn't make a move to pull from his embrace.

Ezra didn't take the bait. He simply pulled her back against his chest. "Moloc doesn't know anything about your normal life, so I am fairly certain he doesn't know you are a student. Even if he did, there are enough powerful beings at the university. He wouldn't dare go near any part of the campus. He's extremely powerful, not stupid."

Brie huffed as she finally allowed herself to melt back into his arms. "Of course it's crawling with magical beings. Fine. But you only get to use it for emergencies and date nights."

"Date nights?" he asked, with a small laugh.

Brie nodded against his chest. "Yes, date nights. I have a suspicion that you never leave the shop except for council stuff, so we should have date nights. That way, if Moloc tries to hunt me down, I'll have you to protect me," she said with a laugh of her own.

Ezra kissed the top of her head and nuzzled his nose into her hair. "I suppose that could be acceptable. We should really get you home, though. We can make plans later."

Reluctantly, they stood, breaking apart except for where their hands laced together. With heavy steps, Ezra led her through the apartment door into the darkened antique shop. Once the door swung closed behind them, they turned to face the Storage Room door.

"Remember how we did this last time? Picture your front door in your mind. Except, this time, I'll step with you to connect the door with a more solid tether. Ready?" He looked down at Brie and gave her hand a gentle squeeze.

"Ready," she responded quickly.

She closed her eyes and thought of her front door, plain white with a few scuff marks accumulated over the years and bronze numbers to indicate her apartment number. Beside her, she felt Ezra lean forward, probably to hit the button on the panel and pull the door open.

"Keep thinking of your door, sweetheart, and step forward," Ezra instructed, tugging her hand to encourage movement.

One step forward, Brie felt the barest hint of a breeze flutter her hair. Her eyes opened immediately. She was standing in the threshold of her apartment. Before her was her living room; Wes sat on the couch. He looked wide-eyed at them, the remote still clutched in his hand. Brie half-turned to look behind her; she could still see the back side of the shop counter in the dim light.

Finally, she realized Ezra was mumbling something under his breath that she didn't understand. The doorway began to glow faintly; then, a slight dinging sound reached her ears as a mobile phone-sized touchpad appeared next to her door with four numbers slightly illuminated. The door ceased glowing, and Ezra ended his muttering.

"Neat trick," Wes said finally from across the room, going back to flipping through channels on the TV like nothing out of the ordinary had happened.

Brie looked at the new panel beside the door before sliding her eyes over to Ezra, who still stood in the doorway. "Four buttons?" she asked.

With his free hand, Ezra ran his fingers through his thick hair nervously. "Yeah, well, one is to get outside normally. Two is the shop. And three... um... three is to my place." He looked away from her, a blush creeping across his handsome face.

Brie laughed lightly. "Is that the magical way of giving me the key to your place?" she whispered so only he could hear.

He leveled his gaze at her. "Something like that. And number six in the shop will go here. So more like a key swap." He leaned forward and kissed her gently, keeping it chaste since Wes was still in the room. "Goodnight, sweetheart," he whispered as he pulled away.

"You didn't tell me where number four goes," she said with a smile.

His returning smile was small, but his eyes shone. "Haven't decided yet. You pick."

"Goodnight, Ezra. See you tomorrow," Brie said as their hands dropped. Ezra's smile widened into a full grin. Then, with a step back, never taking his eyes off her face, he entered the shop again, and the door to her apartment swung shut.

Brie stood at the door for a moment, half tempted to hit the number two button just to see if it worked.

"Sooooo, did you have a good shift? Because it looked like you had a really good shift," Wes said from behind her.

Whirling around, Brie saw the smug smirk on Wes's face, and she couldn't help the creeping smile on her own face. "Yeah, it was pretty great," she said a little breathily. "I should get to bed. It's been a day." Brie moved away from the door reluctantly and headed toward her room.

"If he hurts you, I have the right to kill him, yeah?" Wes called out as she walked past the couch.

"What happened to team 'Don't Fuck Your Boss'?" she teased.

Wes shrugged. "Disbanded after I got drunk with the guy. But I'll still kill him if I have to."

"Of course, you get first dibs. But I don't think that's going to be an issue." Brie's smile grew to cover her entire face; then, she walked down the hall to her room, closing the door behind her.

The next week at the shop was excruciating. Winter solstice was coming up, and the shop had an uptick in customers. There were also more tourists trying to come in for some holiday shopping.

By eight o'clock, Brie was ready to flip the "open" sign, lock up, and enjoy the silence. It was tempting. Maybe she could find Ezra, and they could find other ways to occupy the rest of the night. She had a few things in mind.

The bell above the door tinkled again. Brie let out a loud groan and lightly dropped her head onto the counter. Why couldn't everyone just go away for a while?

"Is that how you greet customers here?" She heard Wes say as she looked up. Her brother walked to the counter carrying a takeout bag. The faded gray shirt he wore said "Geology Rocks!": a remnant from the geology club his first year of undergrad. Even with the bad pun, he was a welcome sight.

"That shirt belongs in a museum," she quipped, taking the bag of food Wes held out to her.

"So do you," Wes replied with a grin. "That's not all for you. There's something for Ezra, too. I didn't know what to get him so I just got him your usual, sans the extra pickles." He turned in place as he spoke to look around the shop.

It occurred to Brie that although she had been working at Spirit Antiques for months, this was the first time Wes had been inside. Funny how that happened, especially since he spent so much time and energy trying to convince her to quit. Brie was incredibly glad that he had failed to persuade her.

"So this is it, huh?" Wes returned his attention to her.

Brie gave him a brilliant smile. "This is, but the real magic is back there." She motioned to the Storage Room door with her thumb. "Want to check it out? We can bring this to Ezra. He's working on inventory again."

"Sure, show me the magic room you talked about." Wes rounded the corner and followed her. The door clicked after she pushed the number two button, then with a push, the door swung up, and she let Wes walk ahead of her through the door.

Then she ran straight into his back.

Wes stood rooted to the spot, mouth wide open and eyes darting around, trying to take it all in at once. "Holy shit! It's bigger on the inside, like for real. How big is this place?" His wide-eyed stare turned to Brie for answers.

She could only shrug. It wasn't like she actually had an answer. The Storage Room was a little touchy about showing its ends. "Depends on the day." She walked past Wes to the end of the short platform. "Can we get a lift to Ezra, please?" She directed her question out toward the room.

Two seconds later, a large rug pulled up in front of the platform, low enough that they could both climb on. "The Storage Room thinks flying carpets are the best means of transportation. Doesn't matter what you ask for; most of the time it'll just be a flying carpet," Brie said as she sat at the head of the carpet. Wes clambered on behind with considerably less grace.

Wes had barely finished situating himself before they zoomed off, careening sharply around corners, picking up speed in the straightaways. Ezra wasn't far though. After only a few moments, the carpet came to an abrupt stop.

Ezra stood before a large shelf with a medium-sized wooden crate pried open next to him. In his hands, he held an iPad with which he was documenting the inventory.

"Hey, babe. My brother brought us food. Want to take a break?" Brie held up the plastic bag of takeout containers.

Ezra raised a brow in question. "Babe?"

"I'm workshopping pet names. Now, food?" She dismissed him with a hand wave.

"Sure, food sounds great. Thank you, Wesley." He threw a small wave at Wes, who nodded back. "We can take it to the break room to–" He was cut off by an ornate wooden table followed by three matching chairs walking around the corner of the shelf.

Brie laughed. "I think the Storage Room has other ideas." She waited for the table and chairs to finish their trek to the trio before she set the plastic bag down and plopped onto one of the chairs.

Wes stared at the furniture that had just stopped moving. He crouched down to study the legs and ran a hand up the length of one. "Okay, that was just straight-up strange. What is this, Beauty and the Beast?"

"Which one of us is the Beauty and which one is the Beast? And I want you to think hard before you answer because you have to live with me." Brie gave

Wes a pointed stare, though it lost some of its edge as she tried to stifle her laughter.

"I would like to abstain from answering that question," Wes said as he took a seat. He started removing containers from the bag, placing labeled white boxes before Ezra and Brie. "It's just burgers and fries; hope that's cool with you, Ezra." He leaned back in his chair, nothing in front of him.

Ezra shrugged. "It's fine. But do either of you ever actually eat anything green? I legitimately worry about your nutrition." He pulled the burger closer and removed the few pickles attached to the bun.

"Pickles are green. I'll take those," Brie said as she removed the pickles from Ezra's box to place them on her own burger, which was already laden with what looked to be half a jar.

Wes wrinkled his nose. "I had a kale smoothie once. It was awful."

Brie and Ezra ate the rest of their meal, trading quips with Wes. It was nice for once to sit back and relax, to just enjoy each other's company without worrying about Moloc or school, or even the Morrigan. It was the most relaxed Brie had felt in weeks. She wanted to savor every moment spent with her brother and Ezra.

"Alright, kids, I should head out. I have some studying to do before bed." Wes stood from the table and instantly a new carpet appeared, one that was big enough for the three of them.

"Guess we are seeing you out," Ezra said, helping Brie onto the carpet before settling behind her. Wes scrambled on after him with only slightly more grace than the first time.

When they emerged from the Storage Room, they were greeted by the sight of Apollo standing at the counter texting away on his phone. "I was beginning to wonder if you were even open today, angel man. You sure kept me waiting," he drawled.

He shoved his phone into his back pocket and looked up at the trio. "Well, hello, handsome." His eyes swept over Wes like he was ready to crank up the charm.

Brie immediately went on the defense. "Nope, stop right there, Apollo. That's my brother, and he's off-limits. So keep it in your pants." She leaned over the counter and pointed a finger at him.

Wes put a hand on her shoulder. "Hold on, let the man speak. You were talking about how handsome I am." He flashed a grin at Apollo, and Apollo's face lit up with his smug smile.

"Gross. Get out. Go flirt somewhere where I don't have to watch. Ezra, please make him leave," Brie cried. It was uncomfortable enough to watch her brother flirt, but why did it have to be Apollo?

Ezra was in and out of the Storage Room in seconds and shoved the package into Apollo's chest. "Go be depraved somewhere else, but behave," he whispered to the incubus.

Apollo winked. "Oh, I will behave, darling." Then, he turned his attention back to Wes. "How about a coffee, handsome? My treat."

Brie could practically see Wes melt. "He's an incubus, so just be careful, okay?" she said to Wes, but he was already rounding the counter to join Apollo.

"If you get to make bad choices, so do I. Bye." He waved over his shoulder as the two men walked out into the night.

"Well, I suppose he was bound to get one St. James sibling. I'm just glad it wasn't you," Ezra said, looping an arm around her waist, drawing her close.

Brie wrapped her arm around him in return and rested her head against his chest. "Me too." She turned to face him and went up on her toes to kiss him. He bent his head down to meet her. Brie sighed into the kiss, truly happy with her life in that moment, despite all the madness happening.

When they broke away, Ezra leaned down to touch foreheads with her. "Brie, I want you to stay tonight, please," he whispered onto her lips.

It wasn't like she hadn't thought about it. Actually, she had thought about it a lot lately. It was still so new between them. They had danced around each other for so long, but Brie wasn't one to usually jump into bed with someone after a week of being whatever they were. That didn't stop her from wanting it, wanting him.

Brie made a humming noise. "Are you sure?"

"Yeah, I'm sure. I've never been so sure about anything in my life. It just feels right being with you. Not because of who you were in another life, but because of who you are now. Brie, you bring out something good in me, something I thought was lost long ago. So let me be with you tonight." His face was so earnest, so open. It was easy to nod and let the excitement overwhelm her.

She kissed him again, confident in her decision of what she wanted to do with Ezra later that night.

By the end of the day, Brie was vibrating with anticipation. After months of Ezra being the prominent figure in her nightly fantasies, she was finally going to have the real thing. She made the decision to not worry about how fast it was moving because she wanted him. But more importantly, she felt safe with him.

It didn't help that it had been a while since she had slept with anyone. She needed to relieve the pressure that had been building within her for some time.

At exactly ten o'clock, Ezra stepped out of the Storage Room. Not even bothering to cross the room, he snapped his fingers; the "open" sign flipped itself over, and the door made a snick as it locked. He punched the number three button and flung open the door.

Without a word, he grabbed Brie's hand and pulled her through the door. She let out a surprised noise, but then the door was shutting behind her, and Ezra was there crowding her space and kissing her.

There was nothing soft and gentle about this kiss. It was pure hunger, and Brie reveled in it. She pushed up on her toes to deepen the kiss, winding her arms around his neck as he pulled her flush against him. His tongue traced the seam of her lips and she gladly opened to welcome him inside. He wasted no time in devouring her.

His hands slid down her hips and around to cup her backside. Without thinking, she jumped and wrapped her legs around his waist. Ezra caught her with ease and backed her up against the door, pushing her up against the unyielding wood. Brie loudly moaned as he started to move his lips from hers and began to trace kisses down her jaw to her neck. When he reached the curve of her neck, he began to suck at her skin. Brie's loud moan would have embarrassed her if she had been capable of conscious thought.

Ezra pulled away to stare at her. "Couch or bedroom?" His voice was so ragged that it only further turned her on.

"Bedroom, now!" she cried out before Ezra started to kiss her again. Without breaking the kiss, he carried her away from the door and navigated his way to the bedroom.

He set her down next to his massive bed, kissed her once more, then broke away to whisper in her ear. "Take off your clothes and get on the bed." It was a command that Brie was eager to follow for once. She quickly removed her boots and socks and shimmied out of her jeans, leaving her panties on. The forest green knit sweater went next, dropped without ceremony on his floor. She stood before him in nothing but her bra and panties, suddenly a little shy. Heat flooded her face, and she cast her eyes away from his, toward the ground.

He stepped close to her, lifted her chin with his finger, and forced her gaze up to his. "Is this too much? We don't have to do anything you don't want to." Goddess, did he look concerned. How could he even think for a second she didn't want this?

"I want this. I really, really want this," she said, reaching out to touch his chest.

Ezra gave her a closed-lip smile. "Good. Now, sweetheart, I said take off your clothes." His husky, commanding voice sent a shiver up her spine, and she could feel herself growing damp between her legs. Yeah, his voice was definitely a turn-on.

She wasted no time as she slid off her bra and let it and her panties drop to the floor with the rest of her clothes. Ezra stood watching her, still fully clothed. His eyes swept over her, from her face down to her bare breasts. They lingered there for several moments before continuing their journey down to the apex of her thighs. Brie had never felt so exposed in her life.

"Fuck, you are so beautiful." The reverence in his soft whisper was almost enough to undo her. Then his hazy eyes turned sharp with a wicked glint. "Get on the bed and lay down." The commands were back and Brie felt the thrill of it race through her body. She didn't hesitate to follow his direction; in seconds, she lay flat on her back, head nestled on his incredibly soft pillows. Ezra placed one knee on the bed at the opposite end and slowly made his way up the bed toward her legs.

Whereas she wore not a stitch, Ezra was still fully clothed, and somehow, that was even more erotic in Brie's mind. She was so exposed to him. It was such a rush. It took her a moment to realize Ezra's intention as he moved himself between her legs. The urge to snap her legs shut was strong, but her desire for him was stronger. She didn't move an inch as he settled himself just above her.

He took his time, just staring at the very center of her. His breathing grew even more ragged the longer he looked. Brie could clearly see the sizable bulge in his jeans; it was all for her.

One long finger traced her fold, back and forth, driving her crazy. When he slid his finger into her entrance, her breath hitched in her throat. She wanted more. As if he read her mind, he chuckled and slid a second finger in, pumping both lazily in and out of her dripping folds. She thrashed under his touch, wanting more, unsure she could continue on with him touching her like that.

Brie didn't have any more time to think because his mouth was on her. All thought, all consciousness fled from her to focus on the sensation of him drinking from her. His name was a strangled gasp on her lips. He chuckled from between her thighs. It was too much and not enough all at once. She writhed against him. As she tried to arch her back, one of his heavy arms came to rest against her lower abdomen, pinning her down.

Her vision completely whited out as she reached her crest while she screamed his name. Her whole body felt lit up with electricity. As the feeling subsided, it felt like an effort to move; all of the tension within her melted away.

Ezra sat up with a smug grin on his face. *Bastard knows how good he is at this.* Brie's thoughts were hazy.

"Enough teasing, sweetheart. " His eyes sparkled with desire, pupils so wide there was hardly any trace of emerald. His clothes came off in record time; it was just them with nothing separating their bodies.

Then he was there, lining up his impressive length with her entrance, his eyes unblinking on hers. Brie placed a hand on his chest as he hovered above her. "Do you have a condom?" It was torment having him there without him being inside her, but she would not compromise on this, even if it meant stopping.

"Condoms. Right. Yes, just a second." He pulled away to reach into his bedside table and pulled out an unopened box of condoms. He pulled one out and threw the rest of the box on the table.

"You planned for this." Brie's laugh was so breathy she barely recognized it as her own. Her concentration was scattered at best.

"I did. Just in case," he said as he rolled the condom on. Ezra lined himself back up with her, then he was there, pushing into her. It was the most glorious feeling as he pushed inch by slow inch. The feeling of fullness was on the edge of overwhelming as he bottomed out, and they stayed locked together, unmoving for several long seconds. Brie sucked in her bottom lip as her body relaxed around him; she gave him a subtle nod.

It was all he needed to start thrusting. It was not gentle. They would have time for gentle later. This was about claiming and forgetting all they had been through, all that they would still face.

Their moans grew louder, echoing around the bedroom. Ezra's arms wrapped around her, pulling her up onto his lap. She wrapped her legs around him as he plunged into her. Her forehead fell onto his shoulder. She pushed herself down as he thrust up, riding him to her next peak. One hand slid between them; he was giving her that last push, touching her just enough to have her shrieking again as her orgasm broke over her. Three more erratic thrusts, and he joined her, a claiming growl, loud and guttural, escaping his throat.

He gently lifted her off his softening length, and they collapsed onto the bed side by side. Ezra moved from the bed to dispose of the condom in the bathroom but was back quickly. He slid beside her and pulled Brie close, wrapping her in his arms. Brie snuggled close to his chest and rested her head there.

One of his hands skated up and down her spine, soothing. "Are you okay, sweetheart?" He pulled back enough to see her face, but no farther.

Brie looked up at him with sleepy eyes, and for a moment, all she could do was stare at his beautiful face. Beside it being the best sex she'd ever had, she had never felt as comfortable, as safe with anyone as she did with Ezra. He still stared at her, waiting for an answer, though. "Yeah, I'm great." She snuggled close to him again, content to listen to his heartbeat start to slow.

They lay tangled together, enjoying the feel of the other's body.

"Do you want to sleep?" Ezra finally asked, his hand stilling on her back.

Did she want to sleep? There was no class tomorrow due to exam prep, but she needed the sleep. Then again, it was still early enough, and he felt so good beneath her fingers.

"I have a better idea," she said, kissing his chest. Ezra took in a sharp breath as she began to kiss her way down his body.

His eyes rolled back as Brie reached her destination between his legs. She intended to reciprocate his earlier generosity. They had all night, after all.

CHAPTER 20

$\mathcal{A}$ s much as Brie wanted to stay in bed all day with Ezra, especially because of how they had woken each other up, she needed to get at least a little work done. It took all her willpower to walk through the portal back to her apartment.

Her dreams or memories had been very Ezra-centric the previous night. Things with him were going to be odd, for lack of a better word. Knowing what it was like to kiss him, as both Bridget and the Morrigan in her previous life, was beyond strange. She needed something to take her mind off of him until she saw him that evening.

Packing up her bag, she made her way to the campus library. With finals coming up, she expected there would be tons of other students around. Luckily, she was up early enough that most were still in bed or had just left to head to bed when she arrived.

Setting herself up at a table by a window, she took her time pulling out her laptop and various books. It had snowed overnight, and the whole campus was covered in a dusting of white powder. Brie gave herself a moment to stare out over the expanse of white before turning on her laptop and focusing on emails from her students.

As the morning progressed, the library became gradually busier. The tables around hers were full of harried freshmen facing their first batch of finals. But nobody bothered Brie.

Around noon, Brie stood from her chair to stretch out her back. Hunching over her laptop for hours had made all her limbs stiff. Satisfied that she was at a decent stopping point in her work, she packed her bag to get lunch before starting again. Before leaving her spot, she sent a quick text off to Ezra, hoping he wasn't in the Storage Room, so he would see it sooner rather than later.

She sent "See you in a few hours" with a heart emoji. *When did I get so sappy and romantic?* she wondered.

She walked down two floors to where Wes was working at the desk. "Hey, I'm about to head out and get some lunch. Do you want anything?" She leaned against the desk and looked down at her brother.

Wes looked exhausted. Brie wasn't sure if that was due to a late night of studying or a late night with Apollo. Truthfully, she really, really didn't want to know. "Go home and take a nap when you get off work. You look like shit." She was determined to be the only St. James sibling with a sleeping problem.

"Thanks, asshole," Wes grumbled, rubbing his eyes. "But yeah, I will. I hate this time of year. Too many needy people and too much work to do in general."

Brie leaned over the counter and ruffled his hair. One part of her palm rubbed against the shaved part while the other side got his smooth locks. "Poor baby," she mocked, "don't work too hard. Love you." She adjusted the strap of her messenger bag and turned from the desk.

"Love you, too," Wes said as she walked toward the door.

The bitter cold chilled her instantly; the library had been warm and cozy. She hurried across campus, intent on spending as little time outside as possible.

"Hey Brie, wait up!" a voice called from behind her.

Brie stopped and turned, not even trying to suppress her groan. "Hi Craig," she huffed out once he was standing in front of her.

Craig beamed at her, not picking up on her tone again, it seemed, or just ignoring it completely. "What's up?" he asked innocently.

Brie stopped herself from giving him a massive eye roll. "Not much. I'm off to get something to eat before I get back to work."

Craig didn't even miss a beat. "Cool, I'll join you. Let's get that bagel place just off campus. It's my favorite."

Brie cursed herself. She had walked right into that one. So she shrugged noncommittally because she was already intent on going there anyway, and at this point, he would follow her there no matter what she said. It wasn't like she couldn't just ditch Craig once she had her bagel sandwich.

"So, any curveballs on the final I should be aware of?" Craig asked with a large grin.

"Are you really fishing for exam questions now?" Brie answered sarcastically. She kept her pace brisk, but Craig had no problem matching her step, chatting while they walked.

When they reached the bagel shop just across the street, Craig stopped suddenly. Brie stopped half a step past him and turned.

"Hang on a minute. I... uh... need to get something out of my bag," Craig said, moving off the sidewalk to a space between buildings so he wasn't blocking the walkway. Brie followed him and crossed her arms in annoyance while he rummaged through his backpack one-handed. She knew she should have just kept walking, but she didn't.

"The cafe is literally right there, so you can just catch up," Brie huffed, reaching her limit with him.

He must have found what he was looking for because his eyes snapped up to look at her. "I'm sorry, Brie."

"Sorry for what?" Brie noticed a sudden change in Craig's face. The easy grin from earlier was gone. He looked pained instead. He pulled something from his bag, letting the backpack fall over the ground before shoving the thing into Brie's hand. He forced her hand to close around the object and held onto her closed fist.

There was a bit of pain where Craig wrapped her fingers around the object, but before she could say or do anything, the world around them disappeared.

Gone was the snowy afternoon and bustling street. Now she saw only blue and darkness. Her feet landed hard, and Craig's grip on her hand fell away. She dropped the item he had placed there. She looked down and saw a shard of glass now smeared with a bit of her blood.

"Craig, what did you do?" Brie asked, trying to keep her voice from shaking.

Next to her, Craig kept his head down, refusing to meet her gaze. "I'm really sorry, Brie. I had to. But he promised me you wouldn't be hurt."

"He?" she asked, fear starting to creep in. She had a pretty good idea who *he* was. It took all her effort to stave off the overwhelming terror in her bones.

Craig's gaze moved from the floor to some spot over Brie's shoulder. She didn't want to turn around. She knew what she would find there. Still, she slowly turned. Her eyes landed on a heavy desk; behind it sat the warlock, Moloc Vangren.

"Miss Bridget St. James, we meet again." His voice sent ice traveling down her spine. The smile accompanying it was terrifyingly cruel.

"What the fuck, Craig?!" Brie yelled over her shoulder, not daring to take her eyes off Moloc even for an instant.

"Please, Brie, just listen to him, and then everything will be fine. He promised we could be together after he gets what he needs." She could hear the fear in his voice. Still, she didn't turn to face him.

"You idiot! He wants me dead! Why couldn't you just leave me alone? He's not going to give you anything!" She didn't care that she was yelling at him. She didn't care about hurting his feelings now. Not when she was staring down her own death.

She heard Craig shift behind her. "No, he promised..."

If possible, Moloc's smile became even more cruel, his stare piercing. When he spoke, it was not to address her this time.

He laughed first. "Foolish child. Empty promises mean nothing to me. You have done your part, and now," he turned his attention back to Brie, "Morgana, I shall take great pleasure in ensuring your spirit stays good and dead this time. But first..."

Without so much as a warning, his gnarled hand shot out; behind her came the sounds of choking. Brie broke her stare on Moloc and whirled around to see

Craig suspended several inches off the ground, grabbing at his throat, which seemed to be held by invisible hands. His face was already a shocking crimson, quickly shifting to purple.

"Let him go! You want me. He's just a kid! Let him go!" Brie found herself screaming now, watching helplessly as Craig kicked the air.

"As you wish, Morgana," Moloc crooned.

The snapping sound filled the room like a thunderclap. Craig's body collapsed onto the ground.

The scream caught in her throat. Brie could only stare at Craig, his eyes wide in horror, his mouth open as if still struggling for air. But his head lay twisted at a wrong angle, off to the side. She couldn't tear her eyes away from his broken form. It wasn't like when Maddy died, her body peacefully laid out as if in sleep. This was horrifying and brutal. She had never seen anything like it.

Images came unexpectedly, flashes of battlefields as she had seen in her dreams. They were the Morrigan's memories. Brie knew that now. She turned away from Craig's body and shut her eyes tight to drive the memories from her head.

"Don't tell me one body is enough to frighten the great Morrigan?" Moloc chuckled bitterly. Brie opened her eyes to look at him. He still sat at his desk. The hand he had held up to kill Craig now rested there.

Brie tried to harden her gaze, but she couldn't stop the tears from forming. It only made Moloc laugh more.

"You, who strolled through battlefields of blood and gore and reveled in the wars consecrated in your name. Mortality has made you weak, Morgana. You were such a formidable foe and now look at you, cowering at one insignificant death. Hiding behind old-world charms and angelic magics when you were once worshiped as the Phantom Queen. How far you have fallen, Morgana." Moloc finished his speech with a mocking frown, fingers now steepled on the wood of his desk.

Brie felt something akin to anger start to bubble up inside her. He was mocking her. "My name is Bridget. And I think mortality works just fine for me, thanks." There was a fire in her voice, though it came from something deep, more ancient within herself.

The grin returned to Moloc's face. "There's that spark. I see her behind your eyes now. I see Morgana's soul fighting for control. Let her free, so I may face the Morrigan once more."

At first, Brie wasn't sure what he meant. Then she felt it, an all-consuming hatred that was not her own. Her whole body felt like she was made from an inferno. Images flashed in her mind, memories unlocking themselves as her former incarnation fought to be remembered, to be present.

Battles and wars unnumbered.

Washing the bloody armor of heroes long forgotten.
Flying high above the world on crow wings.
Ezra's smile in their forest home.
Moloc.
Moloc binding her in a circle, a bright gem clutched in his fist, binding her body to the mortal plane. The low chanting of an incantation as he threw handfuls of grave dirt onto her. As he trapped her in mortal flesh. The glint of a silver knife in the sunlight above her, plunging downward.

Brie was barely aware of clutching her stomach where a phantom knife had stuck ages ago, where Moloc had delivered a simple killing blow to the Morrigan. She pulled her hands away, expecting to see blood, but it was only a memory.

"Stop it," she choked out, tears flowing down her face. Moloc watched with unbridled joy.

When the memories finally began to fade, Brie slumped to her knees as the tears continued. "All this time, Ezra thought it was his mother who killed the Morrigan. That she was the only one with the power to bind a god, but it was you," she screamed, her eyes flashing to Moloc.

Across the room, Moloc rose slowly from his chair and walked around the desk. The long fur coat he wore swirled around his ankles as he approached her. Once again, his hand raised, and Brie felt her body leave the ground. He didn't choke the air from her, though, but that didn't bring Brie much solace. Her feet dangled limply several inches off the ground, so she had to look down at Moloc as he advanced on her.

"And he was a fool for doubting my power then and more a fool now for believing he doesn't belong to me! Killing you quickly would bring me little joy. I want to make this hurt even more than the first time. And when I'm done with you, I'll leave what's left of your body on the steps of that little antique shop to remind Ezra of his place," Moloc sneered, his ice-shard eyes blazing.

The fire that was building within Brie was quickly extinguished by Moloc's chilling words. Fear flooded her senses. Brie was just starting to learn about her power. She had no way of controlling it to help her now. Her mobile phone was in her messenger bag, lying below her on the floor. Not that she knew where she was, even if she could call someone.

"We have a long night ahead of us, Morgana. I look forward to breaking both this body and the spirit within it again," Moloc said as he began to walk, his magic pulling Brie behind him.

Brie felt the fire growing again as the power inside her began to take form. She would get out of this. The golden glow started at her hands and moved to her forearms. She could feel the power pushing against the magical bond Moloc had on her body.

He whirled around and snarled. "There will be none of that!" He pulled a drawstring bag from a pocket in the fur coat and poured a small amount of powder into his hand. With a gentle breath, he blew the powder onto Brie. Instantly, the power within her receded, and darkness began to creep along her vision.

The last thought that flitted through her mind before the darkness completely consumed her was that the shell phone was still in her coat pocket, where she always kept it.

It was ten minutes after six, and Brie had still not shown up at the shop. Ezra told himself he wouldn't use the door to her apartment unless it was an emergency. He hadn't heard from her all day, and she was late, which wasn't like her.

Debating with himself a minute more, Ezra decided to check on her. He pulled his shell phone from the pocket of his jeans, internally rolling his eyes at himself for calling it a shell phone like Brie wanted.

"Brie, sweetheart, are you there?" he asked into the glowing shell.

Nothing. The shell phone remained silent. Ezra tried to taper the concern rising in his mind, the million different scenarios where something was incredibly wrong with Brie. He tried the shell phone again.

"Brie?"

Then a small voice responded from the glow of the shell. "Ezra?"

Alarm bells went off in his head. Her voice sounded weak, nothing like her usual self.

"Brie, are you okay? What's wrong, sweetheart?" It was an effort to keep his voice even and not panic.

Another long pause before her weak voice came through again. She sounded so tired. "Ezra. He'll be back soon. Please. I don't... I don't know where I am. It hurts, Ezra. It hurts so much."

Now he was in a full-blown panic. "Sweetheart, what happened? Where are you?"

"I don't know, Ezra. I... he's coming. Don't say anything or he'll know." Her voice was even more faded, hurried, and then it was gone.

Ezra wanted to scream, to beg her to keep talking, but she told him not to say anything. Reluctantly, he closed the shell phone, not knowing what else to do.

Moloc had Brie. He was certain of that. There wasn't any other *he* there could be. Ezra didn't know where Moloc kept himself while he was in the city.

"Fuck!" he yelled out to the empty shop.

His mobile phone rang, startling him. He wanted to ignore it, but he answered it anyway.

"Hell—" he was cut off quickly.

"Ezra! She's still in the city. There's a warehouse of some kind. I'm still trying to figure it out," the frantic voice of Lily said quickly.

"He has her, Lily, and I don't know what's going to happen to her. I need your help." His voice was just as frantic despite his efforts to remain calm.

"I'm down the street. We need a plan," Lily said, then hung up.

Less than five minutes later, she burst through the shop door with Wes and Apollo behind her.

"Where's Brie? Where's my sister?!" Wes yelled as the door slammed behind him.

CHAPTER 21

"Anything, Lily?" Ezra asked for what was probably the twentieth time in the last ten minutes.

Lily sat in a chair the Storage Room had provided, her eyes closed in concentration. Wes and Apollo stood off to the side, watching carefully, while Ezra paced like a caged animal, ready to leave the moment Lily could pinpoint Brie.

"It doesn't work like that, Ezra. You need to be patient. I'm doing the best I can," she shot back, annoyed, though her eyes remained shut.

Ezra resumed his pacing, keeping his eyes trained on Lily as he did.

"Have you tried her mobile phone?" Apollo asked, his tone serious for once.

"No, Apollo, I didn't think to try the most basic line of communication, a mobile phone. How stupid of me. Remind me why you are here again," Ezra responded, voice dripping with sarcasm.

"Ignore him. He's been spending too much time with Brie. I've been calling her since two, when she didn't come home from the library. Her voicemail is full, but I'm still trying," Wes said, checking his phone again.

"I was out with Wes when Lily called. It just seemed right to come help the little lamb. Why don't you try the glow shell thing again?" Apollo asked Ezra, ignoring the glower shot his way from the angel.

Ezra paused and shook his head. "She said not to because Moloc was coming back. There's no way to know if he's in the room with her or not. Fuck! I wish there was some way to find her using the stupid shell phone." He held the mentioned shell phone in his hand tightly, but his gaze was lost somewhere on the shelves of the Storage Room.

He turned suddenly, facing Lily, who still had her eyes shut tight in concentration. "Lily, could you find her using the shell phones? Like triangulation?" His voice was hopeful.

Lily huffed loudly and cracked open her eyes. "I'm a clairvoyant, not a GPS. You've been watching cop shows again, haven't you?"

Ezra mumbled something nobody caught as he shoved the shell phone into his pocket, knowing it wasn't going to be much help unless Brie contacted him.

The group fell into silence, not making eye contact as they waited for Lily to come up with something. It was driving Ezra crazy to have to wait, feeling helpless. It was his fault she was taken. If he could have just cut ties with Moloc, found a way out from their blood oath on his own, Brie would still be safe.

"I... I think I found her. Maybe," Lily announced, her voice radiating through the silence, causing Wes and Apollo to jump. "And it's not good. I'm calling Bertie," she added, pulling out her mobile phone.

"We don't need him. He has nothing to do with Brie," Ezra spat, firmly against the vampire becoming involved.

Lily ignored him and had Albert on the phone before the second ring. "Hi, babe. We have a problem. I need you to go down to Demon's Row. No, I'm fine. It's Brie, she's been taken, and I think she's being held there. Brie. Yes, Ezra's Brie. My friend Bridget! You are way too smart to be asking such dumb questions. Just get down there. Be careful, and call me back."

"She's in Demon's Row?" Ezra asked, stunned.

"That's my best guess. Bertie's going to check it out. He can pass a lot better than we can down there," Lily said, standing up from her chair to stretch out her limbs.

"What's Demon's Row?" Wes asked.

"The name says it all, really. The worst creatures in New Britain live there, not fully allowed in the city proper, so they set up their own area. It's full of demons and dark magics," Lily responded with a shutter.

In an instant, Ezra moved to the Storage Room door. "I'm going. I'm not going to argue with you,

Lily." Lily closed her mouth against whatever argument she had. "I'm going. You can stay here and wait for Albert's call. But I can't leave her."

He was out the door in a second. Lily looked over at Wes and Apollo, then darted out of the room after Ezra. The other two followed close behind.

Brie felt like her entire body weighed a thousand pounds. Just lifting her head took too much effort. She wasn't sure how much time had passed; it could have been an hour or days.

The room Moloc put her in was windowless and mostly bare, save for a plush dark rug, a dimmed lamp made of twisted metal, and a saggy brown chair that she had curled herself up on. For now, she was alone, tired, and drained of energy. She knew Moloc would be back soon to try again.

For however long he had kept her, Moloc had pushed her to release her powers. Through words and jeers. Through magical coercion. And finally, through physical torture. He wanted Brie to unleash the power of the Morrigan within. He wanted to harvest that power for his own before he killed Brie and destroyed the Morrigan's spirit.

She wouldn't let him have it. Every time she felt her body heat up with the magic, and the glow of her body begin, she fought it and pushed it down within herself. No matter what, she wouldn't give anything to Moloc.

She wasn't sure what made her fight so hard against the power being drained from her. Wouldn't it be better to have the Morrigan gone? Not that Brie would have much of a life after. Moloc wouldn't let her live.

The real reason wasn't her fear of death. She was afraid, of course, terrified even. It was the thought that her death and the power Moloc wanted would just be one more thing he would hold over Ezra. That Ezra would never escape him. She knew that with the Morrigan's power, Moloc would enslave Ezra. So she would keep fighting, if only to keep Moloc from exerting that power over Ezra again. She would keep him safe with her sacrifice.

This thought was taking a toll on her mentally, as Moloc took his toll on her physically. Fresh and dried slashes covered her arms where Moloc had cut into her. A bruise was already forming near her right eye from repeated hits. Her whole body felt heavy with pain; she knew it was only a matter of time before Moloc appeared again to continue his work. That had been the cycle so far, torture, talk, rest, torture, talk, rest.

As she waited, she thought of her friends and what would happen to them once Moloc was finished with her. Wes was her brother. He loved her. They had grown up together under Maddy's loving care. They had always been together. She was afraid for him if she didn't make it. The thought of him being alone because of her made her feel sick. Moloc had little interest in Brie herself, so she could only hope that meant he didn't know about Wes. That Wes would be safe.

Then there was Lily, her best friend and teacher in the ways of magic. She was the sweetest person Brie had ever met. Before she was Brie's friend, though, she was Ezra's. *Will Moloc go after her just to continue to hurt Ezra? Probably.*

And what about Ezra? They had just started something, and it was great. She wanted to keep kissing him for a long time, but Moloc was going to kill her and take away all of those would-be kisses. He would do this to Ezra again, just to see him suffer and submit. Ezra was so kind and had been through so much in his long life. He deserved happiness, not another tragedy. Moloc had already taken so much from him.

She wasn't going to let him take any more.

Closing her eyes, Brie took a few deep breaths and turned her mind inward toward the light within herself. The same light Moloc had been trying so hard to siphon out of her. That is where the Morrigan resided.

"Please, help me. Give me your strength. We can't let him do this again. Please," she said to that light, pleading with it.

The light responded by pulsing. Brie felt it move through her whole body. It grew to a thrumming. If she was going to die today, she sure as hell was going to take Moloc with her.

For Ezra.

With newfound resolve, Brie centered herself and waited for Moloc to return, taking comfort in the power flowing through her body, contained, but ready.

Albert Hsu crouched atop the ledge of a three-story building, his sharp eyes scanning the streets and alleys below him. He rarely came to Demon's Row now that he was courting Lily; she had enough light for two, even for one like him.

But there he was, watching for some sign of Moloc or one of his ilk so Ezra could find his stupid human pet. So far, there had been little movement. It had only been dark for an hour or two, and Demon's Row didn't really wake until close to midnight. In the thirty minutes he had already been out, he had seen a grand total of two low-level demons and an imp. None of them had any trace of Moloc attached to them, so Albert had not bothered.

He stepped away from the ledge and walked the length of the building before jumping a large gap to the adjacent building. With an unhurried pace, almost strolling, he made his way to the opposite end of the building to continue his vigil from that vantage point.

Another twentyish minutes had passed with Albert changing buildings and lookouts before he saw her. Helena's auburn hair bobbed into view around a corner. Even without his enhanced eyesight, it would have been hard to miss her in the green dress. It was always a green dress.

Albert leapt from the building, landing on his feet with a bit of a jolt to his knees. Movies made it look so cool, but it took him a few seconds to recover from the impact before he dared to test his knees. Ahead of him, Helena paused at his landing and waited for Albert's approach.

"Helena," Albert said curtly, nodding his head slightly in greeting.

"Albert," she responded with a slight turn up of her lips, managing to look more menacing than greeting. "It's been some time since I've seen you around Demon's Row. Tired of living amongst the mortals already?" Her voice was mocking. Albert balled his fists to keep calm.

"I've been far too busy to cavort around with the local degenerates," he shot back, mockingly cool.

Helena raised one perfectly shaped eyebrow at him. "Too busy with your little witch girlfriend, you mean? How far you have fallen, Albert. To think I used to respect you. We are family, after all."

"Our lust for blood hardly makes us family, Helena. But you are not my concern tonight. I need to find Moloc. You know where he is." Albert kept his voice even and detached, the picture of vampire boredom. He refused to play Helena's game, though he knew she would continue it, anyway.

Helena's smile was icy and would have struck fear into any warm heart. Luckily for Albert, his wasn't. "Now, what business could you have with Moloc?" Her voice was vaguely threatening.

Albert narrowed his eyes. "My own business, which is none of yours. Just tell me where to find him."

Helena tutted at him. "Albert, you should know better. I don't trust you. So why would I tell you anything you wanted to know?"

"Because you want to be left alone to live, the same as me. And with Moloc in New Britain, that can't happen. You tell me where he is, and I'll make sure he leaves town quickly so you can go back to what you call a peaceful living." Albert crossed his arms tightly, waiting. If there was one thing he knew for certain about Helena, it was she needed her independence, and Moloc threatened that. Like so many, she owed something to the warlock.

Her laugh was like ice water through his veins. "Well, you got me there. Just get the old bat out of town and don't tell him I said anything, and it's a deal."

"You have my word," Albert said, not entirely sure he could deliver, but Ezra would kill him if he didn't help. More importantly, Lily would never forgive him if he left her friend to die.

"In that case, you'll find him one block that way." She indicated down the street with one outstretched hand. "First building on the left. There are wards, of course, powerful ones. I could give you my password, but that would give me away. So you'll just have to figure out a way in yourself. Tah!" In a mortal blink, she was gone, though Albert could still see her silhouette against the darkened streets. He didn't bother to pursue her. It would have been useless, anyway. Instead, he walked in the direction Helena indicated and stopped when the building came into view. The whole thing radiated dark magic, even from a distance.

Albert tucked himself into the shadows between two buildings, pulled out his mobile phone, pulled up a number, and waited for it to ring.

"Lily, I found it. I'll send you my location now. The whole place is covered in wards, so I don't know how you plan to get in. Do you want me to stay down here?" He paused and waited for her response. "Okay, I'll be nearby until you get here. Be careful, Lily."

He slipped the phone into his pocket and settled deeper into the shadows to wait.

CHAPTER 22

I t was another hour of waiting before Moloc appeared again. Brie sat in the same chair, no longer curled in on herself, but with feet planted firmly on the ground and back straight. Her arms rested casually on the armrests; she kept her gaze fixed on the door.

She wasn't actually seeing anything in the room. Her mind was turned inward, focusing on the golden light within, drawing on the strength of the Morrigan. The weariness she felt had lifted, and though the physical damage remained, she was no longer bleeding and felt no pain. The only thing she felt now was determination.

One way or another, Moloc would be dead by the end of this night, of that she was certain. That certainty ran deep into her soul. Brie knew this was not her own feeling, but that of the Morrigan. Brie was now just the instrument of the Morrigan's vengeance. That once might have scared her, to be a vessel only and not her own person, but that was before she had stepped into Ezra's world, before she had let him into her heart. She

312

was still mortal. The situation was beyond her control. The Morrigan was her only chance.

In the part of her mind that still belonged solely to herself, she briefly entertained the idea that Ezra would come for her. He would find her and wrap her in his arms, and Moloc would be put behind them. It was unrealistic, of course. Ezra didn't know where she was, only that Moloc had her. Never in Brie's life had she waited around for anyone to save her. She would have to save herself or die trying. She wanted Ezra safe and far away from Moloc. More than anything, she hoped he wouldn't come for her.

She heard Moloc's footsteps on the other side of the door. With a deep breath, she pulled herself deeper into herself and let the power wash over her. Brie felt of two minds. One that was her own and terrified, and one that was bloodthirsty and ready to kill.

When the door opened, it was the Morrigan sitting in the chair waiting for Moloc.

Moloc sensed it immediately based on the sudden glare that appeared on his face with an accompanying smirk. "I wondered when you would appear. You finally decided to get rid of the girl. Good. I wanted a challenge, and she was weak. But you were never weak, were you, Morgana?"

The Morrigan was in control now. She rapped Brie's fingers against the armrest. "I've grown tired of your games, Moloc Vangren. It is time I took my leave." She stood lazily, as if bored, and took a step toward the door. It was a provocation. The Morrigan was not going to let Moloc get away unscathed, and Moloc was not going to let her just waltz out.

A ball of pure electrical energy collided with her abdomen, suddenly sending waves of electrical pulses through her body. It pushed her back into the chair hard. Moloc let his hand drop from where it extended, his cruel grin growing to show all of his teeth.

"I think not, Morgana. You leave only when I say, and I'm afraid that won't be happening. See, I made the mistake last time of not binding your spirit completely. Putting you in human flesh did not take care of the problem entirely. I mean to rectify that mistake this time."

The Morrigan was having none of it. She pushed off from the chair and conjured a beautifully crafted bronze sword from thin air. The sword glowed with the same energy as the Morrigan's spirit.

All Brie could do was experience it from inside her own mind, shoved into a corner while the Morrigan operated her body. She could still feel everything—the warmth of the metal in her hand, the heat of the magic in her body.

"You forget yourself, Moloc Vangren. I am a goddess of war. And this, this is our war." She spat at him, then, with lightning speed, she lunged with her sword.

With a quick flick of his wrist, the air shimmered in front of Moloc. The sword point stopped in mid-air, less than a foot from his heart. The Morrigan grunted against the sudden arrest of momentum, but her arm continued to push against the barrier Moloc had erected around himself.

They remained locked together. Moloc kept his focus on his barrier, causing him to sweat from the strain, as the Morrigan pushed her sword into the barrier with a strength beyond Brie's limits. There was magic radiating through the sword, and bit by bit, it was forcing itself through the barrier. Brie's arm felt every inch of it. The weight of the sword, and the strength behind it, was taking a toll on her human body. She felt her arm begin to shake.

The Morrigan kept pushing through, ignoring the physical limits of Brie's body. There was little doubt in Brie's mind that the Morrigan would break her body just as readily as Moloc if it meant getting her revenge. And she was powerless to stop it.

Moloc dropped his barrier, unable to hold against the power radiating through the Morrigan's sword. The bronze blade surged forward and skirted off Moloc's side. He retaliated at that same moment with another crackling blast of energy. Brie felt herself flying back across the room. She hit the far wall with a sickening smack, and her body crumpled to the floor. The sword managed to stay in the Morrigan's hand. Only Brie was feeling the pain of the blows and the overexertion. The Morrigan felt nothing but her own burning vengeance.

"Human bodies are just not up to the task of hosting immortals, it would seem. But if you joined with me, Morgana, gave me your essence, I could give you war like you've never seen and the blood of enough heroes to slake even your unending thirst." Moloc's eyes glimmered with possibility. For a moment, Brie truly feared that the Morrigan would take his offer and leave her to die. She sat resting her body against the wall, gasping for breath.

With a firm voice that didn't betray how winded she was, the Morrigan spoke again. "You may kill this body, Moloc Vangren. You may kill a hundred more I inhabit. But you will never have my power."

The Morrigan transformed Brie's body into the crow form and took flight. The bronze sword disappeared before it could clatter to the ground. Stuck in her mind, Brie was left whirling, unaccustomed to the rapid shift. She felt no control over the magic, but with each flap of her wings, she felt the pain. Her body was already weary from Moloc's earlier interrogations. With his latest attacks, she was barely hanging on.

No matter how the Morrigan pushed inside her head, though, she couldn't make Brie's body dodge Moloc's attacks any quicker.

Twin beams of black energy slammed into the side of Brie's crow body, now several feet off the ground, heading for the door. Instantly, the crow form dissolved, and Brie plummeted to the unforgiving wooden floor. A loud snap cut the air as Brie landed hard on her right arm. She screamed in pain; her vision blasted to white.

Her body lay close to Moloc now. With a grace and power that betrayed his aged form, he delivered a swift kick to her ribs. All the air from her lungs whooshed out as pain radiated throughout her body.

"You have such power, Morgana, and yet you can barely use it in such a fragile body. But it's time now to surrender your essence to me." His voice was raspy, but there was a definite glee in his tone.

Brie could barely move on her own. She felt her body start to leave the floor as the Morrigan again ignored the pain and made her stand. Her feet lifted from the floor, and it felt as if she was floating. The Morrigan could do nothing to fight it.

Before her, Moloc began to chant low in a guttural language Brie didn't know, but she knew instinctually that it was a binding spell. The Morrigan struggled to move Brie's body, but her limbs merely flopped around in mid-air, her right arm barely moving. She cried out in pain every time the Morrigan tried to will her arms to move.

On the ground below her, a circle of white light formed into the wood and then filled itself in. The glowing circle shot up suddenly, engulfing Brie's body in a column of white light. The light felt like millions of stabbing pin pricks all over her skin. She released a feral scream that rang through the room.

Moloc smiled.

"I can't break through this, Ezra. This is way above my level. I have no experience with wards." Lily tore her gaze from the storage building in front of them to look back at Ezra. His already tight frown hardened further; it was not the answer he wanted.

"Lily, she's been in there for hours. We don't know what he's doing to her. You have to do something," Ezra growled.

Albert stepped in front of Lily in a protective stance and glared hard at Ezra. "It's not her fault your girl-friend was taken. Lily is doing the best she can. Maybe you should be thinking of a way inside instead of putting it on other people."

Ezra growled again and took a threatening step toward Albert, who bared his fangs in response.

"I could use my charms to get the password out of someone. I'm very persuasive," Apollo chimed in, drawing attention to himself and quickly diffusing the standoff between Ezra and Albert.

"You want to seduce a password out of some demon? Why are you even here, Apollo?" Ezra asked angrily.

Apollo shrugged. "I'm here because Lily caught me at the right place at the wrong time. And believe it or not, I've grown attached to Brie. I care about her safety. Anyway, it was just an idea. It's more than what you have."

"This is stupid. Can't we just charge in? Moloc is going to know either way that we're here, so who cares if we set off a few alarms?" Wes half yelled at the group. He looked ready to bolt for the door.

Lily sighed. "Because they're not just alarm wards; there are wards of sealing and some for like, causing some real damage to the person who tries to open the door. Why do you think none of us have actually touched the door?"

Wes crossed his arms, sulking. "Well, I didn't know that. Now I do."

"Why did I even bother to come?" Apollo grumbled, hands on his hips.

Ezra rounded on him. "Because wherever there is a fight and shit going down, Apollo the Magnificent has to be there, apparently. Your one move is to use those hypno-eyes."

"I also kick people in the balls. So that's two moves!" Apollo responded brightly, not letting the dire situation get the better of his good mood. The worry in his eyes betrayed him.

Ezra threw up his hands and huffed loudly. "Whatever. I have a plan. I was just hoping one of you would have a better one because I really, really don't want to do this."

"Do what?" Wes asked.

Lily smiled at Ezra knowingly. "You're going to call your mom."

"Shut up, Lily," Ezra said, not exactly angry. "Fuck," he mumbled to himself. He stepped closer to the door and out of the circle of what he begrudgingly acknowledged as his friends.

It had been a long time since he invoked a god, but maybe his mother would listen.

Maybe.

She was probably going to be pissed, though.

Without thinking further, lest he talk himself out of it, he let his wings unfurl around his body and raised his palms to the sky as he shut his eyes. He silently began the chant of invocation in the celestial language, thinking of Brie as he did so. She was so young and vibrant and absolutely too good for him. The only reason Moloc had her now was because of him, and the soul inside of her that she had never asked for. For Brie, he would do anything.

He stood there, arms stretched out about his head, for several minutes. Behind him, he could hear his friends whispering.

"What's taking so long?" Apollo stage whispered to Lily.

"Apollo, we're standing next to a building totally radiating evil energy, containing the evilest dude ever, and the angel guy is trying to phone the Good Place. It's not exactly an easy connection to make," Wes responded sarcastically.

"Do you think she'll even answer? I wouldn't if he was my son," Albert asked, putting his arm around Lily's shoulder.

Lily responded by lightly hitting him on the chest with the back of her hand. "Be nice, all of you. She'll answer. I hope. It's the only shot we have of saving Brie."

She hit Albert again when he rolled his eyes.

Ezra's arms began to strain. He had to focus to keep the words from tripping over themselves on his tongue. It had been so long since he had done this. It was taking more energy than he remembered to do it.

Then there was brilliant white light surrounding him, so bright he could see it behind his closed eyes and feel it tingling on his skin.

"Arakiel," the voice was both ethereal and comforting.

And there she was, in a flowing dress of white with a rainbow hem, his mother. She hadn't aged since he last saw her, not that she would. Her dark skin was smooth, and her flowing silver hair, not dulled by age, floated around her in waves. She was eternal, but she appeared to him just as lovely and maternal as she always had.

Behind him, he heard gasps from his friends. They couldn't see her, but they could feel her presence, and the light was sure to fill them just as it filled him.

Tears sprang to Ezra's eyes immediately. "Mother," he whispered. She smiled, and Ezra let the tears fall unhindered down his face. "I'm sorry. I—"

"I know, Arakiel. Let go, my sweet boy. You don't have to carry the guilt anymore." Her voice was soothing, like she was talking to a child.

"I'm not coming home, mother. I can't. There's someone..." His eyes flicked to the warehouse door, which looked so polluted next to the white light surrounding him.

"She's a sweet girl and just your match. She'll keep you on your toes." His mother smiled again. "The evil inside is strong, but I can take down these walls for you." Then she turned, and with no further movement, the light expanded against the warehouse, pushing against the darkness.

The resistance was there, where dark met light, then it was no more. The wards and aura surrounding the warehouse were simply gone.

His mother turned back to face him. "The rest is up to you now, Arakiel. I cannot interfere more than this. I love you, my sweet boy."

"Thank you, Mother," he whispered, and she was gone, taking the blinding light with her. Ezra stood alone, facing the now wardless warehouse door, and quickly wiped tears from his eyes.

The group wasted no time getting into the building. What served as an entryway was a long, dark corridor.

Standing on either side of the only door were two transformed werewolves, their eyes gleaming with hunger as they fixed their gazes on the newcomers.

"Five against two, shouldn't be too bad," Ezra said, pulling a sword seemingly from the air. The blade blazed with white-hot celestial flames.

"I did my part with the scouting. I don't even want to be here." Albert inspected his nails as he spoke in a bored tone.

"Ugh, fine. Whatever. Unless you three are out too," Ezra said, looking at the other two from the corner of his eye, keeping one eye fixed on the werewolves. Neither had moved so far.

"If they were in human form, I could, but all wolfed out, I'm also pretty useless," Apollo said apologetically.

"Uh, I've never actually fought a real thing before, but yeah, sure." Wes's voice wobbled a bit.

Ezra cast him a look from the corner of his eye. "Do you even have power? I won't let you get hurt, Wes. Bile would kill me."

Wes ran a hand through his messy hair. "Yeah, just a sec." He joined his hands as if he held something and brought them over his head. With a swish of his arms, he brought them down quickly. Suddenly, a glowing silver blade appeared between his hands. "I can do this," he muttered to himself, though his breathing quickened.

Ezra sighed loudly. "I'm with you, too," Lily said, stepping up to his side. She turned her palms upward in front of her and began to chant under her breath.

From the cement floor, vines crashed through, cracking the floor as they shot out. This was all the incentive the werewolves needed to attack. There were only snarls filling the space as they lunged for the witch and the angel first.

Lily's vines caught one of the werewolves halfway down the hallway, wrapping up the fur-covered body in tangles. The other werewolf slashed at the vines and raced to the end of the hallway, barely dodging Ezra's arcing sword. The smell of singed fur filled the air.

A second swipe of the flaming sword caught it in the stomach. Ezra danced away from a clawed swipe aimed at his neck, and Wes stepped into the space a second after the claw, bringing his glowing sword to swipe upwards. The blade caught the werewolf across the face, from cheek to brow, blinding it in the eye.

Wes tried to dance away as the werewolf howled with rage, but he wasn't quick enough. The large hand of the werewolf shot out with enough fury and force to send Wes careening into the wall. The blow knocked the wind from his lungs, and the glowing sword disappeared from his hands.

Ezra didn't take his focus off the werewolf. He turned his sword outward and pointed at the werewolf just as it turned to lunge at him. Unable to stop its momentum, the werewolf impaled itself on the flaming sword; the blade burning the fur around the mortal wound. Ezra pried the sword from the beast's chest cavity, kicking it away as he pulled.

The vines holding the other wrapped tighter, completely covering the werewolf's body. Ezra walked toward where Wes lay on the floor and gave him a hand up. The two of them and Lily stormed past the tangled werewolf and headed for the door. The remaining two, giving a wide berth around the corpse and the vine-covered werewolf, followed quickly.

Through the door was a corridor stretching far off into the darkness. The ceiling was so high and dark that they couldn't see it. Identical doors ran down the length of the corridor with no indication of which one Brie was behind.

"They're all spelled. Not like the one that was over the whole place. But there's no way I can pick out energies or sound," Lily said, face dropping into uncertainty.

"So we're just going to have to try every one until we find her?" Wes asked with a groan.

"Guess so. Wes and Apollo take the right. Lily, you and I will take the left. Albert, do whatever the fuck you want," Ezra said, casting a glare over his shoulder at the vampire.

They set off down the hall, opening doors. The first few on both sides swung open easily, but they were empty. Nothing covered the walls or floor to even suggest they were used.

However, the fifth door down on the right side was definitely in use, and most certainly not empty. Apollo swung the door open with all the grace of a charging bull to find a room full of goblins and what appeared to be at least one redcap.

"Wrong room," Apollo said, quickly pulling the door shut and backing up straight into Wes, who was coming up behind him.

"Empty?" Wes asked.

Several loud bangs sounded against the door, like many weapons embedding themselves in the wood. "Uh, not exactly," Apollo said, pulling Wes away from the door. "Lily, do you think you could lock this?" He pointed to the door once Lily turned her attention toward him.

Before Lily could so much as lift a finger to help, the door burst open; it was the redcap that exited first. The nominal red cap on its head was crusted with layers of dried blood, and it licked its sharp teeth as if already tasting the flesh of the intruders.

"Help!" Apollo yelled over his shoulder just before the redcap lunged for him.

Every inch of her mind was screaming for her to move her body, do something to stop the pain, but Brie was so tired. Not even the will of the Morrigan could compel her limbs to move now.

Before her, Moloc continued to chant. His eyes were shut in concentration. The magic used to hold her was draining him rapidly.

Without Brie thinking of it, the bronze sword appeared again in her hand, called forth by the Morrigan. It slipped through Brie's fingers before she could fully grasp it. Her body was too tired and slow to realize. Inside her mind, the Morrigan screamed in rage, berating her for her frail form. Brie knew she would die with the curses of the Morrigan in her head and the sound of Moloc's chanting voice in her ears.

She silently apologized to Ezra as tears flowed down her cheeks.

The pinpricks produced by the light seemed to grow more painful; she shrieked again. Moloc's eyes snapped open at her scream, his gaze holding her captive almost as much as the magic. *Please let me die,* she thought, and hoped the Morrigan would listen. She didn't, and so Brie continued to scream, her throat raw.

Still chanting, he turned his hand so his palm was now facing him. He drew his fingers closed as if coaxing something forward. Suddenly Brie felt as if a part of herself was ripped from her in one powerful tug. She screamed again as her body dropped to the floor next to the bronze sword.

Moloc no longer fixed his gaze on her, but instead on a form made of pure golden light above her. From where Brie lay on the ground, she could see it was the form of a woman, tall with long hair waving in an invisible breeze. All she could see, though, was her back. She knew this must be the spirit of the Morrigan, the one that had lived inside her all her life.

It was now the Morrigan who screamed as the binding spell focused on her. Though Brie still lay in the circle of light, the pain was gone. The pinpricks didn't touch her.

Move!

She repeated the word over and over in her mind. But even a small twitch of her finger hurt. She felt so empty, so drained.

This was her chance to escape. Moloc wasn't focused on her. Let him have the Morrigan. At least Brie could live.

With pain radiating everywhere, Brie sat up slowly just as the room rang with Moloc's triumphant cackle. Her hand fell to the sword and her fingers closed around the hilt without conscious thought. She hefted the sword upright and used it to propel herself into a standing position with her good arm. Her vision swam as she slowly got to her feet.

Brie could barely hear the Morrigan's screams now or Moloc's voice. One step, then two. She stumbled. Her feet took her not toward the door, but closer to Moloc. The glowing circle on the ground did nothing to hold her back now, and Brie stepped over it without a glance.

When she was mere steps away, Moloc's eyes briefly swiveled to her. Though he didn't stop his chant, his eyes blasted his outrage.

Brie kept going. Gathering whatever strength she had left, she raised the bronze sword with her good arm and lunged at Moloc. If she didn't kill him now, he would use the power of the Morrigan to subjugate Ezra. Who knows what worse horrors he would loosen on the world with that kind of power.

This is for Ezra.

This time, he was too slow to break off the magic and shield himself. Brie's blade struck true. The shining sword tip slid easily into Moloc's chest, where his heart would be, supposing he even had one. The Morrigan's screams ceased. The glowing circle disappeared altogether.

Moloc's eyes grew wide and disbelieving. "No," the cry fell from his lips, barely more than a whisper. He collapsed forward toward Brie. She released the sword still in his chest and tried to move, but Moloc's heavy body came down on her. They both slid to the ground. A sharp pain spread through her abdomen as they fell.

Moloc lay dead half on top of her. She moved out from under him with the last dregs of her strength. Looking down at herself, she saw the cause of the pain. A jeweled dagger stuck out of her body, Moloc's parting gift in his last seconds. Brie's eyes scanned the room fearfully, looking for the spirit of the Morrigan from her vantage point on the floor.

She was there, pulling her bronze sword from Moloc's corpse. "I can't save you. But this is a good death, an honorable death. Now, release my spirit before you expire, human child." The Morrigan's voice was devoid of all emotion.

Tears fell freely from Brie's eyes now. "I don't know how," she whispered.

"You do. Search your mind. It is there," the Morrigan replied harshly.

Brie wanted to scream at her. She was dying, and the Morrigan only cared about herself. Then the words were there, the magic pulling at the fringes of her mind. Words spilled from her lips unbidden, the words she remembered Maddy making her repeat over and over again until they were drilled into her mind.

"Ikh bin mir aun ir zent ir. Ikh bafray dikh." Her voice was rough and trembling. Fingertips tingling with magic, Brie shut her eyes to it all.

When the words were gone, and the magic dissipated, Brie opened her eyes. She was alone, with only Moloc's corpse for company.

At the sound of the door bursting open, Brie panicked. She didn't have anything left to defend herself with. She couldn't even get off the floor. The only option she had was to feign death and hope that whoever it was would leave her be.

Lifting her eyes just a little to see who had entered, she found that the new arrival was not one of Moloc's men.

It was Ezra.

He wasn't alone. Her eyes slid from Ezra for a brief second to take in her brother and Lily. Two others stood behind them, though she couldn't see them clearly as her vision began to tunnel into black.

Ezra's eyes went first to her and then to the body of Moloc next to her.

"Ezra." She tried to stand, but her legs gave out before she could move. Ezra was there, catching her in his arms and easing them both down to the floor.

He cradled her in his arms, reaching a hand up to smooth the hair away from her eyes. "I came to save you," he said gently.

A ghost of a smile formed on Brie's lips. "You're a little late for that." She lightly touched the knife still stuck in her body, something Ezra had not noticed. His eyes followed her movements; he swore loudly.

"Hold on, sweetheart. Just let me remove this and I'll get you out of here." He gripped the dagger handle and looked up into her eyes. "I'm going to pull and put pressure on the wound. Then I can use some healing magic on you. Are you ready?" At her nod, he gently pulled the dagger from her body, the blade shining crimson with her blood. Brie cried out. Distantly, she heard Wes make a strangled noise behind Ezra, but she couldn't open her eyes. *Please don't watch, Wes*, she silently pleaded, though her thoughts became rapidly more muddled.

Then all went black. Brie knew no more.

CHAPTER 23

5 years ago

Brie held the torch in her left hand. Beside her, Wes and Celeste held their own torches, the three dressed in shades of deep blue. As one unit, they approached the concrete and brick hearth upon which Maddy's body lay, wrapped in blue linen surrounded by juniper logs and chrysanthemums.

Maddy had always loved the color blue.

Behind them, the coven stood silent, with a few drummers pulsing out a steady beat. Brie, Wes, and Celeste touched their torches to the funeral pyre, holding the flames against the branches until they caught before stepping back and tossing the torches onto the pyre.

Then Maddy started to burn, her body beginning the journey back to fire and ash from which she came. The three of them left the sacred circle that had been built around the pyre and rejoined the coven. A soft melodic chanting started from the back. Brie thought it might have been Janice's voice leading it.

The rest of the coven joined with the chant, still soft and reverent, gliding on the wind as Maddy burned. Brie's voice joined in even as tears slid slowly down her cheeks. Wes's hand was in hers, and he squeezed her fingers tightly in his own. Celeste held her other hand, fighting tears to show strength for her coven. Brie knew that the strength was a facade. The day Maddy died, Celeste had completely broken down, and the three of them held each other for hours.

It had been so sudden. One day she was fine, and then it was cancer, aggressive. She lasted four months; then, she was gone. On her last night, Wes and Brie curled up with Maddy in her bed. Wes was already asleep. Maddy held Brie close and told her she didn't fear dying, that soon she would reach the Summerlands. Brie didn't cry; she didn't want Maddy to see her cry.

As the chanting ended, the solemnity of the funeral subsided. They were not here to mourn Maddy's death, but to celebrate her life.

Several tables had been set up, heavy with home-made dishes. Brie and Wes wouldn't have to worry about cooking for at least a week. Pictures of Maddy throughout her life, from youth to family pictures with Wes and Brie, had their own table, interspersed with the things Maddy loved. More instruments were brought out, and the music picked up as the evening turned dark.

Eventually, Brie knew she and Wes would have to go home to a house that was still full of Maddy, yet lacked her physical presence. Since they were both in school, Brie an undergrad, Wes in graduate school, they were both busy. Clearing out the house was going to take a while. Then they would have to go through the process of selling it. They knew they couldn't keep it.

"She would have loved this," Celeste said, coming to stand next to Brie. The coven leader had a plate full of food, but it was all untouched. She had barely eaten since Maddy's death.

"Yeah, she would have. Though she would have hated all the paperwork it took to get the permit for it." Brie tried to keep her voice light for Celeste's sake.

A small smile passed quickly over Celeste's features. "Maddy always hated bureaucracy. If she had her way, she would have said screw the permits and did it anyway." Her voice was strained, but Brie could tell the older woman was trying.

"She loved you so much. You should have had more time together. Wes and I told her for years, but you know Maddy acts in her own time." Brie thought about correcting herself, but didn't.

Celeste turned to her and gave her a genuine, if watery, smile. "I know. I loved her with all I am. And she loved you and Wes more than anything in this world. You two saved her."

Brie looked away from Celeste, back toward the pyre. "Nah, she saved us. The Goddess chose her to be our mom, and she was the best." Inside, Brie wanted to scream how much she missed Maddy, missed her mom, but she was going to be strong. For Celeste. For Wes. For herself.

The weight of Wes's arm landed on her shoulders, and he pulled her close to him. "How you holding up, Little Witch?"

Brie stepped from Celeste and into her brother's embrace. She buried her face in the softness of his shirt. "I feel like Jenga blocks, to be honest, one away from crashing."

There was a small rumble in his chest, a quiet broken laugh. "I feel you. I pretty much feel the same way. We'll get through this, Brie. She would have wanted us to keep living," Wes said, one hand now stroking her hair.

"We will," she affirmed. They stood holding each other for a while. People drifted up to them to offer condolences and amusing stories about Maddy. Eventually, they were pulled into a dance, and Brie imagined Maddy's spirit dancing with them until she faded to ash.

As the stars came out and they danced, Maddy burned.

CHAPTER 24

Tears spilled from Ezra's eyes. Brie lay limp in his arms, eyes closed. She almost looked like she was sleeping, but there was no movement behind her eyelids, no rise and fall of her chest for breath. The wound in her stomach no longer bled, but the blood below them remained sticky and warm.

He was too late.

Behind him, there came several aching sobs, but he barely heard them. The room seemed to shrink to just him and the lifeless body of Brie. With one hand cradling her head, he pulled her close and wrapped his other arm around her back. Tears blinded him now as he held her. Already, he could feel the cold setting in.

A comforting hand landed on his shoulder, but Ezra made no move to acknowledge the owner.

"Ezra, you can do it. You can save her. It's not too late." Lily's voice floated through his consciousness, though it sounded strangled, as if she was fighting to keep her tears at bay long enough to speak.

His voice sounded harsh in his ears when he responded. "I don't know if I can. It's been so long since I did anything good with my powers." He continued to hold Brie, unwilling to let her go even for a second.

"Ezra," Lily's voice now came from next to his ear as she squatted down next to him. "You've never stopped being an angel, no matter what Moloc told you. And you can do this. Brie needs you to do this. Her life doesn't end here, I promise." Her hand lingered on his shoulder, giving it a gentle squeeze.

"Your sight tell you that?" His tone was biting. He was feeling too much right now.

Lily shook her head. "No, but hope did. I have hope that you will bring her back." Then she released his shoulder and moved away to give him space to work.

Tears dried on his face as he hugged Brie close again. He gently laid her on the floor, hand drifting to the mortal wound on her stomach. He focused on the bloodied edges, and he closed his eyes.

Her smile came to his mind, her eyes bright and wide, like when she was making a bad joke. Then the image of her grumpy and grumbling after a bad day of class. She still looked beautiful, even pissed off. More images of her from their brief time together flashed through his mind. The sounds she made when he kissed her, touched her. He couldn't imagine not hearing that again. Brie, so full of life that she practically glowed. He couldn't let that glow extinguish.

It took longer than he remembered to tap into the light within himself, but it was still there, hidden and waiting for him to call upon it. The warmth that filled his body was long forgotten, but still so comforting. Why had he turned his back on this power? It was so pure and felt right when he brought his hands to hover above Brie and let the light gather between his palms.

He knew no fear or doubt like moments before. Instead, there was only absolute certainty that Brie would live. Maybe she would leave him after this, leave his world behind, and just live a normal human life. But she would live, and that was all that mattered to him now.

Once the light had grown to a sizable orb, he pushed it into Brie's body, watching as her lifeless form absorbed the healing light he was offering. He pressed one hand against her cheek while the other rested on her wound as he waited to see if it would work.

Brie's skin slowly grew warmer under his hands. Ezra could feel the skin begin to knit itself back together. His eyes remained shut in silent prayer. They flashed open when her chest rose and fell as her lungs took in a gulp of air. He studied her for a moment, watching as her breathing evened out and a little rigidity returned to her once limp body. Then, slowly, her gray eyes met his, and he felt tears spring forth yet again, hot and heavy on his face.

With an effort, she raised her hand ever so slightly until it came to rest atop the hand on her cheek. "Ezra," she said in a rasping whisper, "you're glowing."

Ezra surprised himself by releasing a soft laugh. Her smile, though still weak, was bright enough to fill the room and beyond, in his opinion.

With slow movements, he helped her to a sitting position, unable to stop touching her even once she was upright and stable. "How do you feel?" he asked tentatively, cradling the back of her neck with one hand while the other held one of Brie's.

Brie chuckled. "Like death. Like I shouldn't feel this good after being thrown around and stabbed. Did you give me the supercharged healing or something?"

"Let's just say you were touched by an angel," Ezra responded with a smirk. Brie let out a loud groan, followed by a cough.

"Ugh, I was better off dead. That was terrible." Her deadpanned response was hoarse; she tried not to smile.

"Well, if you're going to be ungrateful..." Ezra began, making to pull away from her. Brie seized him suddenly by his shirt and pulled him down to brush her lips against his. He responded by gripping her tightly and deepening the kiss.

Brie was the first to pull away, but only enough to rest her forehead against his. "I'm very grateful. Maybe later I can show you just how much," she whispered. Both of their cheeks went pink at her words. It seemed dying had a way of making her bold.

A throat clearing behind them made them jump and look away from each other. "There are other people present, so unless it's an open invitation to the make out session, I would like to get out of here. But hey, if we want to stay here and kiss and feel each other up, I'm okay with that too. Let's just remove the dead guy first." Apollo nudged Albert in the arm with raised eyebrows in a suggestive manner. The vampire threw Apollo a withering glare, stepped closer to Lily, and grabbed her hand.

"We can make out later, sweetie, but first, I'm all for getting out of here," Lily said as she gave Albert's hand a pat with her free hand.

"Um, Brie just died and came back to life, there's still a dead dude on the floor, and apparently, that makes you all horny!" Wes yelled to the room, tears still drying on his face. Around him, they all chuckled weakly. Apollo stepped closer and swung an arm around Wes's shoulder. "Invitation was open to everyone."

"I just died. I'm allowed to have a little levity right now. But I'm with Lily. Let's get out of here. I don't even know how long I've been here," Brie said, struggling to stand before Ezra pulled her to her feet. She flexed her right arm to find it was no longer in pain. Ezra's healing had extended to that as well, it seemed.

"Okay, but first," Wes started, taking quick steps toward Brie before crushing her in an all-encompassing hug, "I'm glad you're not dead. I was worried as fuck!" It took no time for her to return the hug, close her eyes, and bask in the comforting embrace of her brother.

Wes was pushed out of her arms as Lily playfully shoved him aside. "My turn!" she said loudly, wrapping her arms around Brie with a tight squeeze. Both women laughed as they embraced.

Lily returned to her spot next to Albert, who looked at Brie, not with his usual sneer, but with a wrinkled nose. "I'd rather not hug, thanks," he responded.

"Totally fine with that," Brie said with a small smile. They didn't have to be friends; still, she was glad to see him.

"Well, I'm all for a hug." Apollo stepped forward gleefully. Before Brie could respond, Apollo practically draped himself around her; it took only a moment before his hand wandered down her backside.

Brie shoved him away and gave him a slap across the cheek for good measure. "Hands to yourself!" she growled.

Ezra's arms wrapped around her waist from behind as he glared at Apollo over her shoulder. "Keep your hands off my girlfriend, or I swear I will smite you." His tone made it more of a promise than a threat.

Brie turned in his arms. "Girlfriend?" she asked with raised eyebrows.

"Is that okay? I know we weren't labeling it, and things really just started, but—" Ezra trailed off, cheeks pink again.

Her smile covered her whole face. "Ezra, you just brought me back from the dead, so yeah, it's more than okay. You've definitely earned your boyfriend badge!"

"Before you guys start the whole making out thing again, can we leave and, like, torch this place before any of his goons find us?" Wes asked loudly.

They headed toward the door as a group, but Ezra hung back, arms reluctantly slipping away from Brie. He crouched over Moloc's body. One hand placed on the chest of the dead warlock, Ezra shut his eyes and began to chant.

"What's he doing?" Brie whispered to Lily, not wanting to interrupt Ezra.

"Cleansing and releasing. He's ensuring Moloc's soul, if he even had one, the bastard, can't return to this world," Lily whispered back.

The group watched as pure light flowed down Ezra's arm and into Moloc's body. Where his palm connected with the warlock, a glow started to grow brighter before white-hot flames appeared at the point of contact. The fire spread quickly, consuming the body in seconds until there was nothing left, and Ezra's hand met air.

Ezra breathed out the finishing beats of the chant before he rose to his feet and crossed the room to grab Brie's hand. "Let's go."

No further prompting needed, the group hurried out of the warehouse and made their way back to Ezra's shop.

Brie fell asleep almost as soon as they made it back to Ezra's apartment after parting ways with their friends. Ezra removed her shoes and placed a blanket over her sleeping form before he left her alone in his bedroom.

He assured the rest of the group that he would watch over her through the night and encouraged them all to go home and rest. Wes did so reluctantly and only with a promise that he would be back early the next morning for Brie. He didn't argue further, and Ezra reminded him to use the keypad to get to his apartment faster the next day.

Ezra desperately wanted to talk to Brie about what had happened while she was with Moloc, but she needed sleep first. They would have plenty of time to talk later. He was far too wired to lie down next to her as he wanted. So he paced his living room, eyes occasionally darting to his bedroom door, which he left cracked open in case she woke up.

Then his thoughts turned to the reality of things.

Moloc was dead.

After centuries of tormenting him, causing him to doubt everything, and encouraging him to push away from his family, Ezra was finally free of the warlock. It was like a weight had been lifted from his neck, one that he had grown so accustomed to that he had forgotten it was constantly crushing him, and suddenly it was gone. He felt like he was breathing for the first time in centuries.

Dread lingered not far behind. No matter how much he had loathed Moloc, he was the biggest supplier for the shop. There were creatures all over the city who depended upon Ezra, and he loved the shop; it gave him a purpose.

"You know, I think I might know of a good supplier for your place. He's still in the business," a voice said behind him.

Ezra stopped pacing and turned toward the couch where the white garbed form of his mother sat. She did not glow this time and could almost pass for a human woman sitting there in his apartment.

Almost.

There was a tight feeling in Ezra's chest as he looked at her. "It's a mortal world custom to knock before entering someone's home, Mother," he said with a hint of a smile.

She waved him off with a flick of her wrist. "We are not mortal, Arakiel. And anyway, it's been too long since we have spoken. Now that we have, I intend to take full advantage of the time." There was a spark in her midnight eyes that let him know there was no room for argument. Not that he planned to say anything.

Ezra sighed as he sat down on the opposite end of the couch from his mother and angled to face her.

"I have missed you dearly, my son. I had hoped you would come home at some point over the last several centuries. That man drove a wedge between us, and I wanted to give you your space, no matter how much it hurt to do so." His mother began, keeping her eyes locked on him.

Ezra didn't flinch away from his mother, though he wanted to. He should have talked to her before now, but he was afraid. "Mother, I..." He paused and pinched the bridge of his nose. "A lot happened tonight. I want to have this conversation with you, just not now."

She nodded, flowing silver curls moving with the motion. "I understand, Arakiel," she responded with a sober nod. Then a mischievous smile spread across her face. "Now, about this girl—" she began.

Ezra groaned. "Don't start."

His mother chuckled. "I am not saying anything bad. I like her. She has fire and a good heart. But she is still only mortal, Arakiel. Remember that."

He ran a hand through his hair and closed his eyes, resigned. "I know. And without the spirit of Morgana,

346

she's just an ordinary human with an ordinary human lifespan."

"Oh, she's anything but ordinary, I would say." His mother smiled knowingly. "But still mortal." Ezra smiled a little at her words.

"Can you do anything?" His voice was barely a whisper.

His mother sat quietly for a moment, taking in her son's face. "That is not my decision to make, Arakiel. You know that." She didn't smile this time.

Ezra heaved a heavy sigh. "I know. Thought I would ask anyway."

"Chin up, my son. You still have several decades with her, regardless. But, if you do decide to speak with her about it and she agrees, then come talk to me. Now, I think I best get going. She is going to need you in just a moment." His mother stood from the couch. Ezra followed her lead, and the two of them stood for a few seconds with nothing said.

His mother crossed the distance between them. She was as tall as he. "I love you, Arakiel," she said, placing her hands on his cheeks.

"Love you too, Mother," Ezra said before the god in front of him dissolved into light.

He stood alone in his living room for a minute or two, then turned toward his bedroom door again. Slipping inside the dark room, he gingerly perched himself on the edge of the bed next to Brie's sleeping form. Her brow creased. She looked anything but peaceful in sleep.

"Ezra!" Brie screamed, her eyes flying open as she sat bolt upright in the bed, straight into Ezra's waiting arms.

She pressed her face into his chest and began to sob immediately as his arms settled around her. Images of Moloc still filled her head, his taunting laughter still in her ears. And for a moment, she still thought she was there, even though she could feel the solidness of Ezra around her. Her fingers tightened and twisted into the fabric of his shirt.

Ezra said nothing, making a few soothing noises as he rubbed calming circles onto her back while she cried. After several minutes, he asked, "Do you want to talk about it?"

Brie didn't move her face away from his chest. "No. Yes. I do, but I'm not ready. I don't want to think about it, but it's all I can think about." She choked on a sob.

"It will take time, sweetheart," Ezra said while stroking the back of her head. He held her for what seemed like hours, silence falling between them.

As her sobs turned to sniffles, she pulled away just enough to look into Ezra's face. "There wouldn't happen to be something in the Storage Room that could make me forget, would there?"

Ezra hesitated before answering, "There is. But I don't think you want to erase your memories." The look he gave her was soft and understanding, but still, she turned away from it, averting her gaze.

"You're probably right..." she trailed off, looking at the floor. Ezra trailed a hand down her arm to squeeze her hand.

"Sleep would be the best thing right now, and then we'll just take things a day at a time," Ezra said, coaxing her to lie back down. While she laid back willingly, her grip on his hand didn't waver. She clung to him like a lifeline.

"I don't think I can," she whispered, looking into his eyes. Brie felt fear at just the thought of closing her eyes, knowing that Moloc's face would be there when she did. Even with the solid form of Ezra next to her, it wasn't enough to drive the specter of the dead warlock away.

"I have something that could help. I've used it myself when I want to experience real sleep. Hang on." Ezra slowly removed his hand from Brie's and stood. She watched him walk across the room to the dresser. From the top drawer, he pulled out a small oblong wooden box with gold trim. It looked delicate and old. Brie stared at it as Ezra crossed back over to the bed.

"I got this off Hypnos decades ago. He had it made by this famous music box maker in Switzerland back in the 1850s. Hypnos added a bit of sleep magic to it, but it also keeps out any influence from his son Morpheus, the god of dreams. You should sleep without dreams."

Ezra set the box down beside the bed and opened the top so Brie could see the internal mechanism.

Even as the first notes started to play, Brie felt her eyes grow heavy. Her body felt like she was sinking into the mattress's warm embrace. Ezra brushed a bit of hair away from her face before bending to place a kiss on her temple.

"Get some rest, Brie," he whispered, as his lips drew away.

With one last conscious effort, Brie reached for his hand and pulled lightly. "Stay with me. Please," she mumbled.

Ezra didn't hesitate for a moment. "Okay, sweetheart," he said as he shifted further onto the bed to lie beside her. Brie was asleep before he even settled.

With a heavy sigh, Ezra let the music from the little box overcome him, and he too fell asleep, holding Brie close to his body.

"Are you sure you don't want to take more time? Nobody would hold it against you if you needed a semester off," Ezra asked again, looking at Brie with concern.

Brie sighed and leaned against Ezra's kitchen counter before taking a large gulp of tea. "We've talked about this, babe. I can't hide in your apartment forever.

Dr. Fry was gracious enough to pass my work on to another unfortunate grad student at the end of the semester. I've had over a month off for the holidays, anyway. I need to do something other than hang out here or in the shop. You should be sick of me by now."

Crossing to stand before her, Ezra looped his arms around her waist and pulled Brie close. "I could never be sick of you," he said before kissing her.

With one hand still holding onto her tea, Brie brought her other hand up to tangle in his soft hair. It felt luxurious between her fingers.

Ever since the ordeal with Moloc over a month ago, Brie had spent most of her time rarely out of Ezra's sight. Even visiting her apartment was a trial. Ezra wanted to accompany her even with the direct doorway from the shop.

She finally snapped last week and told him if he didn't back off a little, she would move out. Not that she was moved in. She just spent all her time there, had her own side of the dresser and closet, and most of the space in the bathroom.

Still, she tried to stay in her apartment at least one or two nights a week so she could spend time with Wes. Sometimes Apollo was there too, which was a new and annoying development.

With the winter break, Brie didn't have classes to worry about. After she spoke with Dr. Fry, who was very understanding about her situation, she was able to temporarily postpone her thesis work until the new semester.

Without school, Brie spent most of her time in the shop, exploring the items on the shelf or hanging out in the Storage Room, watching Ezra work on something or other.

Once the shop closed for the day, Brie and Ezra spent their nights in Ezra's apartment, with him fussing over her again. He took care of her, easing the pain with his words, hands, and his lips. He was very good with all three.

Occasionally, she would peel Ezra away from her long enough to go out with Lily for coffee or lunch. It was nice to just have some girl time. Lily never seemed to waver in her good cheer.

Lily still insisted on giving her magic lessons, but without the influence of the Morrigan, Brie wasn't having any success anymore. Their time together was frequently cut short by the arrival of Albert, who still was not overly friendly with Brie, but looked as if he would gladly walk into the sun just to see Lily smile. Brie was happy for her friend, despite the cause of her happiness being Albert.

Life would be fine if it weren't for the nightmares she had every time she closed her eyes. Ezra warned her to use the music box sparingly. Too much of Hypnos's power could potentially call upon his twin, Thanatos, which meant an escort to the Underworld.

Brie rarely used the thing after that bit of information. Instead, she tried to find other means to assist with sleep that didn't toe the line with death.

The Storage Room tried to be helpful by presenting her with oddities and trinkets to assist with her sleep troubles. The latest was a rather old eye mask once owned by William Dement that was supposed to counteract sleep deprivation. So far, it had helped a little, but only when Brie woke up from one of her nightmares. It was of little use when she was first falling asleep. The only thing that really helped was Ezra wrapping his arms around her at night, holding her close until she finally fell asleep. It was a lot to ask. She knew Ezra didn't need to sleep, but she still didn't ask him to stop. And he never complained about it.

"I think it might be a good idea if I talked to someone," Brie said, pulling away from Ezra's embrace.

Ezra raised an eyebrow. "Like a therapist?"

She shrugged her shoulders. "Yeah, I mean, I guess. I know it's a good idea for my mental health or whatever, but how do I explain to a normie why I'm so messed up?" After another gulp of tea, she set the cup back down, empty.

Ezra picked up the empty cup and turned it over before it could refill itself. "There are plenty of creatures around the city who are therapists, you know, with real jobs. Not everyone in our world is a grouchy old antique seller," he said with a straight face.

"What, you mean there are people who are actually happy in careers out there and go out and do things with their girlfriend after work and enjoy life?" Brie feigned shock, but couldn't keep the smile off her face.

"We go out on dates!" Ezra retorted, leaning against the counter next to Brie. "We went to the movies just last week."

Brie huffed out a laugh. "And you spent the whole time on edge, glaring at everyone in the theater like they were going to suddenly jump up and attack us. Do you even know what movie we saw?"

His averted gaze confirmed her accusation.

With tentative fingers, he pulled her hand into his and squeezed before turning to look her in the eye. "I'm just worried that something else could happen to you. I need to do better and realize I can't keep you locked away from the world. I'm trying, sweetheart." He turned his gaze down to their joined hands.

Raising on her toes, Brie planted a kiss on Ezra's cheek. "I know you're trying, babe, and that's why I love you." Her whole face turned bright red as she realized what she had said. She couldn't look at him; the floor suddenly was much more interesting.

Ezra looked at her with a soft grin on his face. "You love me?" His voice was a whisper as he put a finger under Brie's chin to lift it to meet his gaze. If it were possible, she turned even more red, her eyes darting everywhere but his face. She hadn't meant to say it, but it just came out so naturally.

"I uh..." she faltered, nervous. Then her eyes stopped roving, and her face hardened into determination, though her cheeks remained flush. "Yes, I do love you. Obviously." Her voice was firm as she finally met his eyes.

Ezra's smile grew impossibly wide as he tugged her into his arms, completely enveloping her body with his own. "I love you, too," he said softly into her ear. He pulled back slightly and kissed her sweetly. The two of them melted into each other, smiling through kisses.

When they finally pulled apart for longer than a second, Brie glanced at the clock. "Ugh, I should get going, or I'll be late." She sounded disappointed.

Ezra leaned forward and rested his head against hers. "I'll be here when you get back. Just use the shell phone if you need me, okay?" She nodded against him. Reluctantly, the two pulled apart from each other. Brie slowly gathered her school things, which she had brought over in the first week of staying with Ezra.

With a parting smile that filled her whole face, she waved goodbye to Ezra and headed out to campus.

CHAPTER 25

Five months later

"I feel like I should be blasting Alice Cooper's 'School's Out.' It seems fitting after the year we've had," Brie said, plopping down on the chair behind the shop's counter, her chair.

"There's still finals to get through. Does this place even have a sound system? I could plug in my phone and scare all the normies away," Wes said with a smirk as he leaned against the counter opposite Brie.

"No Alice Cooper in my shop." Ezra's voice came from behind them as he emerged from the Storage Room, holding a folded paper menu in one hand.

Brie and Wes gave him matching quizzical looks. "Dare I ask why not?" Brie said, taking the menu from Ezra and looking over its contents.

Ezra's eyes narrowed and his face darkened. "He knows what he did."

There was a pregnant silence between the three of them. "Okay, weirdo, I'm not even going to touch that.

What kind of pizza do we want?" Brie asked, looking at the menu she knew by heart.

"I still don't understand how the two of you can eat pizza all the time. There are other foods out there. I have a kitchen full of food right now. Healthy foods that are green and good for you," Ezra said, knowing full well Brie and Wes would argue over pineapple on the pizza, eat all of it, and still raid his refrigerator later.

Wes laughed. "Listen, dude; we're poor grad students. Pizza is a luxury food for us. We eat it when we can. Otherwise, it's ramen and cold ravioli from a can."

Ezra raised an eyebrow. "You have a working stove on which to heat the ravioli, Wesley. I've seen you use it. And I pay Brie enough that you two could afford real groceries."

"We eat real food, too. Sometimes. I made Wes eat a salad just the other week." Brie piped in, laughing.

Ezra rolled his eyes as Brie took out her phone to place their order. He couldn't help thinking how nice it was to hear her laugh again. A real laugh this time. She used to laugh and sass him so easily, but with everything that had happened, her heart wasn't in it the last few months.

Therapy was helping, though. Brie came home lighter. She thrashed and cried less in her sleep now. She was even able to focus on her thesis again after the first three months. It was progress. Slow, but progress all the same.

Ezra didn't go to therapy even though Brie encouraged him to. Instead, he had more frequent visits with his mother, and they worked on repairing their relationship after so many centuries of not speaking. It was annoying and great at the same time.

He took his mother's suggestion for his new supplier, an old family friend. Jaxius was a reckless fae who, at some point, ingratiated himself with the god. He had a tendency to end up with items that were of questionable legality and were usually boosted off someone else without their knowledge. But he was ancient and had contacts and access to rare magics and artifacts. It had been a big boost to the shop.

The best thing of all was that his business came with no strings attached, and no false promises whispered in his ear. He accepted cash or barter only. It was a new and welcome turn from dealing with Moloc for all those centuries.

Ezra stood by the counter and thought of all that had changed in the last several months as he watched Wes and Brie squabble over toppings while Brie was on the phone. He was free from Moloc at last, had reconnected with his mother, had great friends, a booming business, and a wonderful girlfriend who no longer had the spirit of his former lover within her. He loved her with all that he was.

Ezra realized his life was good.

Except Brie would continue to grow older, and one day she would die, while he would be left just as he is. His mother said it wasn't her decision to make, but Ezra couldn't bring himself to broach the subject with Brie. After all, six months together was entirely too short a period of time to ask someone if they wanted to spend forever with you, even by mortal standards.

After she graduated, he told himself repeatedly. Then if she agreed, he would contact his mother since only she could bestow the gift. That is, if Brie still wanted to be with him. He was still a grumpy old angel, after all. She was so young and vibrant.

He was still thinking about it as he lay next to Brie that night. "I can hear you thinking, Ezra," Brie mumbled sleepily as she shifted to drape her body over his chest. His arm wrapped around her automatically, resting his hand on the space between her shoulders. "What's on your mind?" she asked, not opening her eyes.

Ezra stared at the ceiling before responding. "Just remembering stuff I need for the shop. Nothing too important." He lightly ran his fingers up and down her spine, hoping the soothing gesture would lull her back to sleep. Brie arched her back into his touch and stretched out more on him.

"Liar." She yawned as she reached up to run her fingers through his hair. When it came to Brie, there was very little he could get away with. Ezra sighed heavily, kissing the top of her head.

"Sometimes it's scary how well you can read me, and you're not even fully awake." Brie giggled sleepily at that and then nuzzled closer to him. "Don't worry right now, sweetheart. If it's still bothering me in the morning, we can talk about it." He hoped that would placate her enough to go back to sleep. All of it would still be bothering him in the morning, but if he were lucky, she would forget all about it.

"Mmkay. I have that meeting with Dr. Fry first thing, so aaahhh—" she yawned in the middle of the word before continuing, "after we can talk. Love you." She planted a small kiss on his chest where she rested her head and within seconds was breathing deeply in sleep again.

"Love you, too," Ezra whispered, stroking her hair. For a time, he just watched her sleep and enjoyed the feeling of her in his arms. If only they could stay like that forever, it would be perfect. Better than perfect, really. Now he was back to where he started, thinking about how short her life was and how limited their days were together. He knew he should enjoy each day as it came, rather than thinking about the distant future. But that was easier said than done, and his mind kept wandering to her short mortal life.

At this rate, he was never going to sleep. He would have to talk to Brie about it soon. He just needed to find the right time.

"So now that the Morrigan is gone, what about you two? Like, was your whole thing around serving and protecting me?" Brie asked, taking a large sip of wine.

Lily, Wes, and Brie sat in her and Wes's living room. The coffee table was covered in takeout boxes and a bottle of wine. In the background, the television played another episode of *Buffy the Vampire Slayer*, which they had been watching all night at their "no partners allowed" hangout. *It is nice to just chill out with my friend and brother,* Brie thought.

"I don't know about you, Wes, but my coven has been around for a long time doing their own thing anyway. Now that we know the Morrigan is gone, at least for now, we've gone back to just witchy business as usual. It's not really a big deal for the younger ones in the coven anyway," Lily said. She picked up one of the takeout containers and started picking up vegetables with her chopsticks.

Wes looked thoughtful for a moment. "I really don't know. My family has always been intrinsically tied to the Morrigan, from what I know. I imagine if she pops up again, like she did with you, then one of my family members out there will be there too. So I guess I'm retired from guardianship. Not that I did much to begin with."

Brie gave him a playful punch on the arm. "Hey, you did plenty. You've been the best big brother a girl could have. I wouldn't be here today without you. So don't sell yourself short." That elicited a smile from Wes.

For a time, they went back to watching the show, finishing up the rest of the food. Once they were all lying around the room, digesting, Brie brought up the Morrigan again. "Do you think she'll come back again, and like, you know, inhabit someone else?"

Neither Lily nor Wes said anything at first, and Brie thought they might just ignore the question before Lily spoke up. "I don't know much about reincarnation, but it seems, from what I do know, her spirit is now free. Taking on another human host would just trapping herself again, so I don't think the Morrigan will do that. It's likely that's the last we'll see of her on this plane for a while until she can reconstruct her immortal body."

The other two nodded. It made sense to Brie that the Morrigan, once free of her human prison, would want to stay away from the mortal world, at least for a while.

So when the Morrigan appeared in the shop the next day, it took Brie completely by surprise.

The shop was empty except for Brie and Ezra at the counter, studying a stuffed raven.

"Do it again!" Brie squealed, clapping her hands together.

Ezra laughed and poked the raven's beak for the third time in five minutes.

"NEVERMORE!" it shrieked in a croaking voice, eyes flaring.

Brie was set off into another fit of giggles, ending in a snort. She was in such a good mood that the loud snort didn't make her feel the slightest bit embarrassed.

"Poe was a real dick, you know. He owed me money when he died. Hell, he owed everyone money, the old drunk. He gave this to me in '49 while I was visiting Baltimore. We went for a drink in Fell's Point. He tried to pay with this, but it turns out they don't take stuffed ravens." His laugh was full-bodied, and he smiled broadly at the memory.

"NEVERMORE!"

Brie withdrew her finger from the raven, laughing loudly. "You're talking about Edgar Allan Poe? I'm sure he was a lot of fun to be around. You've met so many influential people in your long-ass life, and you probably thought they were all dicks."

"It's true. I just hate people. But I—" Ezra stopped abruptly, his whole body going rigid. Brie looked at him in confusion; the smile on her lips became hesitant.

"Arakiel." An ancient ethereal voice sounded from the doorway, though the bell had not sounded.

Brie and Ezra's eyes shot to the other side of the shop. Standing at the entrance, the door shut behind her, stood the Morrigan. She was still in spirit form, golden and translucent, but crisply defined, a tall, muscular silhouette with piercing eyes that showed no color. Her hair and dress billowed in a phantom wind. She looked like golden Victory as she strode across the floor, feet bare, until she stood before the pair.

"I thought you had gone, Morgana," Ezra said, his voice flat, like he couldn't pick one emotion, so he just dumped them all.

"Is this how you greet me now, my love?" the Morrigan asked in a sweet, mocking voice.

It wasn't an intentional move, but Brie found herself inching closer to Ezra as she wrapped a hand around his bicep. Possessive. Her eyes didn't leave the Morrigan.

At the movement, the Morrigan's eyes cut to Brie. "Hm, how sweet." The mocking tone remained, and there was no hint of humor in the Morrigan's eyes.

Ezra placed a hand over Brie's reassuringly. His eyes remained on the Morrigan as he spoke. "What are you doing here, Morgana? Get to your point."

The goddess appeared to pout slightly. "And we used to have so much fun together. What changed, Arakiel?"

He ground his teeth and squeezed Brie's hand softly. Brie returned the squeeze, grounding them both. "A lot has changed, Morgana. The most recent being your lack of concern about letting the woman I love die."

"I thought I was the one you loved, Arakiel," Morgana shot back playfully. This was all a game to her.

His free hand clenched into a fist. "You're not capable of being loved or loving anyone, Morgana. I realize that now. You don't belong here anymore."

"Love isn't necessary for what we can do together. Come with me, beyond this small mortal plane, and let us explore what it truly means to be gods together." The Morrigan lifted her hand, offering it for Ezra to take.

He just stared at it, his face blank. Brie still held onto his arm. She squeezed it again for comfort before schooling her features into a hard mask. She released him and stepped around the counter to face down the Morrigan.

"I'm not going to let you take him. So you need to get the fuck out of our shop." She planted her feet in a defensive stance. Not that she planned on fighting. She would lose terribly if she did.

The Morrigan sized her up with appraising eyes. "You have no power, mortal. And you cannot possibly offer him more than I can. You have already died once. And one day soon, you will die again, withered away to nothing but dust. But he and I will live forever. We are alike."

Brie would not allow herself to be cowed by the glowing goddess. She had been an unknowing and unwilling host to the Morrigan her whole life, endured memories that she thought were nightmares since she was a child. She was not going to let the goddess take away her love.

"He doesn't belong to anyone but himself. You don't care about him. You only care about his power. You're no better than Moloc," Brie spat.

The Morrigan grinned, but it was cold and mocking, like everything else about her. "If that is so, then let him decide. Arakiel, my sweet, I offer you an eternity of power, unchecked at my side. While this mortal corpse offers you a few pitiful years while she grows old and boring. Which shall it be?"

All eyes turned to Ezra. Brie cursed herself for taking her eyes off the Morrigan, but she couldn't help it. Without a doubt, Brie knew her love for Ezra was strong. She was fairly certain that he loved her fiercely in return. But she couldn't offer eternity like Morgana. Maybe a small part of her thought he wouldn't pick her. So her eyes swiveled to his; he was looking only at her, not even acknowledging the Morrigan.

Ezra stared at her for a long time. Brie felt her heart rate speed up, her heart thumping so loudly that she was surprised no one else heard it.

Ezra spoke, not tearing his eyes from Brie as he addressed the Morrigan. "Get out, Morgana. You're not welcome here." A small smile tugged at the corner of his mouth, and Brie couldn't help but return it. By some unspoken agreement, they decided to ignore the Morrigan and keep their gazes locked on each other. This seemed to further anger the Morrigan, who was already fuming over the rejection.

"I hope you enjoy your miserable life in your tiny shop, Arakiel. And when your mortal dies and this place crumbles around your head, I hope you remember what you could have had," the Morrigan shrieked.

Finally, they broke their stare, turning toward the Morrigan. Brie reached into the pocket of her emerald green dress and pulled out a weave of worn yarn with a smoky quartz within its tangles.

"It's time for you to leave now, bitch. Morgana, I banish you from this place. I banish you from our lives. I banish you from our thoughts. So mote it be." Brie held the charm toward the Morrigan. It pulsed with a pale pink glow, warding off the banished spirit.

The Morrigan stared in disbelief as her glow began to fade, and she began to disappear. "This is not possible. You have no power. How are you doing this, witch?"

Brie smirked. "You're right. I don't have powers now. But that doesn't mean I'm powerless. The biggest trove of magical objects is just beyond that door and we serve all kind of crazy beings her. I stay prepared just in case. You can thank Isobel Gowdie for this little charm. See you in hell."

The Morrigan shrieked once more, then disappeared entirely.

Brie continued to stand facing where the Morrigan vanished. Warm arms wrapped around her middle from behind. Ezra rested his chin on the top of her head.

"Going to chase all my potential suitors off like that?" he asked, a grin in his voice.

Brie turned in his arms, throwing her arms around his neck. "Did I overstep? I should have let you handle her. I'm sorry." She averted her gaze.

Ezra lifted one hand from around her waist and tilted her chin up. "Hey, you have nothing to apologize for, sweetheart. You stood up for me, and you had every right to banish her after what she did. I'm proud of you." He kissed her softly.

"I love you," she whispered to him between kisses.

"I love you too, sweetheart." He pressed his words onto her lips. When he broke away, he quirked an eyebrow. "So, our shop?"

Brie's face colored brightly in embarrassment. "I meant your shop. I'm just a little attached to this place."

Ezra smiled softly. "And it's attached to you. It's just as much yours as it is mine. I think we plan to keep you." He kissed her again, and she smiled against his lips, content.

EPILOGUE

Three years later

"Congratulations, Dr. St. James!" Wes yelled, throwing his arms around his sister. She returned the embrace, wrapping Wes's frame in the sleeves of her black graduation gown.

"That sounds so weird," she said, releasing Wes with a laugh.

"It's what you've busted your ass for. Be proud." Wes smiled brightly.

"I know. It's just weird that after all these years of hard work, I finally got my Ph.D. A lot has happened this year, you know." She looked down at the silver Claddagh ring with a shining ruby heart on her left hand. She had worn it as her engagement ring. Now it was her wedding ring, and somehow it still felt odd around her finger.

Wes grabbed her hand in his own. "You worked hard for both this and your dude. And now you get to enjoy the benefits of being a doctor of history and a misses to a cantankerous angel forever." He pulled her along as they walked to join the rest of their make-shift family.

Gathered together in a loose circle talking was their family. Brie stopped a few feet short, dropping Wes's hand as he joined the group to stand next to Apollo, who snaked his arm around Wes's waist. Brie looked at them all: Lily, Wes, and Apollo. Of course, since it was daytime, Albert was not there, but he would be at the party later.

There was Ezra's mother, dressed in white with rainbow cuffs, keeping her godly glow in check. Brie had only met her a few times over the years, but she was motherly in a way Brie had only known with Maddy.

And then there was Ezra, her best friend, her lover, her husband, standing tall, dark hair tousled just so, and a small smile just for her as their eyes locked. He had been reconnecting with his mother and building up his life without Moloc's influence. She was so proud of him.

This mismatched group was her family. Hard to believe all of it came about because she took a part-time job at a run-down antique shop years ago.

Ezra excused himself from the group and made it to her in a handful of long strides. "Congratulations, wife," he said softly as he pulled her into his arms and kissed her.

"Thanks, husband," she responded once he let her go. Her hand moved down his arm to twine their fingers together.

"How does it feel?" he asked, giving her hand a squeeze.

Brie exhaled loudly. "Calming. Now that my dissertation defense is over and the wedding is done, I feel like I can finally relax. I'm so ready for that honeymoon you promised." She smiled brightly at him, which he returned with one of his subdued smiles.

"I can't remember the last time I closed shop for longer than a day. But it will be nice to get away with you. And it's just us, right? We are leaving the..." he paused and turned to look at the people behind them, "squad behind?" Brie laughed.

She wrapped her arms around his neck and stepped in close. "It'll be just us. And hopefully, very little clothing." Her eyes sparkled as she smirked at him and brushed her nose against his.

"I like the way you think, Dr. St. James," he said before kissing her again.

"We're of the same mind." She laughed.

"Get a room!" Apollo called out, "I'll join you if you like."

Brie and Ezra groaned and begrudgingly pulled apart to walk over to the group. "Stay away from our room, Apollo, or I will have to hurt you," Ezra growled.

"Promises, promises," Apollo quipped back with his cocky smirk. Next to him, Wes gave his arm a light punch.

"Hey, your boyfriend is literally right here," he said. Apollo turned his smirk toward Wes.

"I wasn't leaving you out. You can join, too, darling," he said, jumping back a little to avoid a swat from Brie.

"When you're all done flirting with each other, I think we should get lunch," Lily said with a toothy smile. She led them out of the hall to their parked cars.

Brie quickly pulled off her cap and gown as she and Ezra approached their roadster. She had insisted they needed a car since Ezra's SUV was never seen again after that fateful Samhain. Somehow, they had ended up with a flashy fast car.

"Can we just skip the lunch and party and go home?" Brie asked, only half-joking as she sat down heavily in the passenger seat.

Ezra grabbed her hand over the center console and kissed her knuckles lightly. "As much as I would love that, I went through a lot of work planning this party. So you have to go."

"I'm pretty sure Lily did all the planning," she retorted, fighting a smile.

Ezra frowned. "Maybe. But I did help a little, and I'm hosting, so it counts. You still have to go."

Brie laughed as Ezra pulled out of the parking lot and headed toward the restaurant. "I love you," she said.

Ezra eyed her from the side, a small smile on his face. "Love you too, sweetheart."

Lily placed her hand on Albert's solid shoulder as she brought her foot up to take off her heels. "Why do you bother with shoes at all, my love? You always take them off, and I always end up holding them," Albert said, his tone stern though his gaze was soft.

Lily handed over one shoe while she switched to take off the other. "Because it's polite to wear shoes in public, and holding onto my shoes is just one of the infinite reasons I love you so much. And I would love you even more if you took these and then got me a cup of that punch over there." She beamed at him, and Albert, as always, was completely helpless against her smile.

"You are lucky you are cute and that I am utterly besotted with you," he grumbled, brushing away a few of her curls to kiss her forehead before walking off to grab her a drink.

"I still don't get it, but if you're happy, Lily, that's all that matters." Brie came up behind her friend.

Lily grabbed Brie's hand with a smile. "He does make me happy. And since I started practicing more moon magics, our schedules have synced up more. Bertie and I take care of each other. But speaking of happiness, how's married life treating you?"

Brie took a moment to search for the right words. "It's been... honestly; it doesn't feel like anything has changed all that much. I mean, sure, the name thing with him and the ring. But there wasn't this big moment where suddenly everything felt different. I don't know what I was expecting."

The laugh that bubbled out of Lily's mouth was unexpected. "Oh. my dear sweet Bridget. Marriage has been and always will be just a legal contract. It doesn't change your relationship or the love you have for each other. All it means is that now half the shop is yours."

With a small laugh, Brie gave Lily's hand a squeeze. "Yeah, I know. Although, Ezra has been a little off since the wedding. Not like distant or anything, just a little quiet," she said, furrowing her brow slightly.

"Ah yes, because he was always such a chatterbox before," Lily retorted with a laugh.

"Fair. Quieter than usual, how about that? He does that sullen stare thing like he's thinking too hard all the time." She tried to mimic Ezra's expression, something she was getting better at pulling off. Lily snorted.

"You know what you could do?" Lily said, bringing a finger to tap her lip in mock contemplation.

"What's that?" Brie responded, knowing full well she would receive a smart-ass response from her friend.

"It's this new thing; everybody is doing it now. It's called TALK TO YOUR HUSBAND!" Lily practically shouted the last part, but only Albert acknowledged them with a quick glance. He was waiting in the wings to bring his girlfriend her punch.

"Gee, thanks, Lily. Why don't I just try that?" Brie groaned.

Lily responded by booping Brie's nose. "Good. Communication is key to any good relationship. Speaking of communication," she stopped and caught Albert's eye, "my vamp guy is giving me the come hither look, and I'm ready to let him take me back to his lair."

Brie made a face of mock disgust, then laughed "Ew! Go on. Go to your blood-sucking menace. Don't forget to stop by tomorrow to pick up the moon-flower you ordered. We're not heading out until the afternoon."

Lily left her, shooting finger guns her way in acknowledgment before joining her boyfriend across the room. Brie stood alone, occasionally sipping from her glass of whiskey, sporadically until Ezra sidled up to her side.

"Having fun?" he asked, wrapping an arm around her waist to pull her close to his side. She smiled up at him and nodded.

Before he could say more, Brie's eye caught Dr. Catherine Fry walking through the door. When she spotted Brie and Ezra, she made a beeline to stand before the couple.

"Good evening, Brie, Ezra. Could I have a word with you both? Privately?" she asked, her voice even. Brie nodded and looked at Ezra. He raised an eyebrow, but said nothing. Instead, he led the two women toward the Storage Room door, pushed the number one button, and walked into his office.

Once the door clicked shut behind them, the couple turned to face the professor.

"First off, Brie, I am so proud of you. Watching you flourish these last few years has been a privilege I have had so few times in my long years of teaching. Whatever you choose to do next, I know you will be brilliant." Dr. Fry's eyes were shining with pride at her now-former student. Brie couldn't stop the small smile even if she wanted to. Just hearing that someone was proud of her still made her feel light as air.

Dr. Fry stood for a moment, saying nothing as she smiled at Brie. Then her face turned more serious. "Secondly, I have something I want to give you. To both of you, really. Call it a wedding present."

"Auntie Catherine, that's not necess—" Ezra started, but Dr. Fry held her hand up to stop him.

"I'm sure you'll think differently once I've told you what it is." She lowered her hand and turned her attention to Brie. "I have been on this earth a long time, longer than I ever wished to be. When I was tasked with watching over Ezra, I saw my immortality as both a blessing and a curse. I see now that it really was a blessing. But my job is done now, and I am tired." She paused and looked into their faces. "There's still a long life in me and I want you to have those years, Brie. If you want, I would like to bestow the blessing I received onto you."

There was silence between the three of them now as Brie and Ezra soaked in her words, comprehension dawning on them both slowly. It was Ezra who broke the silence. "Auntie Catherine, are you saying you want to give Brie your immortality? But that means..."

Dr. Fry's smile was soft and understanding. "Yes, Ezra, it means I will die. And I'm ready. I've already discussed it with your Mother, it was her idea, and we agreed. My immortality will end, and I will live out the rest of a normal human lifespan. But it's up to you, Brie. I can give this gift to you freely, and you will remain as you are forever. Or you can choose to live out your mortal lifespan as you see fit. It's up to you. You don't have to answer right away."

Brie said nothing, her brows knitted together in concentration. She avoided looking at either Ezra or Dr. Fry, instead keeping her gaze fixed on the floor. Dr. Fry's offer was unexpected. Of course, Brie thought about her mortality just about every night since Ezra had asked her to marry him. He would never age. Never die. Brie was already getting older, and though still young, her days were numbered. Her time with Ezra had an expiration date.

Often she thought he would leave her in her old age, no longer in love with a withered old woman. Her mortality was something they never discussed. Many times she thought Ezra was about to bring it up, or she thought about broaching the subject, but nothing was ever said in the end. Fear had kept her quiet.

Next to her, Ezra wrapped his hand around her own and held tight. "Brie, you don't have to if you don't want to. I know it's a big deal, and I don't want you to feel pressured to take on immortality just because you think it'll make me happy or that I won't love you when you get old. I will always love you. It's your life, and I will always respect your decisions." His voice had a strained quality to it. Brie knew he was trying not to be pushy or influence her decision. Ezra was just trying to be supportive, as usual even if it pained him to think about it.

It was her choice to make, and for Brie, there was one clear choice.

"Okay," she said to the floor.

"What?" Dr. Fry asked, waiting for Brie to raise her head. She did after a silent moment.

"I said okay. I..." She turned to look up into her husband's face. "I want to do it. I said I wanted to spend forever with you in my vows. I guess it's time to make good on my threat." She tried to laugh, but it came out weak and watery instead. Brie realized she had started to cry, warm tears making paths down her cheeks.

"Brie?" Ezra asked, bringing one hand up to cup her face while using his thumb to wipe away the tears.

"Happy tears, babe, they're happy tears," she choked out. He wrapped her up in his arms, and Brie could feel droplets raining from above her. It was several minutes before Ezra let her go. Brie turned her attention back to Dr. Fry.

The older woman stood smiling brightly, eyes wide behind her coke-bottle glasses. "Take my hands, Brie. This will be easy."

Brie stepped closer and put her hands into Dr. Fry's outstretched ones. Then she felt the warmth that she used to feel when performing magic. It flowed from where their hands met before starting to travel through her whole body. She felt light and energized.

When the warmth subsided, Dr. Fry released Brie's hands, and the older woman sagged a little. Brie lurched toward her, but the professor waved her off. "How do you feel?" Brie asked with concern.

Dr. Fry smiled wearily, "Old. Old and achy." Then she laughed. and Brie couldn't stop the smile on her face. "Now that that is done, I could use my bed," Dr. Fry said, straightening up to look at the happy couple.

Ezra offered to take her home, but she merely waved him off before exiting the office, leaving Brie and Ezra alone.

"So, how does forever sound, wife?" Ezra coyly asked as he wrapped her in his arms.

Brie wound her arms around his waist as she felt the warmth from the magic slowly fade. But looking at Ezra, she saw a future so bright she would never feel the darkness again.

"Forever sounds good to me, husband," Brie responded with a smile.

THE END

BOOK CLUB QUESTIONS

1. What character growth is seen in Brie? Ezra?

2. How does their relationship evolve over the course of the story, both working and romantic?

3. The Morrigan has been a figure in many stories. Here she is portrayed as cruel and disinterested in human affairs. How does her portrayal here differ from other stories featuring the character?

4. Themes were pulled from various mythologies. Can you identify them?

5. If Ezra knew Brie was the reincarnation of the Morrigan earlier, how might their relationship have changed?

6. By the end Brie no longer has the magic of the Morrigan. Though she is now immortal, she still

doesn't have magic of her own. How do you feel about Brie losing the ability to do magic?

7. Found family is a major theme in the story. Did you like how each member was introduced? How do they fit within the group?

8. Several of the items located in Spirit Antiques are from various famous people and an object that they were most known for, (i.e. Hemingway's type-writer). What kind of magical object would you hope to find in the Storage Room?

9. Up until the end, the POV was all from Brie. Would you have liked to have more of Ezra's point of view? Why or why not?

10. What scene has stuck the most with you?

11. The Storage Room is a character all on its own. How did the setting impact the story?

12. Craig is clearly the character who needed to be sat down and lectured to. Are there other characters you felt could use a stern lecturing? If so, who? What would you say?

13. Was Brie and Ezra's connection believable? Lily and Albert?

14. Were you happy with the "heat level" of the book?

15. If each character could have "their song," one that defined them, what would you pick?

16. Did the story unfold the way you expected? And if not, what surprised you?

17. The ending especially deals with healing from trauma. Did you find this believable? Why?

18. Did you feel like Brie was a reliable narrator of the book?

THE MAGIC CONTINUES WITH LILY AND
ALBERT'S STORY AS THEY NAVIGATE A NEW
ROMANCE WHILE DEALING WITH THE PREJUDICE
OF A WITCH/VAMPIRE RELATIONSHIP.

AUTHOR BIO

K ait Disney-Leugers is an author of fantasy stories with lots of romance. Originally from Ohio, she has a degree in history from Ohio University. She now lives in Maryland with her husband and two kids and uses her history degree to be insufferable while watching historical movies and shows.

When not writing in the dead of night once everyone else is asleep, she enjoys playing D&D, trying in vain to get through her giant pile of books, and baking bread to 90s hip hop.

MORE BOOKS FROM
4 HORSEMEN PUBLICATIONS

ROMANCE

ANN SHEPPHIRD

The War Council

EMILY BUNNEY

All or Nothing

All the Way

All Night Long: Novella

All She Needs

Having it All

All at Once

All Together

All for Her

KT BOND

Back to Life

Back to Love

Back at Last

LYNN CHANTALE

The Baker's Touch

Blind Secrets

Broken Lens

Blind Fury

MANDY FATE

Love Me, Goaltender

Captain of My Heart

MIMI FRANCIS

Private Lives

Private Protection

Private Party

Run Away Home

The Professor

FANTASY, SCIFI, & PARANORMAL ROMANCE

BEAU LAKE

The Beast Beside Me

The Beast Within Me

Taming the Beast: Novella

The Beast After Me

Charming the Beast: Novella

Fantasy & SciFi

Brandon Hill &
Terence Pegasus

Between the Devil and the Dark

C.K. Westbrook

The Shooting

The Collision

D. Lambert

To Walk into the Sands

Rydan

Celebrant

Northlander

Esparan

King

Traitor

His Last Name

Ty Carlson

The Bench

The Favorite

Discover more at 4HorsemenPublications.com

Printed in the USA
CPSIA information can be obtained
at www.ICGtesting.com
LVHW042309060924
790154LV00003B/8